LOVE
ON
PAPER

LOVE ON PAPER

Danielle Parker

joy revolution

Text copyright © 2025 by Danielle Parker
Jacket art by Vi-An Nguyen copyright © 2025 by Penguin Random House LLC
Interior emojis, ink bottle ornament, voice message pictogram and
stack of books art used under license from stock.adobe.com

GetUnderlined.com

Educators and librarians, for a variety of teaching tools, visit us at
RHTeachersLibrarians.com

Library of Congress Cataloging-in-Publication Data is available upon request.
ISBN 978-0-593-56531-5 (trade) — ISBN 978-0-593-56533-9 (ebook) —
ISBN 978-0-593-56534-6 (pbk.)

The text of this book is set in 11.3-point Warnock Pro Regular.
Interior design by Cathy Bobak

Printed in the United States of America
10 9 8 7 6 5 4 3 2 1
First Edition

For the mothers. Especially my own.

Chapter One

To be a writer, you need to (a) write and (b) have something to write about.

Or so I've been told.

Allegedly.

Perhaps.

Maybe you're like me—an aspiring writer who is afraid to actually write and unsure if what she has to say is even worth saying, so you're kinda stuck on this wheel, going around and around, wanting to write but afraid to actually do it. A great conundrum, if you will.

"Macy, hello? I said we're here." Dad's baritone transports me back to the actual moment, not the obligatory freak-out happening inside my head.

We're here.

"Here" meaning Penovation in Berkeley, California, one of the nation's most prestigious writing retreats, where I plan to spend the next four weeks.

That is, assuming I get out of the car and, you know, step onto the Berkeley Creative Arts College campus. I bite my bottom lip, tasting Fenty Beauty's Heat gloss as my brow furrows.

"I know that look. What's on your mind?" Dad shifts in his seat and turns off the car. Instead of responding, I scan the busy parking lot, where families are offloading young aspiring writers and their bags.

What *isn't* on my mind?

I can't quite answer Dad's question.

Not yet. I'll make a note to circle back in four weeks.

He rolls down the driver's-side window, and a soft breeze cools the uncertainty building in the car and in my chest. My gaze shifts to the entrance of the campus, where several eucalyptus trees, which must be at least a hundred years old judging from how they reach toward the sky and sway ever so lightly, providing nice added detail to the forest motif that nature has graciously gifted us.

If I get out of the car, if I allow myself to do this, I know I'll be steeped in Bay Area beauty and I'll get to try something I finally think I have the courage to do.

That's a big *if*, though.

"Aren't you excited to be at camp? Getting accepted is quite an honor. I would be thrilled." Dad pauses, savoring his own words. "Or is there something else?"

"First off, it's a writing retreat. Not camp."

"Oh shoot! Sorry—you're right. If there was ever a time and a place that semantics mattered, it would be now."

"I mean, this is campy, but it's not camp. You feel me?"

Dad lets out a soft chuckle and briefly closes his dark brown eyes while throwing an index finger in the air, his favorite move when he's tickled. "I don't, but perhaps it's not for me to understand." Dad pauses for a moment, then dives back in. "It's okay to be nervous, you know. Actually preferable. The nerves will do you good. You've got this, Macy."

As fast as my brain rushes to envision the worst-case scenario—me being unable to write a single word at this retreat—I challenge myself to envision the best-case scenario: me writing lots of words, even good words, that when strung together make something special.

Especially since Mom let it slip (translation: she told my dad during one of her tirades about my "life choices" and "the teen agenda") that she had to gently persuade some of her bookish friends to give my application another look.

The writing samples required for this retreat were so lengthy and over-the-top that most students who saw what was expected to just apply quit before they even started, exercising their better judgment and choosing to lean into being young and on a beach or whatever. I, however, pushed along and wrote what I thought was a solid essay. Only to find out Mom ran a workshop at UCLA two summers ago with one of the current lecturers and *casually* dropped my name and *casually* mentioned that perhaps my analysis of *Their Eyes Were Watching God* wasn't astounding, per se, but that I had a lot of potential, a lot of talent waiting to be unleashed if I could just get into this program. I can imagine my mother batting her unfairly long eyelashes and saying, *Give my daughter a chance. Pretty please with a cherry on top.*

Did Mom have to mention all that to Dad, who can't keep a secret to save his life? No, but she did anyway. They're divorced but love to get together to chat about me. Kinda rude.

Was she wrong about my essay? Also, no. It wasn't my best, but it wasn't my worst—that would be all of freshman year, when I only wrote in third person because . . . honestly, I can't remember why, but I'm glad I stopped.

But do I want to admit that sometimes I write things that seem average to my way-above-average writerly parents? Would they even understand what it means to be just moderately talented? Dad is a well-known author of a beloved children's book, and Mom is famous for her literary fiction—like gets-stopped-in-the-supermarket-and-gawked-at, her-books-are-in-airport-bookstores kind of famous.

Outside of our car, it's hard not to notice the commotion that begins to swell. More writers and their parents pull up, and with them comes the reality of the situation that it's time to say goodbye.

"Is this hesitancy about your mom?" Dad gets very after-school special; he leans in close, and his eyes soften.

"Oh gosh, not now—"

"I know that the two of you . . . your relationship has never been easy—"

"It's fine. Really." I'd rather do anything else than have this conversation. I get how lucky I am to have my parents' help, but sometimes, as in this case, when everyone thinks they know your mom and dad because they know their work, they assume they know you. And that is not reality.

Dad is my favorite person in the world, and even when I want to be mad or a smart-ass in front of him, I can never fully commit to the bit. What would be the point? I'm extra, but I'm not *that* extra. If anyone knows when to call me on my antics with a laugh or an eye roll, it's Dad.

"Okay, you're right. We don't need to have this conversation now. But we will . . . eventually. You can't escape what you're feeling forever, Macy Mariah Bak Descanso. She's your mother, after all."

Ugh. Dad using my full name. If he weren't my main parent, my ride-or-die since he and Mom got divorced when I was three, I would be annoyed with him and his questionable advice. But I know it's who he is. Dad believes in processing.

These parenting conversations never embarrass him. For some reason, turning twelve and starting my period comes to mind. Mom wasn't around when it happened, so he got me a pink cake with way too much frosting, and a bottle of Martinelli's sparkling apple cider. Then he called my aunt Tammy to have that conversation with me while he went to Target to get an ungodly amount of pads and tampons that overfilled the hallway closet. If anything, sometimes Dad wants to talk and share a little *too* much. One day I'll need to tell him that some things should be left to teen hearsay and the internet— a girl's gotta figure some things out on her own.

"Let's get you checked in," he says eagerly. "You've got authors to discuss, worlds to bring to life. Forget how you got here. Writing your magnum opus or the next great American novel is top priority." He winks, and then I wink back, acknowledging a little inside joke we share about who and what is considered literary greatness.

As much as I fear being judged for who my parents are, I have to remember that this is my reprieve. No distractions.

My fingers fiddle with the door handle. I could stay in my dad's Lexus, and we could talk for hours, as we've done so many times before. But something forces me to move. Slowly, I open the door.

To be a writer, you need to write. Or maybe you just need the opportunity to prove to yourself, and possibly your super-intense mom, that you can measure up. That you belong at one of the country's best writing retreats. That your story matters.

Chapter Two

We stand outside the dorm, a tall light grayish building with an assortment of flags decorating the windows. Dad gives me an ultra-tight hug, and as his eyes begin to mist, I hit him with a squeaky, almost childlike "Daaaaaaaaaad."

He dabs the corners of his eyes and straightens. "Okay, okay. It's just that—"

I know where this is going, and I cannot have any waterworks in public. My voice gets stern, and I age twenty years in an instant. "DAD."

"You're right. Four weeks is a long time apart, though, isn't it? No, this is good. We are both doing things that'll help us learn and grow as individual beings, and I am grateful for these opportunities." He closes his eyes.

"Yes, same, but way less wordy. We'll be fine." I grab the handle of my yellow wheely suitcase. Around us, students are heading through the dorm's double doors. No one else seems to be having this type of emotional moment with their parents. They all sort of fly the coop. Or maybe they aren't first-timers, like me. But this is on-brand for Dad. He's very in touch with his emotions—most starred reviews of his books say so.

"I'll be on the cruise, but there'll be internet. Email me, okay? Or call. You can call. My cell will work. I mean, it should, shouldn't it? What's the deal with international waters?"

I have no idea. Dad's idea of summer fun is a cruise with his colleagues that starts in Seattle and goes to Alaska, then Canada. The first time he brought it up, it quickly prompted Mom and me to agree on one thing for the first time in a long time: our suspicion of large boats and strangers. Being trapped together in the middle of the ocean without Wi-Fi or DoorDash? Hard pass. But Dad insisted. And who am I to kill his joy?

I take a deep breath in and exhale with a smile. "No news is good news."

Dad nods, but who knows if he believes me. I guess I get it. He can't help but be highly protective of his only daughter. But I'm a capable seventeen-year-old. For the most part.

"All right, one more kiss for good luck." I tilt my forehead toward him.

He grabs my shoulder and, in a stern-but-loving voice, drops gems of advice. "Learn a lot. Write your heart out. Take chances. Be brave. Find a story that surprises you, maybe even scares you. And dig deep into that." There is a reason why Dad is one of the favorite professors at the local community college back home in Santa Cruz. His ability to give you the most perfect pep talk you never knew you needed is unmatched. "And, Macy, be nice." He smiles, his crooked front tooth shining.

With a hand to my head, I salute him. "You already know." I take two steps toward the entrance while Dad stays steady, symbolic on all accounts. I inch forward; then I throw up a hand and wave goodbye. Dad doesn't move. Knowing him, he'll probably stand there for another five minutes or so just to make sure I'm good. Gotta love the man.

Against my will, or because of it, my feet carry me inside. With each stride, Dad becomes smaller and smaller, until he's out of the frame completely.

Once I cross the corridor, where the AC is working overtime, the cold air snaps me back to the present. The lighting inside is intense, the brightness level turned up by 1,000 percent. Without fawning too much, I scan the building, the walls like a large paper collage made of various flyers and announcements, reminiscent of every movie with a doe-eyed high school lead on a college campus. The elevator pings open before I push the button, so I'm unprepared when greeted by the smell of body odor and vape pen. Exactly how I imagined a creatives retreat should be, so that's comforting.

The doors close and we beam up to the fifth floor. With a quick tug, I grab my suitcase and walk as if I know where I'm going. My feet are heavy, but with each step I become more confident. I'm officially a Penovation fellow. I belong here, with or without Mom's meddling.

I travel down a long hallway where each door is decorated with names on a silver plate. Different types of music blare out of the rooms, like a radio on scan, shuffling through various stations. I eventually make it to the final door, which reads *Macy and Fern*.

My fingers give the wood a gentle push, causing it to creak. I shouldn't be nervous about rooming with a stranger, but I am. When I envision college, I think about opting for a single room. The whole idea of living with someone super random and hoping for the best seems risky.

What if they sleep with their eyes open? Anything could be possible in this scenario. Truly, anything.

"Oh yay! You're here. Macy?" An upbeat voice calls out from beside a desk.

Another step forward, always forward. "Yeah, Macy." I enter, my eyes wide as I take in the space. The room is two iterations of itself—one side empty, waiting to be decorated and given life, the other vibrant, thanks to several flowery wall tapestries, Instax pictures, and a large Mexican flag. The bed is meticulously made, with a light green duvet and matching pillowcases. On the desk sit a small salt lamp and a mason jar full of Sharpies, and a fuzzy throw blanket hangs from the back of the chair.

"Hi, hey." My roommate pauses and holds up the welcome packet and points to a page that says *Introductions,* then lets out a dramatic breath. "I'm stepping into something new here, and—whew, I don't know why I got so nervous."

"You got this. I believe in you." I do my best to sound chill and not like I was also anxious an elevator ride ago.

"I'm Fern Alvarado. My pronouns are *they* and *them*. Please call me Fern, I'm not big on nicknames. Though I am thinking about evolving Fern to Ferns because, you know, I contain multitudes." The moment the words leave their mouth, there's a lightness, an undeniable happiness on their face—honey-brown freckles glowing, brown eyes beaming. Hell, even their curly hair seems to have more bounce and energy after that introduction.

"Honestly, that wasn't so bad!" Fern says.

"You did great! A perfect ten."

Fern makes a heart with her fingers. "Thank you! And I'm not even done, buckle up. I'm an ENFJ, but the older I get, the more I think the lowercase *e* for *extrovert* is turning into a capital *I* for *introvert*, meaning I'm very into my alone time, and I need it to recharge. I'm a Scorpio sun, moon, and rising, so a piece of advice: don't cross me because I do love to hold a grudge. But also, don't take my reclusiveness personally."

Fern extends a hand with a small heart tattoo on their thumb. We shake, and Fern smiles, revealing dimples in their cheeks. Fern wears a black beanie that seems homemade and a green floral shirt that has a variety of ferns on it. Nice. I know we just met, but I can tell I've won the roommate lotto.

Fern gives me a slight nod—I guess it's my turn. I usually hate exercises that reveal who you are, but Fern was so willing to share that I can't help but follow suit.

"I'm Macy. My pronouns are *she* and *her*. I also don't do nicknames. I'm pretty sure I'm an INFJ, if my memory serves me right, which it often doesn't, so be wary. I'm heavy on the introvert. I know that I'm a Pisces, I think. Wait. No, that's right. I'm a Pisces. I don't really know if I believe in that astrology stuff, but I do love the moon, because aren't we all going through different phases?" I pause, trying to remember all the details in Fern's introduction that I should offer back.

More small bits come to mind. "I'm a *Chicago Manual of Style* type of writer. I think people and things should come with more footnotes. I'm quite literally obsessed with Paper Mate Flair pens; they are superior, the color palette unmatched— I could give a presentation on their greatness. I prefer tea over coffee, but I really love when tea is blended with ice and whipped cream. That's the ultimate drink."

Fern throws up their hands energetically and nods. "Amazing. I would love to hear your pen presentation before we go home."

I exhale, their energy and demeanor helping me to relax a bit.

"Well, I guess I'll have to read your birth chart later," they continue. "There's so much to go over. But for now, roommate and best friend for the next four weeks, is it cool if you take that side of the room, and I take this one? I kinda already started the renovation, so I need you to say yes. Please." In tandem, we turn to Fern's side, which has received more than a renovation. It's an Urban Outfitters's wildest dream. I survey their space; one of the large tapestries on the wall reads, *Grow through what you go through,* with plants behind an Old English font. There's something on the ceiling that makes the wall look like clouds, and behind the clouds are soft lights that twinkle to their own beat. Near the door, there's even a medium-sized plant. I face Fern, pointing at the thing.

"Oh, it's not real, but it's good feng shui." Fern seems to already have mastered the ability to read my mind.

"Okay, perfect, because I could kill a succulent in a greenhouse." We both laugh.

I grab my suitcase and bring it to the closet and take in my side of the room. The walls are off-white, patchy, and peely in some spots. The furniture, which is old but functional, matches, giving the room a practical-but-don't-get-too-comfy vibe.

"So, this is home for the next month," I mumble, unzipping my suitcase to access my Hello Kitty packing cubes. Mom gave them to me a few years ago as a Christmas gift, and while I hated them at first (not the print, because who could hate Hello Kitty? But the weird idea that my packing would need more packing), I've learned to appreciate them now. Packing cubes do seem to bring order to my chaotic organization. I grabbed enough clothes to get me through two weeks without folks realizing that I'm cycling through the same variations of black pants, white tops, and some type of denim piece to layer. What really tie my outfits together, though, are my platform shoes, of which I can never have enough. I unpack the platform Converse, Vans, Dr. Martens, black Steve Madden Mary Janes, and even Uggs and place them at the bottom of the closet.

My dad, who runs ten miles every three days, for funsies, suggested I bring my sole pair of running shoes, which have, at max, seen ten steps. *Just in case,* he insisted. In case I accidentally decide that now is the perfect time to begin cardio activity? He's funny. Still, I brought the trainers anyway, to appease him. I stuff those in the very back—out of sight, out of mind.

"What's your forte?" Fern calls from across the room. Over my shoulder, I see them moving something on their desk, ever so slightly, clearly looking for the right angles. "Tell me what books you're taking on a deserted island. Or tell me what you wrote about to get in—what repressed trauma did you put into essay form?" Fern snorts.

I take three similar but slightly different white Madewell tees and drop them into a drawer before replying. "Hmmm. I'm definitely in my classical literature bag. So, on my island, I'd have *Sula*, *The Woman Warrior*, and *East of Eden*. I know folks go hard for *Beloved*—and don't get me wrong, Morrison did what she had to do with that one—but *Sula* is the story I think that more folks need to get into. I'm really into exploring friendships—well, examining relationships in general." I pause to see Fern's reaction; are we best friends after I've shared my top books, or do they think I'm super boring?

"Ugh. I'm so into it."

Relieved, I say, "I can talk Morrison all day. I love literary novels. My dad's an English professor, and his love for the written word rubbed off on me. Heavy." Fern seems impressed, their chin lifting.

"Dope." Fern pulls out their chair and flops down, their eyes narrowing on me. Instantly, my skin heats. "You look . . . familiar."

And this is where I should walk out and leave. The dreaded question, the one that I've endured too many times in my life, has come to expose me.

I scratch the back of my head. "Um."

Fern jumps up from their chair. "Wait, why do I know you from somewhere?"

My chest starts to tighten, and my breathing picks up.

When talking to other book people, it's quite a thing to have a face that looks so similar to another face that is pretty famous in the community.

I turn away, stuffing the last of my pants into the drawer.

Fern takes two big steps closer to me. "I'm usually really good with placing people." Then Fern closes their eyes. "Give me a second, and I'll have it."

I believe Fern too. This is how it usually goes—I'll be doing nothing out of the ordinary and then boom! People will make the connection.

Fern claps their hands, exhilaration in their eyes. "I've got it! That famous writer? You two have the same—yes, that's it! You're Mina Descanso's daughter."

Chapter Three

"Holy shit yeah!" Fern yells out, hands in the air, a victory won.

I am indeed Mina Descanso's daughter. And every time someone connects the dots, time slows down, and my legs get restless, and I'm never sure how to make the interaction not awkward.

Obviously, I'm proud of my mom. She's one of those super-intense, super-motivated people who at least twice a year is on some type of list (People to Watch Out For, Who's Who?, Movers and Shakers). You may also recognize her from those archaic-but-still-happening "twenty-five under twenty-five" and "thirty under thirty" articles that magazines and news-papers put out for reasons unknown to me. She's that girl, and has been for a minute. She used to say that she'd be president if she hadn't paused her life to become a wife and a mother, a joke that Dad and I never really knew how to take.

My eyes scan the tattered brown carpet, hoping to avoid this conversation for a little longer.

"Ooo-ooh! What's going on here? I hear swearing."

I turn to the door and see several eager faces peering around the frame.

Fern gives them a nod to enter, and the door fully swings open. Mental note to see if this is dorm life protocol. Are we all supposed to be up in each other's business? Another note: make sure the door is closed and locked after Fern goes to sleep.

Without another word, new faces strut in—two girls with immaculate makeup and similar-but-different layered earth-toned clothes, straight out of an Aritzia ad, and two guys, one in a matching black sweat suit and pristine Nike Pandas, the other in Levi's overalls and Crocs.

"Gina, Lily, this is my roommate, Macy." Fern turns to me. "I know these fools from last year's intensive. Black sweats, I forgot your name—"

"Luke," he responds.

"Luuuuuuke," Fern says again, eyes closed, knees bent, committing the name to memory. "Luke, this is Macy."

Luke steps into the room, practically side by side to Fern. I do my best to match the names to faces, but it's hard—my flight level is accelerating, and I start thinking about calling Dad and getting out of here. Maybe I can try being a writer another time.

Luke lifts a finger. "Wait, did you say Mina Descanso? Last year's Booker Prize winner?" He cranes his neck toward me, and I do my best to stay still, like he's a brown bear and I have to play dead. Standing dead but, you know, no sudden movements.

If anyone knows my mom's face and sees me, they know we're related. Not a complete copy-and-paste situation, but freakishly close, two similar fonts. I don't know the percentage of the world's population that shares their mix, but Mom and Dad are both half Black and half Korean. Dad was born in Korea to a Black American mom and a Korean dad, whereas Mom has a Black dad and a Korean American mom, both from Los Angeles. This genetic makeup thus also makes me half Black and half Korean, with my face not unlike my Mom's. I'm not complaining—it's a solid face. Brown skin that loves the sun, brown eyes, and a full set of dark black eyebrows that I have repeatedly over-waxed and that, despite my efforts, have grown back with a vengeance each time.

My parents met when Mom was studying abroad in Korea their junior year of college. It had the potential to be a fairy-tale love story, and it was for the first two chapters. But then things started to get a little . . . dramedy. The story became less romantic comedy and more Tyler Perry cautionary tale. Those two have been married twice . . . and divorced twice . . . and both times to each other.

Because I resemble my mom so much, people think that I am her, and therefore must think like her too. As if we aren't separate beings.

After hearing my last name, some people think of my dad,

whose sole book hit all the lists and won all the awards. Subsequently, he went into hiding. And for years, readers have been asking him for a second book. Dad is one of those rare creatives who hit a home run the first time at bat, like that Lauryn Hill album he always plays. Whenever folks learn who my parents are, they ask if I'm a writer too. I guess I understand, the apple falling close to the tree and all. But I'm different. I'm me. Whatever that is at the moment.

"Nah, she won the National Book Award for fiction." The words are hardly audible as they come out of my mouth.

"Oh wow, that's incredible. What does the award look like? Does money come with it?" That's Lily.

Luke shakes his head, amazed. "Sick. Do you write like your mom? Are you like her? You've gotta be, right?"

"I'm nothing like her." The words fall out, and they are sharp. I can practically hear Dad telling me to tone it down. Now.

My comment makes the room go painfully silent, a mutual teenage understanding that parent stuff is complex.

We stand, staring at each other, until Gina chimes in. "I also heard that the woman who won last year's Pulitzer's niece is here. And another kid with writer parents, that Caleb guy, whose parent had an Oprah's Book Club pick. Do you know him, Macy? You nepo babies stick together, right?"

There's so much to unpack in that last sentence, I don't even know where to begin. So I don't speak. Instead, my cheeks heat up and my mouth hangs open.

"Kidding!" Gina chuckles.

Luke clears his throat and takes a step back. "Okay. Well. I'm going to get a snack before our first session. Keep your door open a smidge and holler if there's anything I need to hear. I'm right across the hall."

Gina and Lily wave bye as I continue to stand like the last tree in a windstorm.

We are quiet for a moment, making sure our neighbors are actually gone. Fern gets close and gives my shoulder a jostle. "You good? I know we just met, but I thought you were about to have an out-of-body experience. I was afraid you might spontaneously combust."

I let out a shaky breath. "I . . . they . . . I'm still figuring out what it means to be their daughter and a writer on my own merits. Plus, my mom and I, we . . . it's complicated."

Fern nods empathetically. "Parent stuff is always the most confusing. But you belong here, I know you do."

"But how do you know?"

"Duh, because we all do. We all have important stories to tell if we allow ourselves, regardless of who our parents are."

I might have been shocked a moment ago, but right now I'm speechless. "Okay, I see you being wise beyond your years." Dad's always saying something similar to what Fern is telling me, but somehow, hearing it from them really hits different.

"Double duh. My parents are not remotely creative—my mom works at a bank, and my dad manages a grocery store. But I'm not gonna let that stop me. We gotta at least try to fulfill our dreams, right? Right. I'm the only one who can tell my story. And if I'm brave enough, I will." Fern shrugs.

A teeny, tiny drop of Fern's faith floats to me and makes me feel maybe—perhaps—sorta—that I can stay here and have something worthwhile to say.

"Come on, you can debate me later." Fern grabs their bag and then darts to the door, holding it open. "Right now, we have to get to our first lecture, and as much as I love a fashionably late entrance, we should be on time for this chapter."

Chapter Four

As if we've been best friends forever, Fern links their arm into mine, and we find our rhythmic steps toward the lecture hall. It's only been a few hours since the fellows started moving in, but social groups begin to form faster than I can blink. Inside the large, very high-tech, and fancy auditorium, folks are seated together, laptops on desks, writing guides from our suggested reading list nearby. We are five minutes early but that is too late. The only seats available are at the back of the room near two large speakers. The rest of the class is bringing that "early bird getting all the worms" energy. I can't help but notice the other writers—everyone sorta resembles each other, with large wire-frame glasses, layered gold jewelry, Fjällräven backpacks, and conviction on their faces, as if they know how talented they are. And they should—this retreat is notoriously intense.

Fern and I take our seats the moment the lights dim and soften, just a bit.

An older woman with fluffy white hair steps onstage and glides to the microphone. Behind her dark, boxy glasses, her eyes explore the room in a long, dramatic sweep before she begins speaking. Not sure any of us breathes.

"Good afternoon, students. I'm Dr. Linh Tien. Welcome to the beginning of a very definitive chapter in your life." She pauses, her voice rich like a jazz singer's. A ripple of claps wades through the room, and the intensity of what I can only imagine we are all feeling at this moment—hope, fear, and possibility—bubbles inside of us. "A warm welcome back to the counselors and faculty onstage. I am eager to be this year's liaison, and I look forward to finding the next literary talents in the room. I've read your applications—I know why you're here."

Silence. We are definitely not breathing.

Dr. Tien spends the next few minutes going over expectations, the integrity of writing and using our own words, the power of storytelling, and overall what we can expect to learn professionally and gain spiritually from being with fellow writers. This buildup plus Fern's pep talk have me ready and—dare I say—able? At the perfect place at the perfect time? About to step into my life's most important chapter?

Without saying anything more, Dr. Tien grabs a stack of white paper and begins floating around the room. My heart is a loud bass drum inside my chest.

The first paper we receive is a suggested reading list. Dad always says reading and writing go together like babies and pacifiers; I guess Penovation agrees.

Dr. Tien grabs another handful of papers and makes her way around the room again. After another moment, Fern turns and passes me my copy.

Dear Reader,

It is with heavy hearts that we announce the passing of our beloved friend and author Betty C. Quinn.

A private person who shared little about her personal life, Ms. Quinn's professional literary life was legendary. She began writing seriously at the age of twenty and by the age of thirty-three had published her first novel, *The House of Love*. Then, she did the remarkable and often unthinkable: Ms. Quinn began publishing a novel a year for the next forty years.

Her specialty? Romance novels, of course, for both teens and adults.

Ms. Quinn called the genre of romance her joie de vivre.

A true believer in the transformative power of love, Ms. Quinn wrote stories that defied the odds, created characters who warmed the heart, and delivered endless unexpected and swoon-worthy happily-ever-afters.

While she was drafting her first nonfiction work, a guidebook on love and writing from lessons learned over her storied career, she began experiencing health complications. Unfortunately, her forty-second and final project will not be published.

If this news is finding you today, Ms. Quinn would beg you to fall in love with someone. Immediately.

And if you can't find that special someone who captures your heart, Ms. Quinn would beg you to find a good book. In her famous words, "A rom-com a day keeps the doctor away."

Without waiting to be called on, someone shouts, "Um, Dr. Tien. Can you explain this a bit more? I don't get what this has to do with—"

She raises her eyebrows and circulates around the room again, handing out another paper.

The Betty Quinn Foundation presents:
Writing Romance

Greetings, Fellow Writers,

Welcome to the beginning of a new chapter—yours as a dynamic storyteller. Over the next four weeks, you will be immersed in story craft, and by the end of your time here, you will be well versed in the art of romance writing. You'll learn to write for teens and adults in all subgenres so you can figure out your preference as a budding writer. Though, if the latter, keep it clean!

With your critique partner, you will spend time exploring various works of art as well as be challenged to write daily in an effort to build your confidence and to hone your craft.

This year, we are proud to offer a rare and unique opportunity—publication! Five student stories will be selected to be a part of an anthology to be released within two years of the retreat, compliments of the Betty Quinn Foundation, in tandem with Random House Children's Books as publisher. Submission winners will also be invited to be a part of the book launch and publicity tour.

Final story requirements:

- No more than 7,000 words
- A young adult love story, of course
- Honest, authentic, and original (see student handbook around plagiarism and author integrity)
- To be submitted no later than 3:00 p.m. on the final day of the retreat

The Retreat at a Glance:

Week 1: The First Draft: Get It Out
The importance of the first draft. We'll get our thoughts out and on paper so that our stories can come alive.

What questions do you seek to ask? Remember the who, what, when, where, why.

Week 2: Location, Location, Location
Finding the best time and place to tell your story.

Week 3: Say Anything: Why Dialogue Matters
Say what you mean and mean what you say.
Explore the different ways dialogue can reveal a character's personality.

Week 4: Revisions: Do It Again, but Better
The art of revisions: how to kill your darlings and polish your work.

Final story due on the last day.

Post-retreat:

Five writers will have their story published by Penguin Random House.

"Wait, is this for real?" A squeaky voice wails from the middle of the room.

Dr. Tien stands at the front as the lights turn back on. "This is for real. Writers, we are thrilled to announce the focus of this year's retreat: romance. As well as the once-in-a-lifetime opportunity for publication. As I stated earlier, today begins a definitive and goal-worthy chapter if you rise to the occasion."

Chapter Five

"You all can pack your bags now. I'm the king of swoons," someone declares, but I can't make out who, the studious composure we had as a group a moment ago now replaced by chaotic chatter.

"I am not joining the damned mob of scribbling women, where I'll have no chance of success." I don't know the name of the person speaking—it's some guy with too much gel in his hair—but this reference I know. He's pretentiously paraphrasing the man who wrote *The Scarlet Letter.*

"You're hot, tall, and, from that Rolex wealth. I'm sure you'll survive!" Fern shoots back without missing a beat.

"Okay. I'm telling y'all right now that everyone can't do enemies-to-lovers." Lily rubs her temples while shaking her head.

Before I can catch a breath, there are acrylic nails gripping my forearm. "I don't know a thing about romance. What do I do? Writing 'I'm not like other girls' stories is *not* part of my five-year plan. How will I get an agent now?" Gently, I uncurl her fingers.

"I need my arm back, but you'll be okay!" I offer before she exhales sharply and scrambles out the front door. I haven't begun to understand what this means for me, let alone anyone else. Thankfully, Dr. Tien gives us a ten-minute break to process everything she's shared, which is good because my brain cells are in overdrive.

Imagine being published before you can even legally buy a drink. There's something alluring about seeing your name, your words in print. Your book on shelves?! My eyes close, and I start to envision the cute posts I'll make for Instagram: me at an event, signing books. Hell, maybe even a chat with Oprah! You never know! Sounds extreme, but dream big or go home, right? Can I rise to the occasion?

But also . . . *romance.* Gulp. Writing . . . love stories? This is where things get a little dicey, and my self-doubt starts to creep in, hard. What do I know about love stories? Other than kissing and an obligatory scene in the rain? I've had one sorta-serious relationship, and that ended when I found out he was only chumming it up with me to get to Dad for his own personal gain. That is, he wanted feedback on his middle grade Black boy wizard story. Side-eye.

Also, my parents . . . they're no help. Can't use them as an example of anything but toxic love, or ask for their advice, since there's a total of one kiss among their books.

Give me any other genre—mystery, thriller . . . hell, I could even try to write a nonfiction piece—but romance?

Fern stands in a group with a few students I've seen in

passing, all of them smiling, clearly not having an internal panic attack like I am. So, I snag a chair at the side of the building and pull out my phone to see a message from Mom.

Whoever taught my mom how to leave voice memos, count your days. As of late, Mom has given up texting and using emojis that don't make sense in context (she is notorious for using the dancing lady in the red dress) and now abuses the voice memo button. To me. Ad nauseam.

Random thought?

Thought that appears, then disappears?

Something she wants me to remember for her?

A voice memo.

Not sure why I thought she'd quit this behavior on my first day of the retreat.

I'm hesitant to lift the phone to my ear, but I do because I can't stand not knowing.

▶ ılıılıtlılııtlılılıtlıtlııtlıılıtlııtlı

Macy? Hi, it's Mom.

Your father told me you've arrived at your retreat. Good, good. This is good. I also received an email from Literary Lunch—it's not what the name makes it out to be, nothing involving food, just literary gossip, or teas, as you would say. Anyway, the email mentioned your retreat and the opportunity of publication with the Betty Quinn Foundation.

I was thinking, and this is an excellent space for you to begin your career as a serious writer. Before you say anything, yes, career *is the right word. You know me; I thought deeply about word choice, and*

*career is the only word that makes sense. Besides, what else would
you call this next step for yourself? Wait—I'm digressing—don't get old.*

Where was I going with this?

*Oh yes, I wanted to give you, albeit unsolicited, but what are mothers
for? I wanted to give you some advice to help elevate your time at the
retreat.*

*First, dedicate yourself to your craft. Dedicate. Don't forget why you
are there and what you plan to do. Friends and activities are fun, in
moderation of course, but be mindful where you put your time and
energy. You know what I think about talent and luck. Dedication is a
stronger currency.*

*Second, speaking of dedication and time, learn to discern what
uplifts you and what distracts you. Alcohol? Marijuana? Most likely
distractions. You're almost eighteen, so you'll have to make these
decisions yourself.*

*Remember what both your father and I tell ourselves: first drafts
don't have to be good; they have to exist. You're my daughter, so
I know you have that perfectionist bone in you, but get the words
out. Don't be afraid. Or be afraid but write anyway. Think of the first
draft as the foundation of a house—wait, no, let me think of a new
metaphor. Later . . . I'll send another voice memo.*

*There's so much you can do with a first draft. There's nothing you
can do with incomplete, half-finished projects. Which leads me to
my final point. Yeesh, this is turning into a long memo. Can you save
these? You've got to be able to. Make sure you save this one.*

Okay, where was I—oh yes, finish what you start, got it? I know it sounds easy in theory, but in practice it takes discipline. Don't let this be similar to your knitting or your pottery. You can do it, Macy. Don't just make one sock or form half a bowl. Whatever you want to do, you can. Do it with integrity. Honestly, honey, I didn't mean to get so preachy, it all sorta came out. But I'm glad you're at this retreat. I know there's something big in store for you.

Oh, oh, last, laaassst one, I promise. Saying and doing are two different things, you hear me? I won't belabor that point, but I can repeat it—saying and doing are two different things. I've gotten way too far ahead of myself. I'm trying to only point out one or two areas of improvement, moving forward. They say a person can actually only receive that much info regardless. Okay, sweetheart. Thanks for listening. Audio message me back? No, don't. You'll be too busy writing the next great American novel I presume. Learn a lot and replay this message when you need guidance.

Talk soon.

Siri, play—oh heavens this isn't—

Am I still recording?

Why isn't this turning off—

Mom's message fills me with dread. Things that are so easy for her—advice on how to be excellent—make me worry because I know how hard writing is for me. The little grains of hope I had from earlier are suddenly gone.

Dr. Tien steps outside and waves us back in.

"Oh, it's on! We out here, writing love stories, working on our craft. Making folks fall in love. Falling in love with folks? Telling our stories. Expressing ourselves. Pushing our inner romantic to the limit?" Out of somewhere, Fern appears and gives my back a pat, clearly invigorated by this news. "And you're telling me there's a chance that my story could be published? I'm about to write something so tender, so poetic, so lovely. Shakespeare could never. Say absolutely less, Ms. Quinn!" Fern is beaming at me; I swear I see literal gold light in their face.

Meanwhile, everything inside of my stomach is turning and swishing around, and I would pass out if that were my body's way of handling things. Instead, a sweat builds on my forehead and a tightness constricts my throat.

The nerves have spiked.

Chapter Six

Back inside, Dr. Tien starts a slideshow, revealing some of Quinn's most iconic covers to help us familiarize ourselves with her work, of which there is a lot. Forty plus book titles, and each cover is stylish and unique, possessing a personality of its own. The first five book covers are simple, with nice fonts, but by book ten we're getting handsome models with longing stares and looks of desire that are definitely gonna make your cheeks warm and have you throwing the books in your checkout cart. Her more recent book covers are what I can only describe as cartoony but cute.

After about five minutes, Dr. Tien goes on to discuss the extensive personal library that's been bequeathed to us for the retreat to use as inspiration and reference.

I'm trying to think about the last time I read a romance, or the last time I actually got swept away in something . . . of that nature. My thoughts tell me it's been a while, that maybe

I've been actively avoiding anything to do with love, and I'm about to self-analyze when Dr. Tien claps her hands, interrupting my wandering thoughts. "Please check under your seats for your picture, and you may begin!"

Under my seat?

My hand moves to the hard plastic and finds a piece of paper stuck to the bottom of the chair.

Gently, I rip it off.

A hamburger? An In-N-Out hamburger, no less—delicious, but confusing. "Wait, what? What are we doing?" I turn to ask Fern, who already has their backpack on.

Fern's eyes are wide with glee. "Icebreaker activity. The images should make a pair—you have one half and gotta go find the other, and its owner will be your critique partner for the retreat."

How did I miss that?

I nod to Fern. "Got it," I say, though I only partially mean it. Fern throws up a peace sign and disappears into the crowd.

"Find your partner," I mumble. "Okay, should be easy, right?" I've taken two steps down the stairs when my shoulder bumps into someone.

"Sorry." I throw up my hands to find a stunning Asian girl with jet-black hair cut into a sick bob with super-blunt bangs. She's got a septum piercing, and her skin is flawless. She may be the most beautiful person I've ever seen. Definitely the coolest. Note to self—consider a septum piercing for more of an edge? Even though I hate needles and wear clip-on earrings because when I decided, at the brave age of fourteen, to

35

finally get my ears pierced, I could only endure getting one done. So, my left ear is pierced while my right ear is not.

"All good. You Mickey Mouse, by chance?" She holds up her card, Minnie Mouse, and I flash mine.

"Is Mickey a carnivore?" I ask.

She grins, eyebrows rising. "Good luck."

I nod, taking another step down. She disappears behind me as we sift through the people searching for their other halves.

Why do we need partners again?

When I reach the bottom of the steps, my feet do a quick spin. Out of despair, I smack my note card onto my forehead, holding it up with one hand, and do another slow rotation around the room, eyes closed. If I can't find my partner, maybe my partner can find me.

I should have heard the shoes, but I didn't.

Because when I open my eyes, he's right in front of me.

"I think we're a match." His voice is moody and deep. He holds up the golden French fries on his notecard and keeps a straight face.

Oh no.

Caleb Bernard is an inch away.

Nope.

The Caleb Bernard whose family is rivals with mine.

He's . . . my other half?

Chapter Seven

"I. Uh. What?"

"I think this means we're partners—critique partners," Caleb says. His voice is different than I thought—it's got more baritone with bounce, like he's a radio DJ with the energy of a game show host. It's nice. I try to remember if we've ever talked, in real life, and the answer must be no. My brain is firing a thousand different synapses at the same time and could possibly short-circuit trying to keep up with all that's happening today.

"But wait—you're actually—you're a writer too?" Not the most brilliant question, but the one that needs answering.

Caleb shrugs. He's a lot taller than I remember from that SoCal Fiction Symposium my dad made me attend last summer. He's gotta be at least six feet, with several inches to spare. Up close, I make sure to really check him out—he's got dark brown eyes and full lashes that are dramatic and alluring.

And he's glowing? Has he always been . . . glitter-like? His dark brown skin shines, not a blemish in sight.

My heartbeat picks up. I don't necessarily believe in love or whatever, but I do believe in hot people, and he's one of them. Objectively speaking, at least from this angle.

He's also the son of my family's only enemies.

"If I can't write, does that still make me a writer?" Caleb sighs.

"Why can't you—" I begin.

"Never mind. It was rhetorical." He holds up his paper. "There's a QR code with questions we need to go over on the back. You wanna work on them outside?" He motions toward the door and takes two big steps, not waiting for me to respond. Long legs mean he's a fast walker, so I do my best to snap out of my disbelief and keep up.

Outside, the morning fog has begun to fade away, leaving streaks of sunshine that pour down onto the blue metal table benches. Caleb picks one closest to the door and takes a seat.

The expectation is that I should sit next to him and have a discussion. Once this thought lands in my brain, my feet slow down, and I try to remember everything I know about the kid, which is a lot and not much at the same time.

For mysterious reasons, our families dislike each other— think Montagues and Capulets. No one knows *why* they originally had beef. All folks in the literary world know, including the family members, is that there's beef—and enough to go around, apparently for generations.

I know of Caleb because, like mine, his parents are

successful writers. So yeah, as littles we'd be at bookish events, in the back, sitting patiently while our parents did their things on various stages. One time at the Los Angeles Times Festival of Books, I think we played tag together behind the kettle corn booth. Random interactions like that.

We don't follow each other on socials or, you know, talk to one another. If we have mutuals, I don't know them.

I'm about a foot away from the table, but I don't sit. Caleb pulls out a spiral notebook from his backpack and grabs the pen from behind his ear.

"Macy, are you gonna stand and stare the whole time? There are at least twenty questions on this thing." He doesn't look at me while he speaks.

Slowly, I make my way to the table. Caleb is scribbling in his notebook.

Without making it awkward, I do my best to sit down quietly. As though if I'm silent then none of this is weird.

Except it's *weird*.

He knows my name. Does he know about my family the way I know about his? What else does he know about me? Does he hate me? Are we in a fight too?

Caleb writes down one last thought, then finally glances up at me, smoothing his extremely faded black shirt, the Haitian flag printed on the front. He's in long shorts and black Crocs with too many Jibbitz on them. Cute or not? I can't quite decide. His fashion sense, that is. Again, objectively speaking, from a scientific standpoint, his face is nice— symmetrical!

"You know my name?" is all I can think to say.

His eyes bulge, and his facial expression is somewhere between annoyed and incredulous. "Of course I know your name. I've even met your parents—a long time ago, but I have."

"I see."

Caleb's eyebrows lift. "Number one—ask your partner three questions in order to get to know them better."

"Does it really say that?" I peer over as Caleb holds up his phone to prove that it does indeed say that. Icebreaker activities are cute in theory, until you're paired with someone you probably shouldn't ever in your existence talk to.

"Feel free to go first," Caleb says, leaning in.

I shake my head. "No, no. Why don't you?"

His hand sways in the air. "I don't want to be rude. By all means."

A standoff, but I don't budge.

Caleb exhales. "Fine. It's sorta about you—it's about your family, so it kinda counts."

I blink fast, intrigued. "Go on."

"Okay. Is it true that your grandfather was in the Witness Protection Program, and that's how you got the last name Descanso?"

I don't even try to hide the shock taking over my face, my eyes wide and my mouth fully open.

"Sorry, I . . ." Caleb's apology sounds sincere, but what kind of "get to know you" question is that?

"Did your . . ." Then it clicks. "Is that what your parents told you? Is that what people are saying?"

He rubs his temple, a blank look on his face. "Yes and no.

Kind of. Maybe? Not all people. Some people." He throws up his hands.

My eyes roll. "It's not like that. Definitely not Witness Protection Program, but my great-grandfather—" I have to stop because I can't say anything else that could turn into another piece of gossip. But he's not all the way off; my great-grandfather did change his last name, but not because of the Witness Protection Program. I mean, I don't think.

He smirks.

Then I remember. "Well, is it true that your dad is the real reason my mom's book wasn't chosen for YOU-KNOW-WHO'S book club?"

Caleb's arms straighten as he scoots back. "Ah, ah. You're going too far. Is that what your family thinks? My dad would never. One, he's not petty, and two, he's busy." Caleb stares at me.

"Okay, just thought I'd ask . . . since we are, you know, getting to know one another or whatever. Wanted to clear the air." But the air is now murky and a little stinky, like rotten eggs.

Caleb keeps a straight face while I do my best to mimic the same. Except it's more nerve-racking to *stare* at each other, so instead I take out my phone and pull up some suggested questions.

What inspires you to write?

Why do you write?

What questions does your writing aim to answer?

Who are your writing influences?

*What's the difference between writing for
yourself and for an audience?*

I immediately close the screen; those questions are not helping me feel confident. In fact, they only make things worse. I am here because I want to change someone's life, like Toni and Zadie did mine, but I'm unsure of my writing. I want to write but am worried that I'll never be as good as my parents. I want to stay because of my own stubbornness, but having Caleb as my critique partner is . . .

"Questions are thorough, aren't they?" Caleb's voice is calm again; whatever tension existed a moment ago is gone.

"Why do I write?" my voice squeaks out. "That's so deeply personal." My body sags. And at the same time, it's a question I should have the answer to, shouldn't I?

Caleb lets out a little laugh, which accentuates his very high cheekbones. "I'll share mine if you share yours," he says, holding my gaze. Our eyes lock and my face gets hot.

"Fine. You go first." I let him speak so I can buy myself some time to try to figure out how to answer at least one of these questions.

Caleb tilts his head to the side, and there's something about the shape of his face. Again, it's very symmetrical, and his jaw seems prominent? Striking? Yikes, I have absolutely gotta get better with descriptors if I'm going to write the next great American novel, or at least a short story. Or even a solid paragraph.

"I write because there's so much I need to feel, and it's the best way I can express myself. I write to laugh, to understand more about life. Sometimes I'm terrible with articulating my words; I always think of what to say too late. But with writing, I'm always on time." He closes his eyes. "Well, that would be my old answer. Like I said, I can't write anymore." His eyes open, but he's not there. He's been replaced by something cold and nonhuman.

"Well, if you can't write . . . what about the assignments and . . . the prize?" I sound like a kid who has just discovered that Santa isn't real.

He shrugs, eyes still empty. "I'm only here because Dad insisted because . . ." He looks off over his shoulder. "Because of my mom."

And then it clicks. I don't need an icebreaker activity to remind me of what I know about Caleb Bernard. I know that his family lives in the south, I think New Orleans. That his parents are both Haitian, and his dad wrote a searing mystery focused on volunteerism, a combination of volunteering and tourism, and its effects on Haiti and other Caribbean islands. I'm pretty sure it won a big award.

I know his mom wrote steamy romance novels with extraordinary love interests—think astronaut and president trapped on a mega yacht or something similar. I know she loved to wear bright colors. My mom, who only wears shades of gray and black, commented on a purple-and-gold sundress she was once wearing in a social media post. From what I recall, Caleb's mom also had a laugh as loud as her clothes. She commanded a room. She was sunshine walking. I can see her clearly, and the thought makes me smile.

Until I remember that she passed away last year.

At this, I immediately straighten up and put on a serious face.

"What?" Caleb asks. "Why are you looking at me like that?"

I am a terrible liar. I get it from my father. "I'm not—I'm . . ." See. Any normal teen would be able to scoot their way out of this. "I'm sorry about your mom," I whisper. "Fuck cancer."

Caleb holds my gaze, and for a moment, his face softens. I'm unsure about what I've done. Was bringing up his mom a bad idea? I know I would react in some kind of way, especially coming from a family rival. But also, I *am* sorry. I think we are the same age, seventeen, and losing anyone, particularly a parent, right now, has got to be one of the worst things possible.

I swear his eyes are watery—glassy, even; but he doesn't make it obvious. He grabs his notebook and stands. "Fuck cancer" is all he says before storming away.

Chapter Eight

After a disaster of a first session with my critique partner, I'm relieved to find that the rest of the afternoon is exploratory—we are urged to check out campus and the nearby hikes. I pass on the nature walk. There are also several cafés and two dining halls near our dorms. Checking those out is more my speed, so Fern, Lily, and I have an impromptu picnic lunch next to a group of college kids in summer school playing ultimate frisbee. We stay on the grass too long, the sun bronzing our skin and making us sleepy. That is, until Fern gets a text from Luke about a bonfire in the works. After reading it, Fern blasts up from their seat, practically pulling the blanket we're lying on out from under us.

"Hey!" Lily yelps.

"Sorry, got too excited." Fern holds up their phone. "Bonfire at dusk. Up, up. Up you go. We should have started to get ready an hour ago."

At this, Lily also begins moving three times her normal speed.

"I don't know if bonfires are my thing," I declare as Lily and Fern pass me empty chip bags and candy wrappers from our lunch.

Fern waves their hand in the air. "They are objectively everyone's thing. Plus, new rule is we do everything while we're here. Open mic night? Art performance? Slam poetry reading? Welcome bonfire? Yes. It's the summer of yes. Okay, technically we are only here four weeks, but take this energy into the whole retreat. Summer of yes." In step, Fern and Lily fold the picnic blanket quickly, and before I can finish stuffing our trash in the bin, they are on the main path, jetting toward the dorms.

Fern takes two hours to get ready, which is about an hour and forty-five minutes more than it takes me to throw together my outfit of jeans and a shirt. While Fern does who knows what, I'm at my desk watching my favorite episodes of *The Office*, reciting the lines under my breath like an extra on set.

An additional twenty minutes pass before Fern holds up something silver and sparkly.

"Ta-da! It's my party backpack." Fern presses a button, and SZA bounces out of the cutest and somehow loudest travel Bluetooth speaker I've ever seen or heard. The speaker is shaped like a cat but spray-painted gold, with rhinestones on the ears.

"What's in there?" I close my laptop.

"You mean, what's not in here? I've got everything—glow sticks, deodorant, gum, an old edible, maybe socks? Oh, and these are mandatory." Fern busts out Fenty body glitter and facial diamonds and ushers me toward them. In an instant, we are sparkly versions of ourselves. If I had to compare us to something, it'd be homemade Christmas ornaments.

After thoroughly bedazzling our bodies, Fern says the magic words. "Okay, now we are ready to go!"

Fern guides us through campus, where everything looks foreign in the evening. But what's new? I have no sense of direction. Fern skip-walks to a playlist full of today's hits, and I practically have to jog to keep up.

We go through an overgrown path, shrubs and tree branches sticking out and brushing our bodies. Finally, after what feels like hours, we reach our designated spot in the woods.

"Oh wow" is the only response I have once we arrive. A large fire roars in the center, where most of the group has taken up residence. There are several picnic tables and, across from them, an amphitheater, where a handful of students have formed a small circle, drinks in hands.

"This is so sick," Fern exclaims.

Most of the other writers, plus some extra college folks taking summer classes, have to be here. There are way more bodies than I saw in class.

"I'm going to grab a drink. You want one?" Fern points to the extra-large coolers, where some guy in a Warriors hat and jacket is guarding what is probably beer. He seems friendly enough, tossing one out anytime someone approaches.

"Nah, I'm okay. Beer makes me gassy." Too much information? Perhaps, but still true.

"A considerate queen. Our shared space thanks you in advance," Fern says, then dips into the action.

I move to get closer to the fire, where a small group is roasting marshmallows on sticks. Now, s'mores are something I must have. As I approach, I can tell I'm walking into a heated conversation by the serious expressions everyone wears.

"I know this for a fact," someone roasting two marshmallows says.

"I need more proof, more evidence. Can someone here cosign?"

The fire is bright, but I can't make out who has the provisions—I need a stick and a s'more as fast as possible.

"Macy, right?" two-marshmallows guy asks.

"Yeah?" The rest of the eyes in the group turn toward me.

"I'm Martin. Martin Corral. My dad is your dad's publicist." Martin has spiky dark brown hair and a long face that makes him look mature. Have I seen him before? Should I know who Dad's publicist is?

I fake a smile. "Fun, but where did you get the—" Martin cuts me off. The graham crackers, the chocolate, who can I beg for necessities so I can have a s'more?

Martin blows on his perfectly roasted marshmallows. "Tell me you know about Betty Quinn's unpublished final manuscript. The one hidden somewhere?"

If I wasn't the focal point before, I absolutely am now.

"Sorry." I shrug. "I don't—"

Martin does a dramatic spin. "Are you serious? Both of your parents are supposedly in it."

"What?" My mouth hangs open. I wish someone would stuff a s'more in it.

"Come on! Betty Quinn wrote this epic anthology on writing romance from everything she learned in her decades-long career. With excerpts from authors, like your parents. She'd been hinting at it for years. Years. Hence, our final submission and her push for this anthology. Despite the flack about story collections, she appreciated the melding of minds. And I agree with her. Anthologies are like the gift that keeps on giving. One book, tons of presents."

Should I know any of this? This isn't ringing any bells. But again, I am not into romance like that.

"Oh" is all I can manage to get out.

Luke, from earlier, steps forward, marshmallows on a stick. "Rumor has it that the unpublished manuscript is here in Berkeley. And we need to find it. If you know her work, you know she was always leaving Easter eggs, little clues. Remember the cat in the Heartbreakers series? The cat showed up in the movie of another book. I can't remember the title, but real ones know. She loved that kinda stuff."

I'm clearly not getting a s'more tonight, but I am getting curious.

"Why do we need to find the manuscript exactly?" I ask. Martin's jaw drops to the ground. His s'more almost goes with it.

"People. Please. Keep up." Martin glances at me. Apparently,

I am people. "Winning a spot in the retreat anthology is cute, but it's small potatoes comparatively. Finding a manuscript from one of the most prolific romance authors of the modern era? Now we're talking endless possibilities—perhaps you get to finish the book, add a foreword. If anything, you become an instant hero to people who auto-buy her stuff. If not that, think about the boost it'd give to your career, long term. This is a big deal. We're talking about Betty freaking Quinn—she sold millions of books, which have been turned into plays and movies and coffee mugs. Not to mention the Heartbreakers series, which is like, super iconic. My family and I watch all three movies every Valentine's Day. Anyway, finding this would be huge. Automatic agent, interviews, publicity. You'd become a household name. You could position yourself and your career in a lot of ways."

"Wow. You're good. Your dad must be good too," Luke says, fawning over Martin.

"He's the best." Martin looks at me again for affirmation, and I give him a thumbs-up.

"So, where do we start?" Luke rubs his hands together.

Thankfully, Fern reappears with a handful of graham crackers and chocolate. "S'mores?"

"Immediately. If not sooner." I'm salivating here.

The conversation shifts, something about the best burritos in San Francisco. I'm only mildly interested as Fern and I assemble our treats. I take a marshmallow and am beginning to roast it when there's a roar of applause. We pause, and there in the center of the amphitheater is Caleb with a microphone in hand.

Martin points. "My roomie might know more. I heard his parents are in the anthology too."

"You've got to be kidding me." Folks crane their necks and move toward the pit. Caleb plugs the microphone into a large amplifier, reverb rustling through the trees for a few beats. I'm staring at Caleb, and I can't seem to see anything else. He sings? Can he dance too? Why does he—

"Macy—you're going to start a forest fire, like quite literally. MACY!" Martin yells at me, waving his stick in my direction.

"Oh shit." My marshmallow is basically ash, totally melted and black, turning into char. I throw it all into the fire, then watch the flames eat it alive. I stifle a sigh.

Slightly deflated, I turn to watch Caleb again, who brings the mic to his face. "All right, y'all. You know what to do. Sing along and help me hide my voice. I might be atonal." There's a big laugh from the crowd before the music comes on.

The intro to Willow Smith and Tyler Cole's "Meet Me at Our Spot" starts, and goose bumps sprout on my skin. Unbeknownst to Caleb, this is one of my favorite songs. Romantic and angsty. Not to mention a viral hit.

The guitar starts playing, and once again, there are claps and cheers. But this time, a smidge louder than before. The forest has come alive. Then Caleb starts belting. And he's right, he may be atonal. He's on beat, but whew, his singing voice should probably be reserved for the shower or the car, when he's by himself and no humans or animals are around. But right now he doesn't give a fuck. Both his hands are wrapped around the mic, and he's giving his best rock star performance. There's something cathartic about singing at the top of your lungs, badly in his case, but it's freeing. He looks happy. Happier than he did this afternoon when we were together. He even dances, a two-step that involves some jumping, and moves around with the words, like he's onstage and we've all paid a lot of money to attend his concert.

When I wake up
I can't even stay up . . .
Meet me at our spot

Suddenly Caleb's voice is drowned out by everyone around us. I even find myself screaming the lyrics so loudly my throat gets scratchy. We are one with the music. Hands are in the air, waving around, including mine. He guides us in what feels like a ceremony.

When he's done chanting, he throws the mic high up in the air. Caleb catches it, thankfully, and everyone around him goes nuts.

Who could go next? Who would want to top that?

A brave girl grabs the microphone as Caleb takes another bow then bounces offstage. He runs up toward our fire, eyes red and knees wobbly.

"What'd I miss?" His words have a slight slur to them, and his body floats and sways like a buoy at sea.

Is he drunk? *His mom died like months ago, Macy, can you blame him?*

"Tell me you know something about this missing manuscript, for the love of all things." Martin wastes no time.

"All I know . . ." Caleb wobbles once before finding his balance, then glances at me. "Mace . . . critique partner, your"—he burps, clearly from too much beer—"your parents . . ." He holds up his hand and points to me. "Your folks are the whole reason the thing got canned." He throws his face back and closes his eyes.

"Oop. Not him charring your families' beef," Fern whispers to me.

Martin's jaw unhinges again, and he spins on his heels, cell phone in hand, his dad probably on speed dial. My palms get sweaty. Is Martin's dad going to call my dad? Since Caleb just spilled some questionable tea, insinuating my parents are responsible for killing Betty's final dream, are they going to hate the Bernards even more? Is that even possible—how deep does their past go? I bet that Martin is doing all he can to uncover as much as he can, to achieve publishing domination.

Regardless, my new objective is clear: unearth Betty Quinn's mystery draft.

Chapter Nine

Fern and I stumble back to our dorm around two in the morning.

"You want one?" Fern points to several cups of instant noodles. I shake my head no.

"You're gonna regret your answer in about five minutes," Fern says. They might be right. Oddly enough, I'm not hungry. Instead, I flip open my laptop and see an email from Dad.

To: MacyMania911@gmail.com
From: MrDescanso@gmail.com
Subject: Ahoy!

Dearest Macy,

Daddio here. Writing to let you know that we've set our sails, and all is well! Did you know that the walls of the cabin are magnetic? Cool way to hang things, right? Silly me, though, I hung my jacket out to dry and guess what? It belongs to Ahab and Ishmael and the seas now. Rookie mistake, truly. Thankfully, it was an old thing that I don't mind donating to the ocean gods.

How are you? How is THE RETREAT?

Should we both send pics of the food we've eaten?

I remember Mom saying that the cuisine on your end is better than most. If anything, I can send you a few restaurants to visit in Berkeley. I know some hidden gems.

Please tell me that you are having a wonderful time, that you're meeting new people, and that you're discovering new parts of yourself as well. So far so good on this end. I hope the same for you.

I miss you already, and I love you.

Dada

Dad's email makes me smile. And since I'm no closer to sleep, I respond.

To: MrDescanso@gmail.com
From: MacyMania911@gmail.com
Subject: Seas the day

Yo captain, my captain!

How do I know that this is you and that you

haven't been replaced by a pirate, or worse, a bot? We should have thought of a code word—ah well. Here's hoping this is the man I call father.

Things on my end are . . . going.

The food is rather delicious. They have unlimited frozen yogurt, which is straight dangerous for me. My personal goal is to have it for every meal, including breakfast.

I'm also trying to step out of my parents' shadows for once, and of course, I get recognized before I even have time to introduce myself. Le sigh.

But I'm glad to hear you're off to a good start.

Before I forget, what do you know about Betty Quinn and an anthology you and Mom supposedly got canceled??? Also, I know this is a little taboo, but why do we hate the Bernards again? Their son Caleb is here. And if I have to defend our family's honor by any means necessary, I shall. Just say the words.

Love you,
M

The smell of instant noodles, chemicals, and chicken wafts in the air, making my stomach rumble. Fern was right, I regret saying no. I glance at my screen to see that Dad has pinged me back way too fast.

To: MacyMania911@gmail.com
From: MrDescanso@gmail.com
Subject: A fish out of water

First off, we don't *hate* anyone, not even the
Bernards. There's a complex history there, which
I should probably let your mom discuss with you.
Preferably in person, you know how so much context
can get lost via email or text. Now, do we maybe
dislike a few people? Perhaps. Again, ask your
mother.

And sorry to say, but I don't know much about
Betty Quinn. Again, sounds like your mom's forte.
Why don't you reach out to her? I think she'd be a
great resource here. And this just came to me . . . Yo
captain, my captain. Why didn't I think of that? It's
got Dad pun written all over it!

P.S. Go to bed!

To: MrDescanso@gmail.com
From: MacyMania911@gmail.com
Subject: Pain in the boat

Chapter Ten

If I got irritated every time Dad brought up Mom to try to get us to talk or get along better, I'd be grumpy AF, which is not how I want to go about this life. But I am a little annoyed, and I'm a little unimpressed by his answers. I bet he knows what Mom knows, why we hate—sorry, dislike—the Bernards, and could tell me. Instead, he's using it as an opportunity for Mom and me to connect, which is sneaky.

The next morning, I do the unspeakable—I take Dad's advice, and I text Mom.

> **Macy:** hiiiii. I'm here. So far, so good. But there are rumbles. What do you know about Betty Quinn?

> **Mom:** Can you be more specific? Also hello dear, did you get my voice memo?

Macy: Yup. Thx. What do you know about BQ and . . .
a missing manuscript?????

Mom: I'll never understand why you can't spell
out certain words.

Mom: Your dad mentioned that there was talk of
this old tale. Leave it alone. Focus on your writing
and your goals for the next four weeks.

I'm not even mad. Of course Mom would mom by keeping me on track while she avoids telling me anything real or juicy. But since she's on the line, I try one more time.

Macy: k, last thing before class . . .

Macy: why do we hate the Bernards again?

My phone shakes, and instead of a bubble on my screen, there's a photo of Mom's beautiful face—she's calling me! This woman has no texting etiquette. What a great offense. She's calling because she wants to lecture me, no doubt, not because she wants to answer my questions directly. I know her all too well. She does the same thing to Dad.

"Sorry, Mom," I say under my breath as I let it go to voicemail. "I know you wouldn't want me to waste writing time."

Today's morning session is more logistics: We'll start every morning as a group for a lecture. Then we'll have some writing or reading time, followed by lunch. After lunch we are encouraged to work with our critique partners or do something that supports our writing—art museums, more reading, yoga, things like that.

Since I haven't seen my *American Idol* critique partner since the bonfire, I decide to go for a walk and explore. Outside, I follow a small wooden sign to Lake Rose. I didn't even know the campus had a lake on it, but now seems like as good a time as any to check it out.

Five minutes into my walk, the path begins to narrow, consumed by blossoming foliage, and goes around a bend until it opens to a small yet beautiful lake. Definitely man-made, but relaxing and tranquil nonetheless.

The lake is a perfect circle, with a fountain in the middle, spraying water up and out. There are several benches around the perimeter and a small outhouse behind a large tree.

"Okay, I can get into this." I see an empty bench on the other side of the lake, so I start walking there, only to see Caleb sitting next to my target spot, three feet away.

He peers up from his book and we lock eyes.

"Hey," he says.

Two more steps, and I am at his bench. "Hey."

"Well, well. Our second meet-cute."

Is this a meet-cute? Does the other person have to think you are cute for it to fall in that category? Do I want him to? Too many questions muddle my brain. An awkward silence keeps us both from moving or saying a word, but after a beat, he pats the wood beside him. "Why don't you at least sit? Enjoy the views. Get inspired."

I let out a sigh of relief. The invitation is very necessary because that small walk has reminded me how out of shape I am.

"Thanks," I mutter as I flop down.

Neither of us says anything for some time. Caleb is almost monk-like, the silence not seeming to bother him, but it makes me nervous.

"So, how long you been out here?" I gesture at our surroundings.

After a while, he budges. "When did breakfast start? I woke up with a major headache. Sorry about yesterday . . . leaving abruptly . . . things are . . ."

"It's okay," I offer too quickly.

"And last night—that's what happens when I don't eat," he says.

"You get drunk and sing karaoke?"

Thankfully, he laughs. My brain is too jumbled to bring up the other thing, the whole mystery draft. So we sit for a moment in silence, until I can't take any more. I pull out my phone and open our first assignment. "Since we're here, should we, you know—try to do work?"

"You mean our weekly prompts?"

"Y-yeah? I mean . . . if you're up to it."

Caleb nods to himself. "Sure. It beats staring off into the abyss."

"Amazing perspective," I say.

Caleb reaches into his bag and pulls out two packs of gummy bears and offers me one.

"Oh, good call on Haribo."

"They are superior." He smiles.

"The absolute best." I rip open the pack and shake the bears into my mouth.

"Whoa, nice. I usually rip off their heads and put them on different bodies, but that works too."

I nod, pleased. "Gracias." The perfect sugar pick-me-up. "So, what do you think about this first assignment?" Thankfully, everything is online, so even though Caleb missed this morning's lecture, we all have access to the readings and notes.

Caleb brings the phone close to his face and reads, "Go people watching. You and your partner should create a backstory for two people in love. Submit your work to the portal when you're done."

Caleb is talking, but I'm standing.

"No fucking way," I mumble.

Directly across from us, a flute quartet begins to set up, unfolding music stands and chairs.

"Ummmmm . . . ," Caleb mumbles.

"Is this what I think it is? What's going on?" Now they're in a circle, and within a second, a soft serenade comes from their instruments.

"Why would a quartet practice out here?" Caleb asks.

Before I can reply, out comes a tall woman in all black, who begins throwing bright red rose petals on the ground.

"Oh my gosh. . . ."

"What is happening?"

From the path, two more people in black appear, both with cameras around their necks. From behind a bush a woman with a clipboard comes out and points, checking her watch every two seconds. They buzz around the area in an organized flurry.

"Is this someone's engagement?" Caleb's voice is soft.

"Dude. Talk about love on location," I offer.

"What do we do?" we both say at the same time.

"Is it rude if we stay?" Caleb asks.

"*Or* is this the perfect example for our assignment?"

The quartet plays something lovely that travels across the pond. I should recognize the melody, but nothing comes to mind.

"I wish we had popcorn," I whisper.

"Me too. Salty or sweet?"

"Both." I pause because the music stops. "You?" I whisper again.

"Same. Unless there's that fake bright orange cheese popcorn as an option. That stuff is chef's kiss."

"That shouldn't be allowed to be called cheese."

Caleb snorts. "I need delicious, not nutritious."

A moment later, walking down the path and holding hands is a really good-looking couple, solid nines. She's in a yellow floral dress, her hair up high, with bright red lipstick, and he's in a matching khaki set, grinning wildly, grasping her waist tightly.

Caleb and I watch as this moment slowly comes into focus

for the woman, her brain registering what is happening and what this means.

The quartet continues to play as he guides her to the center of a heart made of rose petals. He drops to one knee, and her hands cover her mouth. From where we stand, we can't hear them, but the excitement and intensity are palpable.

My eyes are misty. I want to look away, give them their privacy, but I can't. This is the sweetest thing I've accidentally stumbled upon, maybe ever?

Caleb's mouth is wide open. "Holy shit," he lets out. He grabs my hand for a brief moment. "I can't believe we are witnessing this. Like, one of the most memorable days of their lives." His eyes grow big. I don't respond. Maybe it's his touch or maybe it's his statement, probably a combination of both, so I give my best surprised nod. He lets go of my hand, and I can speak again.

"This is absolutely insane, right?" These two strangers are hugging and kissing, and the only polite thing to do, especially since we spent the last two minutes staring at them, is clap.

"Congratulations!" Caleb cuffs his hands and yells. The newly engaged couple waves, and the flutist lifts her chin and leads the group in a new song.

"So," Caleb says.

"So," I respond back. "What do you think their story is?"

"Hmmm . . . she could be an intergalactic alien hunter," Caleb offers.

"Like a ghostbuster?"

"Yeah. But for aliens."

I pause. "Okay, I can picture it. She's an alien buster who travels the galaxy, and he's giving . . . preschool teacher. Or principal."

"Oh, definitely preschool teacher."

"And they meet . . ."

Caleb turns to me. "Obviously when she has to enroll her adopted alien child in school."

I nod. "Obviously. Then they fall in love after a steamy parent-teacher conference."

"Soulmates."

"And now they are here, settling down on Earth."

"With us. Two of their closest strangers." We both grin. My eyes toggle between the newly engaged couple, Caleb, and the lake.

"When do you think they'll get married?" Caleb nods at the newly engaged as they continue their photo shoot, hand held high, ring up, both of them smiling super hard.

"Eh." I shrug.

"What's that sound mean?"

"There wasn't a sound—"

"Oh no, you definitely made a sound. Like a grunt of disapproval."

The fact that he can pick up on my noises after two conversations should be concerning.

He inches closer. "Go on, this is a safe space."

"Fine. But only because you asked! I don't know. Is marriage still a thing? I thought we all agreed that fighting the patriarchy was one of our top priorities."

Caleb nods. "Yeah, that and saving the planet, right?"

"I mean, hopefully."

I stand before Caleb starts asking any more questions. "I think I'm going to head back." I've met my lovey-dovey quota for the day.

"To tell your mom that I'm not half bad?" His lips part and a mischievous smile illuminates his face.

"You wish." I pause. "I . . . are you . . . what if we agree to not talk about our families?" Because, you know, let's not make this any more complicated than it already is.

Caleb shrugs. "Yeah. Okay. That could work. Because I *have to* be here."

"And I want to try to maybe get into the anthology." As soon as the words leave my mouth, I know I mean it—I want to learn and give writing romance, and this retreat, a fair shot.

Caleb stands too. "I don't want to hold you back. But yeah, that's a good idea. We won't talk about things that could get us distracted from our work."

"Awesome. Then we won't talk about our families," I offer. "And it'll totally be fine."

Chapter Eleven

I'm exhausted from writing up our first story—which we decided to call "Alien Heartthrob Galaxy" (the title needs some work but, for now, stays)—and brainstorming concepts for my short story submission. So after dinner, I'm curled up sloth-like in bed. I barely have the energy to lift my head, let alone swipe on my phone.

"Are you sure I can't change your mind? A mini mixer? We can scope out all the hot people up close?" Fern stands by my desk, persistent. Bless them. "Oh, Lily sent me a pic, and apparently, because who doesn't love a good theme, all the food is bite-sized. Check out the dessert table—mini cupcakes, mini cookies, mini cinnamon rolls." Fern shoves their phone in my face. "Come on. Say yes!" Sugary temptation sets in. There is something rather delightful about food when it takes on a smaller and somehow cuter form. I could see myself really devouring those brownies. But that would require me to put on clothes and have enough energy to talk to folks. Can't do it.

Fern leans in to read my face, so I bat my best doe eyes, hoping it'll work.

"Okay, okay. I'll let you settle in tonight, but starting tomorrow, we are embracing the madness and experiencing all that there is to do here, got it? Summer of yes, remember?"

"Heard. Don't be afraid to bring back some desserts."

"Light work." Fern throws up a peace sign, then closes the door.

How everyone else is handling the mystery draft, the retreat's new theme, and the once-in-a-lifetime prize so casually is beyond me. Unless they aren't, and they're better at hiding their freak-outs. Curiosity begins to brew, and I begin to wonder—who exactly was Betty Quinn? Maybe if I know more about her, I'll have a better chance at thriving here and possibly writing something worthy of publishing.

I flip open my laptop and drop her name into Google. It doesn't take long for the results to populate endless upon endless headlines about Betty Quinn and her many books.

FAMOUS ROMANCE AUTHOR'S LATEST NOVEL TO BE A BROADWAY MUSICAL

ROMANCE AUTHOR GIVES ADVICE ON HOW TO ACHIEVE A SUCCESSFUL AND STEAMY RELATIONSHIP

INTERNET ABLAZE WITH AUTHOR'S HIDDEN EASTER EGG CLUES AT EASTER DAY PARADE

After about a minute of scrolling, I go back and click on the first result, which leads to her actual author website.

Betty's home page is simple: a black quill and a large open book in the background with the same letter about her life that we saw in class. There are several tabs at the top, and I go through each one. No pictures of Betty, nothing about her personal life, just her writing. In an age where nothing seems private, how she managed to stay so hidden is impressive.

Another click, and I've returned to her "books" page. Images of covers—both photographic and illustrated—for each title float on the screen. So many stories—also impressive. She accomplished so much, and I'm over here struggling to come up with an idea for one seven-thousand-word short story.

On the bottom corner of the screen, a green book appears, and on the front as the title it says, *Finish what I started.* I blink—the image stays for a moment and then disappears.

"What the what?" I mutter. My eyes dart back at the screen, and sure enough, the image is gone. I stare, stare, stare, then boom—the book is back. For a brief moment, I think I could be hallucinating, but this is real. The message is on-screen for ten seconds before it disappears. With my phone I track that it's on a loop, appearing every three minutes.

But why?

Finish what I started? What does that mean? And again—*why?*

I'll have to show Fern later. Maybe they know something I don't.

I planned to go to sleep early, so that I could be energized for tomorrow, but I get sucked down an internet wormhole about Betty's Easter eggs in media interviews and in books. So, when Fern gets back around midnight, I'm wide-awake.

"Ack, sorry, were you asleep?" Fern whispers, slipping out of their jacket and shoes.

"Nah, I wish. It'll take me another hour or so. I was being reckless and had two afternoon teas. Plus, three full-sized desserts at the dining hall. And I've been on my phone for the last hour, so my brain isn't getting the hint that it's time to wind down."

Fern turns on a cactus lamp on their desk, then moves around the room in slow, quiet circles.

"Same same, but different. I had all this energy after the mixer, so I went for a walk, then a walk turned into chilling with a group of kids, one of whom had some edibles. So, we started nibbling and talking and . . ." Fern lifts their hands to their brain and "poof" does an explosion sound.

"Go on."

"Wait, first, I can't be slipping." Fern scoots by their closet and grabs a cleaning wipe and rubs their face. Then, with swift skill and precision, they take out their contacts and do a quick three-step skin-care routine. I'm in awe. If I remember to wash my face, I consider that a victory. Let alone take the extra steps to have hydrated, happy skin.

Finally, Fern flops onto their bed. "Okay, I've been waiting for this."

"Waiting for what?"

"Um, duh, sharing secrets until the sun comes up with my roommate. Being instantly connected to you because the retreat gods have pushed us together. Things like that."

I laugh. "Okay, but what was the 'poof' you had?"

"Right! I almost forgot. The 'poof' is that I saw myself winning a spot in the anthology. Then I saw myself writing lots of books, becoming a full-time creative. Why not? My work matters as much as anyone else's. I need to get over myself and my fears and write my own stories. And so what if they are bad at first? They probably should be. I'll keep going and keep trying and yeah. . . . Am I making sense?"

I turn on my side toward Fern. "Totally. I'm glad you got to that revelation. I think that's what we're here to discover, right? The artist within us? Maybe I need some of what you had."

Fern's voice is so full of hope, I almost can't believe that they ever have a moment of feeling anything less. But I guess we all do.

Fern reaches over and taps the cactus lamp. Then everything goes dark.

"Real talk, though—tell me a secret or two to get this party started. Who needs sleep?"

I giggle.

"A secret? I don't know if I have any," I say.

"You're a terrible liar. We all have them. I'll go first. . . . I was born with an extra pinkie finger. Wanna see the scar?"

The rest of the night is spent like this—Fern shares stories about growing up in the Central Valley, their two older brothers, and summers spent at their grandparents' house in Oaxaca. I tell Fern about growing up in Santa Cruz, and funny stories about my parents and their writer friends, until we both fall asleep a little after two in the morning.

Chapter Twelve

The next day after lunch, which is half a turkey-and-avocado sandwich with jalapeño chips, two chicken tacos, and one and a half servings of vanilla soft serve with sprinkles, we have a slight change in scheduling and are urged to meet back in the main auditorium.

Dr. Tien says, "I have a surprise for you all. Follow me." She takes us outside and to a redbrick building behind the main auditorium.

"I know some of you might've been disappointed by our virtual tour. And I've heard whispers about this year's retreat." She pauses to make sure we are all paying attention. Dramatically, her hand waves in front of the sensor, and the double doors open wide.

The silence becomes a wave of murmurs.

Dr. Tien glides into the room and gracefully raises her hand to the walls around us. "It took us a few extra days to ensure everything was in pristine condition." Another dramatic pause. "Welcome to Betty's very personal, very sacred library."

Our heads turn in a collective 360-degree rotation.

There are endless books stacked upon books—this is quite the collection, and I once spent an entire afternoon at the Library of Congress because my parents thought it would be "fun."

Books everywhere—floor to ceiling.

"Students, you have approximately fifteen minutes to peruse. You'll notice she had quite an extensive collection of all genres. Try to recall your first time in a library, or in a bookstore. Try to replay that sense of wonder, knowing that other worlds sat at your fingertips, ready to be explored. We hope you find that excitement and energy now. That as you walk these aisles and examine these books, something in you is intrigued, a curiosity is sparked. And that you carry that spark into your stories, into your writer's life, as a constant, burning flame, and that . . ." But before she finishes her sentence, the group is up, being pulled in one direction or another. This is how the kids at Willy Wonka's chocolate factory must have felt.

I'm overwhelmed with options, so, two at a time, I climb the narrow steps in the center of the room and find myself in a large, extremely bright white space. If the main room was organized and intentional, this area is definitely not.

On the floor are hundreds of storage boxes, scribbled with black marker on the sides in a nice uppercase, bold font.

"Photos . . . Agent wish lists . . . Rejection letters . . . Articles that make me smirk," I read to myself, finally taking in a deep, relaxing breath. Although this room is chaotic, I have to admire Betty Quinn and her life's work—I can't imagine all she had to endure to write so many books. I can't even write one story, let alone many.

I open a rejection letter, the paper soft, preserved in time.

Dear Ms. Quinn,

Thank you for sharing your manuscript THE HOUSE OF LOVE. Unfortunately, after careful review and consideration, I will have to step aside. I didn't love the voice as much as I'd hoped. That said, the story has promise, and I wouldn't be surprised if I end up kicking myself for letting this slip away, but for the time being I must pass.

> All the best,
> Sam Lawrence, Founding Agent
> Lawrence & Gilford Associates

And another one.

Dear Ms. Quinn,

I have read your recent submission and unfortunately, THE HEARTBREAKERS is not a good fit for me at this time.

Wherever you are on your writing journey, I wish you the best of luck with finding that one yes.

Take care,

J. S. Madison

Senior Agent

Apostrophe Literary Management

Dang. There are nine more where those came from. The letters I read are nice enough and professional, but rejection always hurts at first. Didn't Martin say *The Heartbreakers* went on to be one of her bestsellers? These letters are interesting to look back on now, given how successful her career was. Note to self: be resilient in your art and believe in yourself.

I tuck the letter back in and close the box lid. My nose twitches like a rabbit's; the space has a distinct scent, a mix of worn paper and something I can't quite place. Celery? I take several steps back just to see how far this place goes when suddenly we are all interrupted.

"Holy shit!" a voice calls out, frantic and loud.

In three more big steps I'm back by the door frame, staring out to the main room.

"Is this for real? This can't be real." The voice again, with a hint of panic.

"Language!" Dr. Tien responds, climbing up the stairs to Martin.

"What's going on? Are you okay?" All the cool and calm composure fades as Dr. Tien stands next to Martin.

Martin flails his hands in the air before finding his words. "I—I found something in this book." He peers down at the table, avoiding all the anxious eyes on him.

"What do you mean? Something? What something?" Dr. Tien huffs out.

"Maybe ten thousand dollars, easy. Give or take?" he says, holding up a black book, its insides hollowed out, in one hand, and a shitload of cash in the other. "Actually, I'm gonna say more than ten? This is really heavy." His hand bobs and the bills undulate in the air.

"Gotdamn!" Someone exclaims what we're all thinking.

Martin lets the book fall out of his hand, which makes a soft thud on the table. Then he drops the cash, which lands with authority.

"Wait, there's something stuck in between the bills." He thumbs through the wad again, which makes a rainbow in the air, before pulling out a small piece of faded blue paper. "'My first advance,'" Martin reads. "There's a heart and a *B* and *Q* on it too. 'See what you can do with it in this economy.'" He holds up the note like a shield.

Whispers fill the room. Beads of sweat begin to gather on Dr. Tien's brow, and by the *Lord of the Flies* energy that's building, I'd say she's got about twenty seconds to gather control before the class erupts into chaos.

"Google says Betty's first advance was super low—she spoke about this in a few interviews." Gina holds up her phone as if we can see the screen—we can't, but the group nods in agreement. Gina taps on her phone again. "Her first advance was only seven thousand dollars. Probably what you're holding there."

The whispers turn into maximum volume, voices over voices trying to decipher what this means. Why would Betty have left the amount of her first advance in an empty book? Is it a statement or advice about not being discouraged? Before she died, she was making Nora Roberts money. With the agility and speed that I would expect from an Olympic athlete, Dr. Tien has her hands on the book and the cash.

"All students, outside. NOW. Morning session is canceled. I'll see you this afternoon," her voice commands. She puts the cash back in the book and closes the cover.

"Wait, why? I don't get it," another anxious voice calls out.

Gina blinks rapidly. "Because something's not right—there are too many strange things happening here."

My stomach falls, and my heartbeat begins to pick up. *Strange* is one way of putting it. Exciting and exhilarating is how I'm framing this quest. Betty's left us more than crumbs, and I'm catching them. There's a draft out there waiting to be found. We're playing Betty's game. I plan to win.

Chapter Thirteen

The afternoon yoga session gets canceled because half of our class thought they would have enough time to take the BART train into San Francisco to try this pop-up boba shop and make it back by two p.m. Instead, they got lost and found themselves super south, in Daly City.

It's an unusually warm day, so Fern and I both retreat to our room to take advantage of the very free and very cold AC.

"What do you think they're gonna do with the cash? It's a lot of money, no? It's giving suspicious, it's giving unmarked bills, true crime kinda, sorta, in a way," I say. Fern and I both climb out of our outside clothes and change into something more relaxing before sitting on our respective beds. A tie-dyed shirt from middle school and spandex shorts for me, and a matching cream athleisure set for Fern. Then Fern layers it with a cut-off green flannel with a painted plant on the back to give them their edge.

"Dr. Tien is probably going to take the money and invest in Bitcoin or something."

"Nah." I roll up a white sock over my ankle. "She doesn't give me crypto vibes, but I could be wrong. We'll know if she comes to class tomorrow in an immaculately crispy new suit."

Fern nods, then heads to our fridge to grab a mini Coke, their afternoon drink of choice. This reminds me to also hydrate, so I take a very long sip from my very large and very loved Stanley cup, followed by a small bite of a cinnamon roll I took from the dining hall this morning.

"Betty Quinn," I mutter between gulps. "What do we really know about this woman?" I'm tempted to tell Fern what I discovered last night but forgot to mention once we got to sharing secrets.

Fern laughs, turning in their seat. "Eh. I've found money and treasures, even an old dime bag, inside of all sorts of tins and boxes in my abuela's house. Old people stash stuff. They're like squirrels, right? It's their preferred method. But then again, it is a lot of cash. But again, again, maybe it's a lot of cash to us brokies, but nothing for bestselling, award-winning Betty. The rest of the students are loving this, though. The talk is incessant."

At this, I turn in interest, placing the Stanley on my desk. "What is everyone else saying?"

"Oh, they're thrilled. I swear most of the students care more about unearthing her final manuscript than they do about the anthology now. . . ."

Fern comes in close, like others are around and they can't

possibly hear what comes next. "Folks are desperate to find it, even Dr. Tien."

"I've heard. Wild, right?"

Fern shrugs. "I don't even know if I believe it. I mean, I know she was old-school and wrote some of her novels on paper, but she didn't tell anybody where she put it? I refuse to spend this entire retreat running around aimlessly in the hope of getting praise from her fan club." Fern pauses and grabs their laptop. "We have writing to do. We are meeting with our partners soon, and I want to show mine something so I can get feedback."

Fern flips open their laptop, and immediately keys begin clacking frantically. I go to my desk to do the same, open my first document, and begin typing several ideas I've been thinking about:

- The first date of the alien couple—perhaps they are at an intergalactic carnival?

- Or, if it's for teens, focus on the daughter of the alien couple? She travels the galaxy looking for her first crush?

- Betty's got me thinking about clues ⇢ a detective? Falls in love with a suspect? I know that seems obvious but timeless. Maybe?

Chapter Fourteen

The next afternoon, Caleb and I decide to meet for a writing session in the Writers House, a two-story building with a wall of reflective glass and each room cleverly named after a romance writer. We reserved our space online and chose the Katherine Center room. Inside, the building is peacefully quiet and flush with a variety of blooming succulents, a beautiful space to write, no doubt.

I shuffle through the floors, admiring the students already inside, hard at work. At the door to our room, there's a picture of Katherine Center and some of her titles. Even I've seen books like *The Bodyguard* and *Hello Stranger* in our home library. I grab the handle, give it a turn, and find Caleb sitting at the large table, fiddling with a green Nature Valley granola bar. Today's shirt has a big Dominican Republic flag on the front, with holes scattered across the neckline like constellations in the sky, and baggy blue jean shorts paired with his black Crocs.

"Hey." He barely glances up.

"Hey," I mumble before sliding into the seat across from him, tossing my bag on the table. "You're bold, those bars are always like—" I pause as Caleb finally opens the wrapper and bits of grain explode through the air.

"Confetti?" he says, taking the word out of my mouth. His side of the table is covered with granola as he finally raises his head and offers me a piece.

"No thanks."

"I didn't poison it. Promise."

My eyes widen.

"Actually, pretend I didn't say that." Caleb doesn't wait for my response. Instead, his hand is a mini broom as he guides the granola confetti into his other hand. In a move that would frighten all teachers, he leans way back in his chair, extends his NBA-player arm, and drops the crumbs in the trash can by the wall.

I'm watching him like he's as fascinating as a new episode of *Housewives* (any franchise grabs my attention), and upon realizing that, I make my brain refocus, so I take out a new notebook and a pen.

"Writing by hand? Very Betty of you. I dig that." Caleb raises his eyebrows and pulls out his own notebook.

"Yeah, my mom says writing by hand is important in the early creative process." Shit. I brought up family.

Caleb nods. "My dad told me something similar."

The lights flicker once as we stare at one another. Why did I bring up Mom? That made him bring up his dad, and

I know in the backs of our minds we're thinking the same thing—beef. Family feud, and not the game show. Could we ever be more than enemies? Maybe frenemies? Something along those lines.

"The assignment sheet says we should do a writing sprint—are you familiar with sprints?" I'm sure he probably doesn't mean to sound condescending, but for some reason that's what my ears hear.

"Yes, Caleb, I'm familiar with sprints. My mom and I usually do fifteen minutes."

That's a lie.

A nice one, though. Mom and I have done exactly *one* writing session, a fifteen-minute sprint, where you write nonstop. My mom, being the achiever that she is, managed to write and go over her word count, whereas I wrote half as much and doodled in the papers' margins.

Caleb stares at me for a moment. "My dad and I usually do twenty."

"You do twenty-minute sprints?" I don't believe him.

"Yep. Six times a week." He holds my glare.

"You write six times a week?"

"Seven, if I'm really moved by my story."

"Be so for real."

"Why would I lie?"

If he's telling the truth, I'm seriously impressed. Even Mom doesn't write on weekends. At best, she'll brainstorm with incense burning and jazz playing on vinyl. And after her *think sessions*, as she calls them, I'm not supposed to talk to her for at least thirty minutes, so she can fully decompress before rejoining the world.

I clear my throat before speaking. "You're telling me you write six or seven days a week doing twenty-minute sprints?" I search for something in Caleb's face, a smile or a nervous twitch to tell me he's full of shit, but nothing gives.

He only shrugs. "Yep. Yeah, sometimes I do. When I'm really in a groove, that creative lane."

My eyes squint in disbelief; it's who I am. "Okay, go off. We love a productive king."

Caleb raises two fingers to his forehead to salute me.

"How long do you wanna sprint today? Long or short?" I ask, hoping he can't hear the nerves in my voice.

"I'm fine with whatever works for you. You down for twenty?"

I fake a smile. "Twenty works. I could even do twenty-five minutes." Lies. All lies. I don't even have a story idea.

"Twenty-five works. We could even do thirty if you want." He raises his eyebrows.

I nod and pretend to be into this even though the alarm in my brain is blaring code red. Thirty minutes of writing? That's not a sprint, that's a marathon. And I have not trained my brain for a marathon.

"Sure," I say anyway. "Sounds great."

Caleb grins and takes out his phone. "Awesome, I'll set a timer."

"Super awesome." Super awesome? Yeesh. Because there is nothing "super" or "awesome" about any of this.

I slide over my copy of *The Grapes of Wrath,* which I had in my bag, in an unpretentious manner, of course, and Caleb uses the thick book to prop his phone up. The changing numbers stare back at us, and honestly, they are frightening. Usually my writing practice, when I muster up the courage to try, involves me, loud music, angst, and more often than not a looming deadline. I haven't mastered that whole dedication thing. Not yet, at least.

"Ready? Here's a topic: outline a remake to your favorite love story."

I smirk. "Born ready." At this I should probably perish, because my responses have somehow turned me into my dad? I'm surprised that I don't shape-shift, so I begin writing to save myself from further embarrassment from . . . myself.

"All right, let's get it." Caleb starts the timer, determination all over his face.

My eyes dart to my paper. Okay, I can do this. Remember what Mom and Dad say—no bad ideas in a brainstorm. My favorite love story . . . okay.

Therefore, if so, de facto . . . um.

If I had to write a love story, I'd wanna write about . . . my greatest love, which is . . . food?

This is hard!

But not impossible.

I sneak a glance at the timer—twenty-nine minutes left?! Thankfully Caleb doesn't look up; his pencil is skating across his paper.

Maybe he wasn't bluffing about his sprints.

Head down, Macy. Eyes on your own paper.

Stories. I like stories.

Mine will need to be about . . . ?

Shit, I have no idea. What am I even doing here? I can't do this—no, I can do this. Positive self-talk. I just need a little time.

What I'm doing now, this is good, see. I'm taking the first step. Right? You have to start somewhere.

Somewhere over the rainbow.

Wow, really, brain? Stop it.

My eyes glance over at Caleb as he gives me a thumbs-up. I smile, because this is fine, more than fine.

This is me as a real writer.

Is this real writing? Because my paper is blank, and the thoughts in my brain are like a breakfast scramble, lots of ingredients jumbled together.

Another panic moment, and it's clear that I have nothing, so I start writing my name in cursive, challenging myself to keep the letters connected, one long flow. Which is, unbeknownst to me, tiring. If one hand needs a break, try the other! Isn't this good for my brain? Creating new synapses. Get it out, like the syllabus says. I make sure Caleb isn't watching and put my pen in my left hand, which is extremely foreign.

Because what the hell, I gotta do something, there's still twenty-two minutes left in this marathon. No way can I do cursive, not yet at least, so I start slowly, writing, of course, my name.

Macy Mariah—

"Um, pause." Caleb interrupts the chatter in my mind. Long arms reach over to stop the timer. "Are you writing with your left hand? Did you switch hands?"

"Wh-what? No, I—"

"Dude, you totally did. You were writing right-handed before."

"Well, that's because I'm . . ." Oh no, what's the word?

"Ambidextrous?" Caleb fills in.

I do my best to smile. "Yes, sometimes I am that. When I'm writing, I find it helps me think."

Caleb stands up. "You are a terrible liar." In three short steps, he's on my side of the table, hand out. "Show me what you wrote."

Quickly I grab my notebook. "Ugh, no. It's not ready."

"I'm your critique partner. It's my job to read it anyway." His hand becomes a claw as he attempts to grab my notebook.

"While that is mostly true . . ."

"Macy," Caleb demands.

"Ugh, fine. I switched hands. I'm very much only right-handed. And today the words are not coming. I have nothing. Besides, who willingly does a thirty-minute sprint?"

"I know—"

"What do you mean you know? What? *You* suggested thirty!"

"I didn't expect you to go with it." He pauses, hands in the air. "Here. If it means anything, I got nothing too." Caleb glides back to his side and holds up his notebook.

"Are you kidding me?" my voice shrieks.

"Okay but . . . it's low-key good."

He's right, it is good. It's definitely not writing, but for a quick portrait, it's very good.

He's drawn Monica and Quincy from *Love & Basketball*, which, I suppose, is a remix of a love story. Sort of. Damn him.

Caleb steps closer to me. "If you look closely, you'll see it's only one line."

"Stop." I crane my neck to get a better look. "This is exceptional."

"Now . . . my turn."

I hand over my notebook and wait for him to explode with laughter. Only he doesn't.

After a minute, he hands me back my work, or writing, or whatever I want to call it.

"Well. I'm sure this isn't what Dr. Tien or Betty Quinn had in mind," I mutter.

Caleb nods. "Yeah, this writer's block is going to ruin me."

"Writer's block?"

Caleb's face falls and everything goes sour. "Yeah. My talent is gone, and it's never coming back."

"I remember my mom had writer's block once, and she cried, full-on hysterics, for an hour, saying that she'd 'lost her gift,' and that 'she'd never write again,' and that her 'creative flame was barely a spark.' Dad immediately took me out to get ice cream, and when we came back, she had notecards and ideas and three of her beta readers on a Zoom call brainstorming something she said had come to her during her breakdown. She ate her melted cup of rocky road like nothing had even happened and wrote to her agent." I pause, thinking about that time. I must have been eleven; it was during their second marriage. So, is writer's block really terrible? All Mom showed me that day was that break*downs* tend to lead to break*throughs*.

Of course, I can't say that to Caleb now. He's probably not asking for a therapy session.

Actually, he's not looking at me at all.

"What?" I mutter.

Caleb's face is cold. "I thought we weren't talking about our families."

"We aren't. I—"

"But you totally did."

"I know—I did because I was trying to help you."

Caleb grabs his notebook. "I don't need your help."

"But you kinda do, though," I mutter, not loud enough for him to hear, but he glares at me anyway.

"Caleb, my bad. My intention wasn't to remind you of your mom by talking about mine, it just sorta happened."

"My mom loved rocky road too."

"Oh."

We sit in a painfully awkward silence. I pull out my phone and load up Betty Quinn's website to show him the book with the hidden message. "Wanna see something weird?" I offer as an olive branch.

Caleb stares for a moment, his mood shifting. "Oh, I know.

Martin showed me the website the other night." He pauses, clearly considering if I'm worthy of hearing more. He leans in, and I notice several freckles sprinkled across his nose. "Wanna see something even weirder?"

I nod, slightly afraid.

"Meet me in my dorm room in an hour."

Chapter Fifteen

After our session, I head back to my room to freshen up and dance to some loud '90s pop music before going to meet Caleb. Her ears must have been burning, her spidey sense activated at me doing something other than writing, because ta-da, there's a voice memo from Mom.

▶ ılııiltılıılılıılılllıılııılllılı

Hi, honey. I haven't heard from you in a while. That must mean you're very busy, right? That you're probably already finished with your first draft and you're deep in revisions? Haha. I know it's only been a few days. But that isn't to say that you can't finish a draft in a few days. You absolutely can. Again—discipline.

But that's not why I'm sending this message.

I wanted to let you know that I had dinner with Camille Lewis, you know Camille, we went to a new sushi restaurant down the street,

you would love it. We even got dessert, which you would also love.
Camille and I had some sake, which I never do, but I never get to
see Camille so, oh yes—we got to talking about you and writing,
and did you know her son Leo went to Penovation last year? He's
at Princeton now, pre-med, but he likes to write on the side. One
of those Michael Crichton types. Well, Camille passed on her son's
email address to me to give to you, in case you want to email Leo
and ask for tips for your final piece? Or maybe he'd be a good beta
reader? You can never have too many of those.

Okay, sweetie, I'm off to sign some back stock.

Keep me posted.

Rage begins to bubble inside of me—this woman is a piece of work. I've been here less than a week, and of course she's meddling—of course she's doing whatever she can so that I don't fail. Why doesn't she think I can do this on my own? My eyes close, and I try to exhale out all the red I'm seeing. Think of peaceful things—Rihanna's next album, Disneyland, Froyo—be calm within. If I need help, it won't be from her, or Leo Lewis.

Chapter Sixteen

"Hey, I'm here!" I knock on Caleb's dorm room on the second floor.

Once the door opens, I pause. Is this a big step in our frenemy-ship? My feet don't move. Entering his space is private and personal.

"Come in, come in. It's clean, I swear." He holds the door open, so I walk through the portal. It's like I've been given an all-access pass to the inside of boy world.

Hmph.

He's right, the room is clean. On purpose. Maybe he's the type to travel with a bottle of Lysol or a can of Clorox wipes. The furniture and setup are the same as mine, but the vibes, the energy? Completely different.

Caleb walks to the right side of the room and plops his phone down on the bed. On his side of the room, vinyl albums cover the wall—from artists like A$AP Rocky; Tyler, the Creator; Fela Kuti; and Missy Elliott, to name a few. The bed is made with a quilted light gray duvet with matching pillowcases, and on it is a yellow Pokémon Squishmallow that's obviously been cuddled by a stage-five clinger, based on all the lumpy spots.

A sleek black MacBook is half-open on his desk, next to a suspiciously straight row of blue ballpoint pens and one yellow Post-it that says, *You can, and you will,* with a heart next to it. And of course, his notebook. I'm a cultural anthropologist right now, giving everything an intense inspection. But I didn't say I was covert.

He watches me intently, then clears his throat. "My mom's. Her mantra that I've adopted," he says, nodding to the note.

My heart drops into my stomach.

"It's a great mantra."

He fakes a smile.

In two large steps, Caleb grabs Martin's desk chair. "Make yourself comfy, so we can . . . discuss."

He makes it sound so ominous, but I sit anyway.

Caleb stands by his bed frame, his long arms holding his body up. The science doesn't make sense, but his biceps flex and stretch his shirt hem.

Refocus, brain, refocus.

There's a scent. In the room.

Is it him?

It's not me—it seems familiar, and it's alluring and intoxicating, and I want to bottle it up—

"Macy, hello?"

95

I run a hand through the side of my hair. "Ah. Sorry. My thoughts. Sometimes, I feel like I have one, then two, then I . . ."

"Float away?" Caleb sighs, shifting his feet as he pulls out his desk chair. "That's my whole thing these days." He's gazing out the window as he speaks. I think he's about to say more when he abruptly stands up and closes the door.

He meets my eyes now with such seriousness my body stiffens. "I've heard some things. . . . With my writer's block, I probably won't win a spot in the anthology. But what if I—we—could potentially win an even bigger prize? About half of the students here already know about the message on Betty's site. The other half don't care. And maybe a fourth of the students have found what I'm about to show you."

Goose bumps cover my skin. "I'm suddenly afraid and yet intrigued?"

He nods. "There's . . . definitely something else going on."

Caleb takes out a black hardcover book from his bag.

"Here." He hands me the book. "Read the dedication. Then read the acknowledgments and tell me what you see."

My fingers wrap around the book. I hold it gently, like it's a baby. Quickly, I scan the cover, trying to remember what I've seen them do on *CSI*. The front is decorated in cursive font with gold lettering and small pictures of eyeglasses, magnifying glasses, and hearts. The book is called *Something Clever*, Betty Quinn's last published work, a YA novel about two teen journalists who realize they're competing for the same internship spot only *after* they've hooked up at a house party, printed a year ago. Pulled to find more, my fingers flip through the thick paper to the third page.

"Dedicated to the students of Penovation." I nod. Okay, not unusual—perhaps even to be expected; she was known to be generous to aspiring writers. A quick glance up, and I note Caleb widely grinning. I continue to inspect the book, a nice-sized thing of about four hundred pages, the distinct paper smell filling my nose, urging me to sit down, curl up, and read. My thumb finds the acknowledgments section, which is short, so I read it out loud:

" 'Beautiful Earthlings Could Love Ever Vanish Easily Reunite I Love Endings For They Teach How Everything Should Encompass Circular Returns Everything Thankful To Overcome Love Overcomes Vengeance Evermore.' "

I draw in a breath. Nothing clicks. "This . . . doesn't make any kind of sense."

"I'll give you some time. Read it again." Caleb's voice is soft.

My eyes scan the words, and I do my best to focus. "Honestly, the punctuation is the most annoying thing. Why is it like this? It's going to give me—" And that's when something appears. I think I see it, like one of those vanishing messages in special ink, or those trippy pictures that begin to swirl and move after your eyes stare at them for a while. I was obsessed with those in third grade. I blink rapidly to refocus.

Slowly, it appears, more pronounced and apparent than before. "Oh shit." My right hand digs in my backpack, searching for my pen and notebook. I can't unsee it now.

"What did you find?" Caleb asks.

"Each of the first let . . ." My voice trails off once I click my pen and turn to a clean sheet of paper. I take each capitalized letter and write it down. The message unfurls before me:

BE CLEVER I LEFT THE SECRET TO LOVE

Caleb hovers next to me, his chin practically on my shoulder. I can't help but notice how close we are. If this were any other situation, I'd give him a proper shove, but since we're suddenly in the middle of an episode of *Orphan Black*, I let him linger. He smells nice, so the proximity isn't all bad.

"I don't . . . 'Be clever I left the secret to love'?" Am I suddenly Sherlock Holmes?

Caleb wears a goofy grin, like we've won a million dollars. "Ding, ding, ding! You got it! She left the secret—for us." His arms flail in the air. "Here . . . like here!"

I rub my eyebrows. "Do you think this could be the manuscript?" I'm curious if Caleb remembers what he told me, Martin, and half of the students the other night about my parents at the bonfire.

"Gotta be, right?" Caleb's eyes toggle back and forth. "Well, I mean, that's what I think."

An exhilarating blend of excitement and nerves washes over me, and suddenly, for the first time since I got here, I'm a smidge eager to begin. I *need* to find that manuscript—I need the recipe Betty used to cook up forty romances if I want to get a book deal. Plus, I can figure out what my parents, Caleb's parents, and Betty Quinn have in common.

"What are you thinking? Now you're making *me* afraid."

I bite my bottom lip. There's so much adrenaline coursing through my body, I could run a marathon. At least a 5K. "My mom told me to leave this alone. But I'm thinking we need to get back to the library and find the remaining clues before others do. This manuscript could change our lives. I'm thinking we've got a mystery to solve, and you're just the person to help me."

Chapter Seventeen

▶ ılılılılılılılılılılılılılılı

Macy, it's mom again. Still haven't heard from you. I won't take you sending me to voicemail personally. Also, remember that it's personally, not personal. Your dad is wrong.

Camille and I had lunch again, this time Lebanese. Pretty good, you know I love anything with rice. She said that Leo said you haven't emailed him. Why not?

Email him, okay? Get as much help as you can. Plus, I don't want Camille thinking that we think we are too good for her help. Even though we might be.

Okay, I know you're doing a good job.

Bye.

Chapter Eighteen

A few days later, Dr. Tien, in flowy gold pants and a fitted gold jacket, claps her hands. "All right, everyone. Today's group lecture is going to be replaced with a little exploration. We're going to check out Betty Quinn's favorite writing space on campus. She, like many other authors in the area, loved to plan writing retreats here."

Around me, the group nods in anticipation.

The hike, which I call anything that has a slight incline or requires exerting more energy than my usual trot, to Betty Quinn's remote cabin takes about fifteen minutes on a mostly paved trail, then descends into a flat but unmarked gravel road. The trees seem to grow taller and the leaves become more abundant, nature really doing its thing. Every step we take lets me know that we are leaving one world and entering another. The sounds of the city are easily replaced with chirping birds, a light wind, and the rustling of tree leaves. Scenic and beautiful, no doubt.

"We're almost there, folks. Stay with me," Dr. Tien calls out, which is clearly directed toward me, as I've become the caboose of the train. Dad is right. I need to exercise more. Dr. Tien, on the other hand, even in a full Chanel suit, moves with grace and ease.

We arrive at a painted wooden sign that reads, *The Commune,* which is row of several small and aesthetically unpleasant cabins. Dr. Tien leads us to a larger and slightly more dilapidated one.

As a group, we form a circular blob in the middle of the path. I take two steps forward to get a better view.

Hmph.

This is a little . . . underwhelming?

I don't know why I was expecting something more glamorous? Functional? Built better? Like Toni Morrison's Hudson River home. I'd probably pump out masterpieces if I lived on the water too.

Fern steps to my left side and gently tugs my arm. "It's giving horror story, right? Tell me this isn't a crime scene. Is it even architecturally sound?"

All valid questions—questions that we the people deserve answers to.

"This can't really be the place she worked in up until eight months ago, can it?" I whisper back.

No bigger than four hundred square feet, the shack—I mean, cabin—with its old, faded wood, seems to wither under the weight of our stares alone. If I lived here, I don't know if I'd ever invite company over. But perhaps, for Betty, that was the point.

Dr. Tien claps eagerly, smiling all the while. "Because it's a tight fit, we'll go in about five students at a time. Give yourself a few minutes to peruse the space, write down questions you may have, think about the cabin perhaps as a setting for the perfect love story. Think about where you write and how that can affect your mood. Think about some of your favorite novels of Betty's or by others, then look at the stories' locations and see how they affect the plot. Let's spend a good amount of time reflecting, shall we? After, you'll debrief with your group." Several students make their way inside, and to the surprise of almost everyone, the cabin doesn't collapse.

"If I were an extremely wealthy, extremely prolific writer, I would definitely pick someplace more fun to write. Maybe I'd get a room at the Disneyland Hotel, and whenever I got bored, or the words weren't flowing like they should, I'd—bloop—go downstairs to the happiest place on earth." Fern grins at this.

"Can you swing a room for me too?"

It's almost our turn, but something in me still says not to go inside unless I want to end up on the five-o'clock news. After another moment, Dr. Tien waves us in.

When we finally cross the threshold into Betty Quinn's writing world, I'm speechless, eating a big bowl of my own words. The inside of the cabin is beautiful, with dark hardwood floors, antique fixtures, and wood furniture to match—a desk, a rocking chair, and two stuffed bookcases. To the left side of the room, there's a small kitchen with an actual wood-burning stove and a glass case full of antique china inside. Three students hover near Betty's writing desk, so I head into the kitchen, which has a rich lavender-and-honey smell, as if someone has been burning an expensive candle. Near the stove is a white cabinet that I can't resist opening. Once I do, I'm surprised by the variety of teas inside, from loose-leaf to old-but-functional tea bags in tin cans. My hands have a mind of their own, so I open the bottom drawer to find vintage teacups and saucers in an assortment of colors. A black kettle with gold trim stands out to me. Okay, Betty. You were a tea lover, like me. Respect.

Gently, I close the cabinet doors and make my way into the main room as other students circle behind me.

I find my way to Betty's desk, where there's an old, patchy green Underwood typewriter. Out of habit, I press a key and release the click heard around the world, or at least in this tiny room.

"Please don't actually use the typewriter," Dr. Tien cries out. My hand jerks back.

"Sorry," I mumble.

Betty Quinn's writing setup is a dream. Her desk is big and wide, no bells or whistles, nothing fancy, but it has everything one could need to write, well, forty plus books. Propped up are several dictionaries, an old quill pen, and even a copy of her first adult book, *The House of Love.* My fingers flip through the pages for a little peep.

Her fingers ran over the taut lines of his stomach muscles as he called out her name.

Instantly, my face heats up—*oh my*—also, mental note to grab a copy of that book.

"This is your final minute warning," Dr. Tien calls out to my group.

Sixty seconds. I do my best to take in the space, to find something that helps me make sense of the clues or, at least, why she's leaving the clues.

Dr. Tien does her infamous clap. "All right, let's head out."

I give the room one last glance, then I catch something on the opposite wall. The size of a small poster, eleven by seventeen at best. A sign, aluminum in blue and gold, that says *BE CLEVER.*

My eyes are stuck on the light cursive font.

Be clever.

And then it hits, all at once.

The acknowledgments!

BE CLEVER!

Not like actually *me* be clever, although that is always a good idea, but the sign.

My chest tightens as I take a step forward, closer to the wall and away from the front door, hyperfocused on the sign.

"Sorry. Time's up. The next group needs to come in," Dr. Tien barks.

I blink my eyes and burn this image into my brain.

There's something behind that sign, and the only way to find out what is to come back and see.

Chapter Nineteen

After two snack breaks, debriefing with my group, and having lunch, I text Caleb to meet me in front of the Writers House at sunset with his best spy gear. Minutes later, his eyes are wide as he approaches. I nod, speaking a silent language, because we know this rendezvous is about the clues. Why Caleb brought two flashlights—a large, earthquake-sized one and another thin one—to this retreat, I'm not sure. But he has them, as well as a peanut butter sandwich he must have taken and saved from the dining commons. I'm thankful for the flashlights because the path to the cabin is much more menacing and eerie at night.

We're only five minutes in and the walk seems more rugged than earlier.

Caleb grabs my wrist. "Wait, pause. Look up." He tilts his chin and I do the same. "The sky is so . . . perfect."

The stars are beginning to twinkle, and there's a sliver of a moon. The world seems to stop, everything silent. From the corner of my eye, I sense that Caleb is watching me. My chin betrays me, and I find myself turning to him. He's even more attractive up close. His skin glows, and his eyes are radiant. He's his own kind of light source that pulls at my heart. Strong.

A second passes, then another, and the moment has turned into a full-on staring contest.

"We should . . . we should keep going." The words barely escape my mouth, but if I stay here any longer, admiring the shape of Caleb's face, there could be trouble.

"Yeah, you're right. You cold?" He unzips his hoodie.

Wearing his clothes, burrowing myself into his scent, a citrus-and-wood combination that can affect one's judgment, would be double trouble. I shake my head no. Even though the air is crisp, I'm warm, flushed.

The closer we get to the cabin, the more I realize that, um, we don't really have a plan. This all seemed to make more sense in my head, moments ago. I was operating on a "return to the cabin, and it will all work out" kind of energy, but that's beginning to fade.

As we make our way to the front door, I grab the knob and give it a twist. "Shit. It's locked."

Caleb snorts. "Did you think a literary landmark like Betty Quinn's writing sanctuary would be left open?"

"Well, not when you put it like that. . . ."

"So, what do we do?"

"That, dear Caleb, is an excellent question." One that I don't have the answer to. I give the knob another turn for good measure. Still locked. "Do you have a screwdriver? Or a Swiss Army knife?"

"Are you being serious?" Caleb steps beside me. "I have none of those things. Do you?"

I throw up my hands. "I didn't think it was that wild of a question considering the flashlights!"

"Macy, how'd you think we'd get inside?"

"I don't know, a little breaking and entering?" I fake a laugh. But also . . . ? Desperate times call for desperate measures.

Caleb closes his eyes and, when he opens them again, smiles big. "Fine. Only a little. Not a lot of breaking and entering, just a modest amount. Let's check the back."

We scramble to the other side of the house, which has a door that is, of course, locked. There is an old window, with a small ledge for cooling pies, or perhaps placing a plant. On the tips of his toes, Caleb reaches his long arm to the bottom of the windowsill, where, after a couple of tries, there's movement.

"It's happening." He gives the window frame a back-and-forth shimmy as it wiggles up and open. Another inch and Caleb will be able to stick his hand underneath and push the window up enough for us to climb in.

"It's happening!" I repeat.

"Shhh." He puts a finger to his lips and holds up a high five with his other hand. I give it a slap, and he holds my hand. "We're doing this." His skin is nice. Soft. Warm.

"A modest amount of breaking and entering," I say. I pull

my hand back and stuff it into my pocket. My brain is going in two separate directions with Caleb—trying not to touch him now, and trying to figure out how to touch him again later.

After a moment, I refocus. "You've got to lift me up." I'm not really thinking of what that physically entails. "It's the only way."

Caleb's eyes and mouth twitch a bit as he runs through various calculations. Before either of us changes our mind, he's on all fours, tabletop position, transforming into a human stepping stool.

I stifle a laugh.

"Hurry, before I start thinking rationally."

In a swift movement, I step onto his back, jump up, and grab the small ledge. Caleb arches his spine, cat position, and gives me another inch. From somewhere inside of my body, my core muscles that I didn't know I had activate, and my muscles pull me up and over. Another burst of energy, and I find myself in the kitchen sink, then a quick roll and I've landed on the kitchen tile, standing upright, where I belong. From somewhere above, Betty Quinn must be watching out for me.

"You good?" Caleb whisper yells.

"I'm in!" I almost can't believe it. My eyes take a moment to adjust to the dark shadows and fading light. "Come to the front," I shout, hopefully not too loud. I hear Caleb's feet shuffle as I move through the house.

With a quick motion, as if this is my house, my hands

unlock the door. There's Caleb, standing, one arm grabbing the top of the doorframe, smirking.

"Boy, if you don't hurry in before anyone sees us." I reach for his arm and pull him inside.

"Who is gonna see us? Everyone's at that poetry slam." Caleb twirls on his feet as I lock the door behind him.

Oh right. The slam was part of Fern's summer of yes. I'll make it up to them. But also, "Didn't you *shhh* me earlier?"

He steps near me and throws up his hands. "I don't know the rules. I've never done crime before."

"Neither have I!"

"Another thing we have in common."

We pause for a moment, making eye contact that warms my body.

Inside this bubble, we might as well be the only two people left on the planet.

Caleb extends an arm, practically grazing my face. "Excuse me," he mumbles, softly touching my ear and flicking on the lamp behind me.

The cabin begins to glow.

"Oh yeah."

Lights. Electricity. Being able to see would be good. Even though the old lamp does a pretty poor job of illuminating the space, it'll have to do.

Because we are way too close yet again, I take a step toward the middle of the room and point. "There. Right there."

BE CLEVER. The poster glares back at us.

"You think this is connected to the acknowledgments?" he asks.

"I mean, there's only one way to find out."

Without another thought, I pull the chair from Betty's desk and bring it to the wall.

"Kind sir, would you care to do the honors? I mean, I did technically break in, so you doing the inside lifting only makes this fair, right?"

Caleb crinkles his nose like a bunny. "The logic is a little off, but it'll do for now."

"Good, good. Up we go."

Caleb could be a ballet dancer as gracefully as he moves. Effortlessly, he lifts the frame off the wall. He twists an outstretched arm, and I grab the sign, which is covered in a thin layer of dust. Gently, like it's glass, even though it is canvas, I place the *BE CLEVER* sign on the small table near the desk.

Caleb steps down from the chair, and we both stare at the now-empty spot. Our eyes go to the discoloration on the wall. The frame has left its mark, a white square that almost resembles a door.

"Should we see if . . ." My voice is shaky. I'm curious but I'm also afraid. "If something is behind the wall?"

Caleb steps back up, taking his time as he lightly gives each plank a push. The first three don't move, but then, one springs back.

"Holy . . . ," he says.

I move closer, doing my best to understand the hidden space. The wall goes from off-white to black, a small opening about the size of a shoebox. The perfect hiding spot if you needed one.

"Reach inside!"

Caleb's eyebrows scrunch together. "You want me to stick my hand in there? What if there's bones or a mousetrap or something?"

Fair point. I grab one of Caleb's flashlights and turn it on, giving the mystery space a new spotlight.

"You've got to come closer," Caleb says, waving me toward him. He holds out a hand and I take it, stepping onto the small chair, our legs and bodies practically entangled.

I do my best to steady the light. "Okay, be brave," I say. Caleb stares at me for some type of approval that what we are doing is, in fact, not insane, or at the very least, not against retreat policy. I have to fake a smile because, let's be honest, I have no idea what we're doing. But I'm having fun anyway.

"Be brave," he mumbles back. Then he just goes for it, his hand disappearing into the hole in the wall.

After a beat, his eyes widen. "Oh shit," he mutters.

"What? What?" Adrenaline pumps through me as I step down from the chair. He follows me, a thin black binder in hand, which he waves in the air.

"Light," Caleb instructs me as he squats down. I point the flashlight at the floor.

We're silent for a moment, too stunned to actually speak. We are indeed looking at something intentional, something left behind by Betty Quinn. I guess we were actually clever.

It's a thin, half-inch binder that appears to be a hundred years old, the leather sturdy but worn.

Find me here, the front reads, in a big, beautiful cursive font along with the letters *B* and *Q.*

Caleb looks up at me, his face full of wonder. "Is this real? Am I dreaming?"

I nod. "This is really happening."

If ever there was a moment to stop, turn around, change our minds, take a new path, this would be the time, right? Are we invading this deceased woman's privacy too much?

Instead, I bite my bottom lip. "We have to open it."

"Agree," Caleb says, but he doesn't move.

Slowly, I do the honors. I lift the leather, and the pages are soft, the most delicate tissue paper.

"What is this?"

Caleb and I stare at one sheet of paper inside a plastic protective sheet. Numbers. Lots of organized numbers. Looks chaotic but—

"I bet these are GPS coordinates," Caleb infers.

My mouth falls open.

"Do you think they lead to her secrets? Why would she leave them in a binder in her cabin?" I ask.

Caleb and I are so immersed in our confusion and wonder that the sounds from outside, the footsteps, beat in our ears, startling us. We aren't alone. Someone is coming, and they are close. Very close.

Faint traces of an outside light source peek through the window into the cabin.

Caleb points to the binder. "Quick, take a picture of this."

My hand shakes, but without a word I do my best to take several photos of the numbers. Caleb is suddenly Spider-Man, scooping up the binder, leaping onto the chair, and hanging the *BE CLEVER* sign back as if we weren't just here. When he hops down, I return the chair to the desk and turn off the lamp.

"Out the back," I whisper, and he nods, already two steps into the kitchen.

Except my feet are moving in the opposite direction, toward the window and the sound. I have to know. I have to see. I crouch down at the window and lift the smallest portion of the bottom curtain. I can't make out the face that's approaching.

"Come on, come on," I mumble.

"Sssskkkt. Macy. Back here, let's go," Caleb whispers through gritted teeth. He's right, I should go, I should move, but—

"I . . . they're near, and if I can see them . . ." *Show yourself.* "Dr. Tien?"

In a matching Fear of God Essentials sweat suit, no less.

I slip into the kitchen and out the back door as keys unlock the front door to the cabin.

"Macy," Caleb whispers, hand on my arm. "Run."

Chapter Twenty

We don't think. We move, quickly. We're down the hill and through the twists and turns of the path faster than I've ever moved. Every step I take, all of my muscles are burning, pulsing, aching for me to stop. But Caleb keeps pushing, so I do my best to hang on even though my legs are on fire.

When we reach the main campus, I'm sweating like I've been in a steam sauna for an hour, not to mention heaving. Caleb is breathing softly, unaffected by the sudden marathon we've just run.

At the first bench I spot, my body flops down, and I wait for my lungs, which have melted, to save me from the lactic acid buildup in every possible part of my body. I'm pretty sure that a quick run, an easy jaunt, shouldn't leave the average seventeen-year-old this . . . *breathless.*

Caleb turns to face me. "Who did you see? Well, it doesn't

matter who was there. Others are catching on. That means we aren't the only ones playing."

"Dr." It takes everything in me to utter a syllable. "Dr. Tien." Oxygen. Need oxygen. I hold up a finger; I need a moment to catch my breath. At this rate, it'll take me a day or two to properly recover.

Caleb tries to fuse my thoughts together. "Okay, so let's think this through. Martin gabbed about the manuscript. Other students have found the clues, which is to be expected. The front of the binder said, *Find me here*, so, Betty must have wanted us to find something at these locations. Dr. Tien showing up is a little odd, though, right?"

My head bobs as another deep inhale steadies me.

"A lot odd. Or, maybe she's a superfan and knows Betty left behind something extra juicy," I finally say.

Caleb seems genuinely concerned for my well-being, which is sweet, and also a wake-up call. He pats my shoulder. A kind coach. "We'll get you to exercise a bit more. This campus has a beautiful trail and indoor track."

"Absolutely not. Don't even think about it. That was, you know, simply surprising for my body. Usually I can exert energy, if I know about it in advance. You need to give my body a warning. Three to five business days."

Caleb raises his eyebrows in a manner that makes me think maybe I stumbled into a sexual joke. Is his mind in the gutter, or is mine?

I pull out my phone and Caleb swoops in and grabs it.

"Wait, what are you doing?" I ask.

"Putting a reminder in your phone. Call me when you wanna exert energy." He waggles his eyebrows.

If I could disappear, now would be the time. I can't flirt when I literally can't breathe.

"What?" Caleb says all nonchalant.

"I didn't mean to insinuate—"

"That we should be more than critique partners?"

Our hands brush as he hands me my phone back. I clear my throat. "The pictures."

Caleb laughs from somewhere deep in his belly, which makes my skin tingle. I never knew a laugh could be so exciting to my senses.

But the moment is cut entirely too short as a stampede of students run by.

"Come on, come on!" someone yells. It's almost impossible to make out any of the voices. As one student zooms by, two more follow suit. "The clock tower—it's happening." A hand reaches out for Caleb as it flies by equally fast.

Caleb stands. "I think I'm gonna go check it out. I heard there's some ritual, might involve some streaking, might involve some dancing. Hopefully no singing. I thought it started around midnight, but this works too. Join me?"

"Tempting. Very tempting." Which is totally true; this is the summer of yes and all. But there are other pressing issues. "I think that I want to see what happens when I search these numbers, see what I find."

"I get it. Text me? Keep me in the loop?"

I place three fingers to my forehead. "Scout's honor." By the time my fingers are off my face, he's gone, running with another group of flailing arms and loud sounds.

I get up, turning toward the dorm. "Well, this mystery isn't going to solve itself."

Chapter Twenty-One

With everyone out running around campus partially clothed, the dorm hallways are eerily quiet. I've gotten so used to seeing different faces at literally any time during the day that when no one is around, the silence is shockingly loud.

In a move that has become so familiar, I grab my keys and unlock our door. Fern isn't in our room, which makes me feel a little lonely.

But I flip open my laptop, turn to a fresh sheet of paper in my notebook, and pull up on my phone the picture we took when we were FBI-level secret agent spies.

"All right, Betty Quinn. What are these locations you've left, hmmm?"

46.6794538, 7.8644132

37.7871844, −122.4074346

37.8642161, −122.4587593

37.8646099, −122.3018278

39.9072312, 116.4304934

37.8902531, −122.2558409

34.0419994, −118.2354169

36.6178945, −121.9014569

49.2420938, −123.1137812

40.7225526, −73.9882959

I stare at the numbers for a moment before my phone buzzes.

Caleb: Update. Clock-tower shenanigans aren't really my vibe. I turned around immediately after arriving. What was I thinking?

I have to smile.

Macy: I don't know. What were you thinking?

Caleb: That you were better company.

I pause for too long.

Caleb: I'm about to look up the locations.

> **Macy:** Same. I'll do the top half. You do the bottom?

Caleb: Bet

There's something about the first time you text a person. It's like the first time you hold hands or something. There's a vibe and flow to it—there's gotta be a compatibility there, or nothing will work. So far, I'm into the way this boy texts.

With the first location in Google, the return makes me frown.

> **Macy:** First spot is someplace in Switzerland

Caleb: I got a place in Berkeley

> **Macy:** That's promising. Right?

Caleb: It's def closer

> **Macy:** Next spot is in San Francisco

Caleb: Oooh. Dat's fancy. Next spot I have is in Los Angeles.

> **Macy:** Ah. My next one is in Belvedere.

Caleb: The local spots could make for interesting dates

Macy: 💀

Caleb: Okay, this one is near campus—I think one of the lookout points

Macy: She's so international. Must b nice. another one for Berkeley

Caleb: This next spot must be old? Wrong? From the street view, it's a dilapidated building. Seen better days.

Macy: So, you're saying we should go there first?

Caleb: Absolutely.

Macy: I got one in China.

Caleb: Tres bizarre.

Macy: I don't get her.

Caleb: Me either. But maybe that's the point.

Macy: Maybe there's no point.

Caleb: I don't know about all that. Road trip romances are fun, even mini ones.

Caleb: What do you say? Tomorrow afternoon? We check out a couple of these spots?

My phone flies through the air and lands on the other side of the bed as I squeal. Taking this partnership so off campus feels intimate, romantic even. Not that he can see me, but I need a minute to compose myself.

Macy: Sure, after class works.

Caleb: Cool. I'll see you tomorrow, bright and early.

It's not a date after class, per se. But I stare at our text message exchange for a little bit too long. One, because how cliché would it be to find romance at a romance writing retreat with your rival? I may not read romances, but I've watched enough movies to understand the basic beats and tropes.

After my mind cools down, I put the locations in alphabetical order, hoping to see a pattern, but nothing reveals itself. Only addresses for different places around the world.

Betty's favorite places?

More writing spots?

Vacations she took with ex-lovers?

My thoughts are spinning in my brain when Fern busts in the door, glitter on their face, their curly hair wild and free, breathing in a way that can only be described as panting.

"Are you okay?" My first instinct is to mom mode it.

Fern shakes their head no. "I've been running around.

Profound life discoveries." Fern moves through the room like a wrecking ball, bumping into the furniture. After a moment, Fern throws up a hand and takes a long drink from their water bottle, then kicks off their shoes and flops on the ground.

"Let's debrief. Should I go first, or do you wanna go?" Fern asks.

"You go first. I haven't been up to anything." Okay, not entirely true. Caleb and I did break into Betty's cabin and find a list of locations she left behind, but honestly, I can't go around volunteering that information, now, can I? Incriminate my roommate over a misdemeanor? Better not.

Fern is one with the carpet, their arms and legs outstretched like a starfish, face staring at the ceiling. "After dinner, there was a night hike with s'mores after—s'mores are big here."

"Yummmmm."

"Yeah exactly. I had three of them."

"I would have eaten twenty."

"Ta, that's absolutely my plan. Every night I plan to eat at least five."

"I've got to catch up." Giggles escape our mouths.

"I wanna Veruca Salt those damn s'mores. But anyways, I'm there, getting my s'mores on, when a group of kids I don't know, I think one was called Eden and another George? They start saying something about Betty—you know what I mentioned before."

I nod.

Fern lifts their head off the ground an inch. "Okay, good.

124

Good. So, apparently there are benches around campus that are donated by, you know, people who do that kind of thing."

"Folks with money or whatever."

Fern waves a hand in the air. "Yes, exactly. Those kinds of people. Eden said that she and George were randomly sitting on a bench and guess who it was donated by?"

"Betty Quinn?"

"Betty 'here's a random clue' Quinn." Fern leans up on their arms. "And guess what else?"

"What?"

"There's an inscription."

Of course there is.

Fern shakes their head and continues, "George chimes in that the inscription alone doesn't mean anything, it's two words . . ."

"What words?"

"Ugh. I forgot already. But George says that he and Eden started exploring campus, and they found more benches donated by Betty Quinn. With more phrases. They weren't able to check out all of campus because a *90 Day Fiancé* marathon came on, but they did confirm that there are more benches around campus, should you want to find them . . ."

"Wait, which one? Which marathon?" A slight digression, but an important detail.

"*Before the 90*, then *The Other Way*."

"I respect it."

"Same. But I didn't even get to the big news!" Finally, Fern stands. I follow, stretching my arms up to the air and twisting my back, the lactic acid settling in my muscles. If tonight's little run leaves me sore, I'm seriously going to be pissed at . . . myself.

"Tell me."

"So, I went to the little clock-tower thing, which, by the way, was kinda hot. Did you know that people were going to be streaking in their underwear?"

"Did you streak? No judgment, I just need all the details."

"Duh. Does that surprise you?"

I think for a moment. "Actually, no. Not at all."

"Excellent. I see you seeing me, roomie. Honestly, clothes are overrated. And probably not great for the environment. I'd love to walk around here in our birthday suits but, you know, decorum or whatever."

"Or whatever." We both laugh.

"At the clock tower, while in my undies, I start to ear hustle."

"As one should. And?"

Fern is drawing out the suspense. "Martin." A sly smile covers their face, the corners of their lips practically touching their ears. "Martin thinks he found the location of the missing draft."

Chapter Twenty-Two

"Today, we are writers," I declare as Caleb holds open the door to the Jane Austen room for me. This morning we've been given time to write with our critique partners. Which is good, considering our last unproductive doodle session.

"We are writers today." Caleb takes the seat near the window, and I sit across from him. We pull out our notebooks and place them on the table. Unlike the energy we gave each other during our previous writing attempt, our vibe now is . . . dare I say, friendly? Flirty? We are on the edge of something—the nerves doing cartwheels in my stomach tell me so.

Caleb grabs the pen from behind his ear and lifts his head, chin high, before speaking. "Okay. Should we . . . ?"

"Be realistic and . . . start small? Maybe a little brainstorm first? What are you working on?"

Caleb's face instantly tightens, but then, with a small exhale, he relaxes. "I think I have an idea. It's not the best I've ever come up with, though."

I hold up my index finger. "Aht, aht. We just have to write. Nothing needs to be perfect, not yet." I pinch my lips together. Oh my gosh, I sound like Mom.

This cheerleading seems to land with Caleb, because he lets out a teeny grin—I've been noticing that a lot more with him, small smiles that are both infectious and sorta make me melt a bit. Not that I want to make him smile, but I like it when he does.

We lock eyes. "Okay, well, in that case, I was thinking about time travelers. Well, I always think about time travel. . . ." Caleb looks up to gauge my expression. To be a good partner, critique or otherwise, is to be supportive.

"Okay, yes, we love characters with range." I nod and mean it. Every writer needs that little bit of inspiration, that spark, to light the flame and get things started. "Also, no judgment, but what do you mean you *always* think about time travel? How are you defining *always*?"

Caleb laughs, which is also contagious. Then he bites his top lip. "Probably more than I should say without embarrassing myself. I dunno. I guess I'm stuck here in the present . . . wanting to change things about my past . . . wishing for a time machine or whatever. There are some things in my life I wish I could go back and do differently, you know?" He pauses again. "And what's your idea?"

One quick pick at my fingernail. I ask the questions, and Caleb always provides the answers. He's so ready to be vulnerable and open. I admire that about him. His openness makes me nervous because that means I've gotta reciprocate, but we are critique partners. So, I understand the assignment.

"Promise not to laugh." A warning never hurt anyone.

"Cross my heart." He bats his long eyelashes.

"I've been thinking about what I should write for the anthology since day one. I considered taking on the alien story. Scrapped that. Then I started envisioning a girl with some type of truth serum but couldn't figure out where I wanted the romance to go. Where people have to be super honest with her. Painfully honest. Something like that has always intrigued me."

Caleb's eyes narrow. "Go there. Start there. Who would you want to use the serum on first?"

In real life? My mom, obviously.

"I'm not sure . . . ," I say instead. I mean, I'm only kinda sure. "If only I had a truth serum." I sigh. "How about we do a ten-minute sprint?" I offer, to steer the conversation away from a potential family discussion. Not a deflection, because I would never. But because I want to try to write. I think. *Try* being the key word.

"Ten minutes of writing. Our stories."

"No drawing."

"Using our dominant hands."

At this, we are both cheesing, so hard my cheeks could fall off. Caleb whips out his phone, and the numbers on the clock stare back at us.

"Let's do this," I offer, ready to actually give today's writing my best go. Caleb nods, he hits start, and we begin.

My pen meets the paper, and it takes me a moment to figure out where to go from here. I'm the last one in the race, but I begin. Slowly at first, each word afraid to leave me, but eventually, the seconds roll into minutes, and the words spill out and onto the page. I let my characters, a teen detective from Ohio trying to figure out how her childhood best friend ended up with a concussion, and her crush, an egotistical-yet-attractive hockey player, find themselves on an ice-skating rink. Scratch that. Let's make her a persistent sports journalist for their high school newspaper, the *Oaks Grove Gazette*. That ties together more, right?

Now our budding *journalist* and the popular jock—who is a foreign exchange student from Toronto—need each other for a multitude of reasons. She could use him to follow leads. He could prevent her from learning the role he played in his teammate's head injury and blasting him in the paper. And as long as they avoid each other, there's no risk of accidentally revealing how much they like each other. Does it make sense? Not entirely. But is this fun? Hell yeah.

Today's writing reminds me of baking cookies. When we started, I wasn't sure if I'd added enough ingredients, if I'd even mixed everything together right. But when the timer goes off, I look down at my words, and my cookies are edible! I even think I could have spent more time in this sprint. Maybe not twenty more minutes, but definitely five. Okay, maybe three.

Caleb peers up at me, relieved. "Well, how'd you do?" He does a quick turn and dives into his backpack, and I don't know why I'm surprised, but homeboy pulls out Flamin' Hot Cheetos. "Only god can judge me." He raises his eyebrows before swiftly opening the bag.

"The writing actually went, dare I say . . . well?" Caleb pours the remaining bits of his second breakfast down his throat. "Also, are you good? Cheetos this early? You're asking for a stomachache."

"I forgot I had them in my bag, and the moment I saw them, I knew I had to reward myself."

"Meaning?" I lean over the table, doing my best to sneak a peek. Sure enough, there's writing. Lots of writing.

"Well. I wrote. Which is something." He wipes the chip dust from around his mouth. "Ramon and Belinda, two vigilante time travelers, disagree about where to go and who to save next—her ex or the foster parent who kicked them out as kids. Both are in danger, but they only have enough gas in their machine for one mission. . . ." I nod. "So, they have to decide whose mission to complete."

"Oh dang. How will they choose?"

"Haven't gotten that far . . . *yet*. But I know the guy doesn't want her back with her ex."

"Love. Who can deny what the heart wants? But yes, this is good. You're on track with the syllabus, and you're exploring new story ideas. This is progress—we will finish these stories by the time we leave!" My hand goes up and Caleb gives me a high five, one with heat, because our hands stay in the air, his eyes steady, the room suddenly much warmer than before.

My phone buzzes on my desk, snapping us out of our trance.

"My mom," I say when I peep down at the screen. "Do you mind?"

Caleb shakes his head and I listen to Mom's message.

▶ ılıılıltlılıtltlılıtltlılıtltlıltlılı

Macy, it's Mom.

Just a little message to remind you to stay focused. I was thinking, maybe it wouldn't hurt if I sent you a list of books to read to help with your writing? You know that good writers are voracious readers, right? So, maybe I'll send the books through overnight shipping. Oh, wait, I'm sure there's a library there. I can email you a list, a very good list. Yes, I can do that. Promise me you'll go to the library and check out my list.

Okay, I know you're doing an amazing job.

"You good?" Caleb asks.

Impeccable timing, this woman. I close my spiral notebook, my creative bubble popped. The rest of the words to my hockey mystery romance will have to wait. "Yes. No. I don't know. It's my mom calling to check in, make sure I'm on task, kinda annoying." My eyes roll an extra second or two for emphasis.

I'm on task, Mom, I'm on task.

I jump to my feet. "We've written a bit, but now it's time."

"Time for what?"

"To check out a spot on Betty Quinn's list."

Chapter Twenty-Three

Two hours later, Caleb and I find ourselves at the San Francisco spot on Betty Quinn's sorta secret, definitely confusing mystery list of locations after taking a rideshare from campus.

Well, we think we are here. It's not like there's a sign that says, *Betty's clue.* Martin may have found the missing manuscript, allegedly, but I didn't want to call off this outing, and neither did Caleb. I kinda like his company.

I glance from my printout from Google Maps to the large, busting building in front of me, then back to my paper. Yes, I have my phone, but for some reason the printed map made the road trip–mystery combination more official.

"Are you sure this is it?" Caleb does a quick spin on his heels. We are in a high-traffic area. The number of people around us keeps swelling, a growing balloon. The city smells like a mix of popcorn and hot trash.

I shrug. "This is what the internet says."

"Well, if the internet says it's true, then it must be true."

From behind us, a horn blares, and a cable car bell rings. We're in downtown San Francisco—Union Square, to be exact—which is loud and energetic.

"I don't get it. What could be here? Why this very busy tourist destination?" Caleb mutters, shaking his head in his new neon-green San Francisco T-shirt. The first trinket shop we saw, of which there are thousands in this area, he popped in, bought the shirt, and changed. The shirt is his vibe, no doubt. I wouldn't pay twenty-five dollars for it, but I also don't collect T-shirts from places I've visited. Didn't mind the quick peek at his abs, though.

"I guess we'll find out."

"But the Cheesecake Factory?"

Caleb tilts his head back, peering all the way up at the never-ending building. I do the same. The bright lights at the top seem like they could be painted in the sky.

"Shall we?" he asks. But we both already know the answer. We're too deep in this thing to stop now. Betty might have said that we're too clever to let it go. The only way is forward, or, in this case, up.

"Full disclosure," I say as we face one another. "I've never eaten at a Cheesecake Factory before."

Caleb's hands are on my shoulders. "What? Have you not lived in America for like your life? Who among us hasn't been to the Cheesecake Factory? Tell me you're lying."

Intentional or not, this makes me laugh. "I don't know. It's never been my thing. Never thought I'd be into it."

"Never been your thing?" Caleb bends at the knees, like he might collapse on the ground. "Cheesecake Factory is, universally, everyone's thing. That's the restaurant's whole vibe—being for everyone."

I fake a smile that he doesn't buy.

"Okay, come on. Immediately. *Immediately.* We must rectify this now."

Which is how we find ourselves on the eighth floor. As soon as we step off the elevator, I'm taken aback by what's in front of me: big windows and a 360-degree view of the city. From this height, the world looks magical, absolutely unreal.

The wonder of this place must be dripping off my face, because the hostess at the front booth beams like she lives for catching this expression from Cheesecake noobs.

"First time at this location?" she says, grabbing two very large menus.

I nod, and she types something into a small computer and then motions for us to follow her.

"Then I've got something special for you. Right this way. One of the best seats in the house." We walk through the restaurant, passing low orange lights and other tables with patrons.

She stops at a table right in front of an expansive window. "I know I'm biased, but I think this is the most romantic view in the city." Caleb glances up at me as she places our menus down on our plates. She may be right. Maybe this is what Betty Quinn wanted us to witness. She was, after all, writing a guidebook on love. I could see "watch the sun go down from the Cheesecake Factory window" being one suggestion.

I inhale another view of the city, the many different shapes and sizes of the buildings, the people small as ants, and of course, the deep blue water that meets the shore.

"This is absolutely insane." I lean toward Caleb for confirmation that we are both enjoying this experience, but his face is blank. "Um, what just happened? Are you okay? Blink twice if you're alive?"

Caleb kinda blinks. "Yeah. No. I . . ." His bubbly energy from moments ago is gone. He's been replaced by an alien lookalike. This Caleb seems so distraught and downtrodden I don't know what to say; no joke can get me out of this. I stare in silence, first out the window, then down at the menu, and then back out the window.

Several moments later, our server, an older gentleman with a sick mustache that spirals at the ends, stops at our table to get our drink orders. I go for the strawberry lemonade, and Caleb sticks with water. A quick spiel of the specials and then our server disappears. He circles around his section and returns moments later with a basket of bread for the table, and we place our orders. I glance at Caleb, thinking surely carbs will excite him, but they don't. Instead, I grab a large hunk of the brown bread and smoother it with cold butter.

"Holy ships," I mutter, mouth full of food. This bread is delicious. Fantastic? Explosive? A taste sensation inside of my mouth. If Caleb weren't here, I'd take his piece and devour it expeditiously, but I refrain.

But alien Caleb is still so silent. He furrows his brow, deep in thought, and his eyes stare at the white plate in front of him.

I take a piece of the sourdough bread and add more butter, not breaking his trance.

Caleb stays in the sunken place, and after a moment, he finally speaks. "Sorry, I'm just in my head."

"I can tell." I push the basket toward him. "Eat. Food. Food always makes it better. Plus, aren't you like habitually hungry? Where's the Caleb I've grown to adore, and what have you done with him, bad replica?" I should be embarrassed at this admission, but Caleb is rather adorable.

Caleb reaches for the last piece of brown bread and puts it on his plate. "Can we speak about our families? I wanna be able to tell you things."

I swallow and nod.

He gives an appreciative nod back. "When my mom first started chemo, we were at the hospital a ton, which happened to be near a mall that had a Cheesecake Factory in it. So, we kinda tried to make the chemo fun, make the outings fun, and we set a goal to try everything on the menu, at least once." He grabs the plastic book and gives it a wave.

"How far did you get?" I can barely ask.

"Ha!" Finally he lets out a real Caleb grin. "Not far at all. Mom is, um, I mean, was, such a creature of habit. She'd always say she wanted to try new things, but nah. Once she found something she liked, she'd only order that."

Caleb takes a quick sip of his water, the life coming back

to his eyes. "I, on the other hand, loved the idea of tasting everything. I got to be like one of those food influencers. I got pretty far in the menu before . . ." His face falls again as he continues, "Before we had to move her to hospice across town." Caleb stops and closes his eyes, a defense mechanism to block whatever emotions are brewing. But one tear falls, full and fast, down his cheek.

Sometimes I wonder what's worse, holding them all in, or just letting one escape.

I'm an empathy crier. If he cries more, I'll lose it too.

"But I can say this. We did try all the cheesecakes, and for that reason, I'm very proud." His face beams at the memory as he wipes away the trail left by the tear. "S'mores and Dulce de Leche are our favorites," he says, answering the question I was just about to ask.

Caleb holds my gaze, eyes shining like he might actually have found a little peace. Our server swings back around with plates that are so large, I'll actually call them platters. A crispy chicken sandwich with fries for Caleb and a spicy pasta dish for me.

"What about you? What about your parents? Your mom? I think I met her once at a convention. Dad frowned a little when it happened, but your parents were polite, so it was cool."

I let out a little sigh. "My mom? She holds everything so close to her chest, you know? It's complicated. Well, maybe not complicated. Strange? My parents are intense in their own ways. I'm close with my dad, but I don't really know my mom. Which I hate saying out loud given that she's still . . .

around. But I don't *know her* know her. I wish I did, though. I wish we had a better relationship. We try, but somehow one of us always disappoints the other. At least that's how it's been for me."

My chest tightens, and my appetite seems to shrink. I haven't even told Dad that this is what I think about Mom stuff, even though I'm sure by now he knows. Dad loves and defends her ad nauseam. He understands her in a way that I just don't.

"Damn, I'm sorry. That's rough."

I wipe my nose with my sleeve. "Thanks," I mutter.

"If you could ask her anything, what would it be? Or, I guess, what do you want to know about her?"

"Oooh. That's the million-dollar question. I'd still need that truth serum to get the answer out of her, though." I'm stumped when it comes to that woman. I've spent so much time being upset with my mom and low-key hating her for the pressure she puts on me and the way she toys with Dad's heart that I've never thought we could have a relationship where one of us wasn't left angry. As if two weddings weren't enough. There was the time she sent him flowers on Valentine's Day and he interpreted the white roses to mean they were more than just friends. Awkward. Or even at a recent book event, when she called him one of her greatest inspirations—publishing sites and gossip accounts went rabid with the idea that they were rekindling something, which put Dad in a mood for a week.

We sit in quiet for a few minutes, pushing the last crumbs around on our plates, before someone clears our table.

"This is fun," I say.

"I'm glad you're having a good time." Caleb nods. "I am too. I was a little worried I couldn't physically or mentally be here, but this has been the perfect meal with the perfect company." He sticks his tongue out, then grins. "I guess I can be happy and sad at the same damn time. But right now, with you, I'm mostly happy."

Same. I feel good here with him, and this *is* the perfect meal with the perfect company. But I don't say that, even though I'm sure he can sense it by the way my cheeks are burning up and I'm cheesing like I've been breathing laughing gas.

Around us, the orange sky begins to fade to a deep pink, and the city lights brighten as the first stars come out to shine. What was once a soft twilight is now something out of a fairy tale.

Caleb orders two slices of cheesecake to-go, a limited cinnamon roll flavor for him and Oreo for me. He pays the bill, which could signal a date, but I don't let that thought fester. The boy is gainfully employed—I recently learned he works part-time at an indie bookstore. Meanwhile, I don't currently have a job. My parents are hoping I'll continue to learn the value of a dollar through textbooks rather than real life. So, you know, he's got that Cheesecake Factory money.

With our bags in hand, we make our way to the front of the restaurant. Caleb lingers. "This view really is sick."

Our host from earlier smiles. "Absolutely. How was your date?"

"Oh, we're here to solve a mystery," I blurt out. Caleb just laughs.

She stares at us, deadpan. Oh shoot! Maybe the nervous laughs should be replaced by our serious-inquiry voices.

Caleb leans forward. "A mystery about Betty Quinn. You see, she sent us here."

"I'm aware." She holds our gaze, unfazed.

My fingers pull at Caleb's shirt hem. Okay, so this is happening, really happening. We're going to uncover this.

"Is there anything we should know? Why are we here?" Caleb asks.

Behind us, the commotion builds. The front of the restaurant has begun to balloon with hungry bodies.

"Sweet endings are a piece of cake." The same deadpan. Then her black nail taps on a green enamel pin on her vest, two books stacked on top of each other, but I can't see the titles.

I lean in. "I don't get it, what does that mean?" I ask, confusion in my voice and on my face. Her lips curl up, and she's about to respond when a loud ding snaps her out of our big moment.

The elevator door opens and out spill more people.

"Fern?"

"Macy?"

"Martin?"

"Lily?"

There are a few other familiar faces with them, but I don't know their names.

"Why are you all here?" I ask.

"Grubbing."

"Betty Quinn."

"Cheesecake."

"Are y'all on a date?"

The voices crash over one another.

"Who said Betty Quinn?" Caleb asks.

Somehow, the loud space goes quiet. Fern shrugs.

"We all know that there's more to this place than meets the eye." Lily surveys the small circle that's formed.

So, the others know about the coordinates too. Maybe we should've taken the binder with us.

Fern's head turns to the side, sensing a presence before it can be seen. With long, powerful strides, the person joins our group.

"Dr. Tien?" I look at Caleb, then at Fern. "What are *you* doing here?"

Chapter Twenty-Four

The next morning, while getting ready to some banda music, Fern explains that Martin hasn't found the manuscript, and that he only said he did to throw others off track, which sorta worked. Fern also heard from Gina who heard from Lily that yes, Dr. Tien is also on the hunt with us, that Dr. Tien has also spent an unnatural amount of time in Betty's library after morning sessions.

With this new knowledge, Caleb and I decide we gotta check out another spot.

"You know, I think this is going to be awesome," Caleb says as he turns Lily's cousin's borrowed Volvo station wagon into a parking lot that afternoon. This car is Berkeley personified—eco-friendly, long-lasting, a little quirky, with too many stickers decorating the bumper, and functional, with some good-sized dings that only make the car look tough. I like it.

The afternoon sun is high, and fluffy clouds are adrift in a beautiful bright blue sky. The elements scream "perfect California day," where the ocean, the sky, and the sun are all in an agreement to be stunning, showing off their best sides.

"Actually, this is a terrible idea." I don't need to think— I know. This can't be.

Caleb jumps out of the car. "You coming?" He practically sprints to the booth.

"I think I'd rather not!" I shout, but it's too late. He runs back, because apparently now he's The Flash, and opens my car door.

"I think I'm in love with Betty Quinn!"

My eyes glance up again at the bright neon sign, *Berkeley Bikes,* in terror. "This can't be right, can it?"

Caleb whips out his phone. "This is right, and this was the premise for one of her books! The one where the ex–best friends get stuck on a bike trip from San Francisco to Los Angeles? For a charity event?" He scrolls and then shows me the cover for *Let's Ride Away,* which I've heard of. The illustrations of the bike sign on the book look a lot like the *Berkeley Bikes* sign in front of us.

"This was one of my favorites." He claps, causing two seagulls to scatter off.

He's way too eager; all his energy does is make me nervous.

"Which one should we get?" Caleb points to rows of tandem bikes, surrey bikes, and individual bikes in a variety of colors—some with baskets, some without, but they all scream terror to mc.

"Ehhh."

"What? I know that face—what's on your mind?"

"Well, aren't you versed in my expressions," I say.

"An expert. I've been studying you."

"Fine. Here goes." Dramatic pause, because while the truth can be liberating, it's also embarrassing. At least this is, for me. "I can't ride a bike. A literal accident is waiting to happen."

"You can't ride a bike!" Caleb practically screams.

I shove him playfully, my head on a swivel to see who's around. "Oh my gosh, don't announce it to the world."

His hand covers his mouth. "Sorry, that was a big initial reaction. Let me try again." He clears his throat. "Thank you for feeling comfortable enough to tell me your truth." He takes a moment to recover from stifling giggles as my face heats up. "What did you do as a kid? What was your childhood? Not even with training wheels? It doesn't add up, because I could totally see you being the leader of a local biker gang. A very menacing but cute bike gang."

Ugh. My shoulders fall, and all my insecurities from the past seventeen years roll into this activity. This is why I don't like to tell people this very important but random fact about me. Once I tell Caleb about my lack of biking skills, what's next? My middle name? My life goals? The fact that I have a recurring nightmare from when I was a fifteen-year-old barista for two weeks who accidentally served folks decaf coffee? And since the customers could tell after two sips, they asked for the manager, which led me to start crying inconsolably in the middle of my shift?

Instead, Caleb's ogling me like he *wants* to hold my secret, his brown eyes all safe and warm.

Annoying.

"Promise me you won't tell anyone, or shout it out loudly again," I beg.

He gives me his pinkie. I roll my eyes but lock my pinkie with his nonetheless.

"Since you must know, I tried to learn. Really. My dad did his best to teach me, for months. I never got it. Then, one day, I had this big fall. In hindsight, it was probably a normal fall. However, when I was seven, whew, it felt like my world was ending." I exhale, this confession providing some relief. "So, I dunno, I just figured life would be safer if I didn't engage in things that, you know, could hurt me. Like biking. Biking can hurt! I attempted to learn again when I was nine. And again, at eleven." I pause at the memories. "You know, I think I just realized that some things in life are simply not worth trying over and over, because what if the outcome is always the same? Me, sad, defeated on the ground? Bits of gravel stuck to my knee?"

Caleb keeps his eyes low but nods. Some things in life only have one of two outcomes—why risk getting the bad one?

"My mom loved to bike." Caleb's voice is a whisper. I inch closer to make sure I hear him. "She was super fit. Loved to run, then go for a bike ride. The only reason I got into biking was so I could go out with her on the weekends, make it our thing, without my dad or my sister. We'd get up before the sun, ride, and then have an awesome breakfast after. Every

Saturday. For the last three years. When she got sick"—his shoulders sag—"we had to stop doing that, of course." He dabs the corners of his eyes.

"You're crying," I say without thinking.

"She was so healthy, so strong. And way faster than me." He takes a heavy inhale.

"Fuck—and I can't stress this enough—fuck cancer," I tell him, a tear running down my face.

"Are you crying?"

"I mean, I'm actually very sensitive, Caleb! Empathetic—I feel too much." I try to defend myself, and for some reason, this just makes Caleb laugh, which makes me laugh. Contagious.

"My mom would have liked you," he says. "She appreciated complex and sensitive women." He blots the corners of his eyes again, then stands near one of the bikes. "All right, it's clear what we have to do. Mom would want it. I can teach you."

The reality of what he's saying and what he wants to happen sets off a fear alarm in my body. "I really want to for you and your mom, but I'm telling you, it won't work."

But he just nods, agreeing with himself. "This can be good for you, and for me. Maybe something that made me happy before can make me happy again. Even if I'm bawling this whole time, I want to get on a bike. And I want to bike with you."

Caleb's expression is so earnest there's no way I can wiggle out of this, but didn't he hear me when I said I couldn't bike?

"I can watch you bike," I reply, giving it another shot. "Or we can take a photo, and I can photoshop myself in."

"Absolutely not." He's stern. "Plus, I bet that Betty Quinn *wanted* us to bike together. Why else would she have us here? It's very Sarah Dessen."

When the reference doesn't register on my face, he adds, "*Along for the Ride*?"

I shake my head.

"It was on the suggested-reading list."

Probably not the best time to tell him I don't really do suggested-reading lists. I read purely based on vibes. Caleb doesn't wait for me to respond. Instead, he sprints to the bike rental booth and returns with a helmet and a blue piece of metal on wheels.

Every cell, every muscle, and every fiber in my body is screaming, pleading, *Don't you do this! Don't you do this to us! Not! Again!*

But Caleb is holding the bike with one hand, making it seem so safe. "I got you," he says. I hesitate but make my way to the hell on wheels. He's standing behind me, holding the seat steady. Out of the corner of my eye, I see several runners and a group of girls on Rollerblades. They don't acknowledge us or care what we're doing, which gives me a little relief. The path is made for moving. My eyes close, and I take a deep breath.

"Okay, here we go," Caleb calls out in coach mode.

We begin the session, and much as with any other beginner doing anything, it doesn't go well. My feet make two rotations before I stop. We do this over and over until we've officially moved a foot. Snails move faster.

At least I haven't fallen over.

Yet.

Caleb keeps a smile on his face. "You're doing great. Really, you are." He pauses. He always takes a guilty pause when he's lying. I too have picked up on his mannerisms.

"I clearly can't do this." My voice is flat. "Let's go get food or tattoos, or do anything else. Please?" I've gone seventeen years without having to know how to ride a bike. Do I really need to start now?

"You can and you will. What you need is momentum! Every time you get started, you stop yourself. Don't. Let yourself float, let the movement carry you into the next rotation."

"Waaaah. I can't," I whimper again.

Caleb places one hand on my shoulder and, with encouragement, says, "Embrace the fear of falling, Macy."

Our eyes connect like magnets, and suddenly I have a strong desire to bring Caleb's face closer to mine.

We stay in this trance for a long, stretchy moment, as if time doesn't exist.

I move in, just a smidge, as Caleb breaks into a mischievous grin. "Did you feel that?" he asks.

"What?"

"Chemistry."

There is something indescribable between us, but far be it from me to name it.

Caleb leans in, and a soft kiss lands on my cheek. A devilish smile transforms my face.

"But we can't let chemistry deter our mission! Let's go! Back on the bike," Coach Caleb calls out. I hop on and begin again.

Chapter Twenty-Five

After several more minutes of slightly embarrassing one-rotation pedal pumps, I keep my eyes forward, and then it happens. Momentum. Balance. Movement.

I'm biking!

The world passes in slow motion beside me.

My eyes dart over my shoulder, and there is Caleb, running behind the bike, an arm outstretched.

"You're doing amazing, honey!" he shouts.

"I'm doing it! Also, never call me that again!" I scream, the wind wild in my mouth. I'm free, floating. There's a courage in my voice and my body that I've never experienced before. It's liberating.

Caleb cheers, but his voice isn't behind my shoulder like it was a moment ago. A little turn of my neck, and I see Caleb, waving goodbye, a small dot in the distance. Which means he isn't holding me up or keeping me stable. Which means I really am riding alone, by myself. My head snaps forward, and I try to quell the panic storm building in my body.

If he's back there, and I'm up here, that means I'm moving. That means I'll keep on going until I somehow stop. Or fall.

Momentum is a silly thing that continues pushing me forward.

I could stop, somehow, but I don't. My feet are pedaling in an easy groove.

The path twists and turns along the water, and I understand why people might enjoy this. One more minute, and I lift a hand off the handlebars, braver than I've ever been. My brain shuts off, and I enjoy the silence.

Until after another minute, when I remember someone.

Caleb! Where is he?

I need to stop, or he needs to hurry.

Up ahead, the path veers off into a large patch of grass. I do my best to slow down, pumping the brakes two or three times. But I've got *too much* momentum, which clearly can be a bad thing, because when I try to stop, I don't.

In an instant, the bike is moving in a jerky spasm and then I'm wobbling, and of course, I tip over.

It's a clumsy fall, one that's more theatrical than real, but I go sideways, a victim of gravity. The bike flops down by my side, on top of my leg. My eyes close, and my body softens into the earth. The endorphins in my brain are throwing a party because even though I should probably cry out in pain, I'm laughing, happy and proud.

I'm a biker now. I can ride a bike.

I relish this moment, a minor little victory that makes me a winner, even if only temporarily.

After about five minutes of grass lounging, I prop myself up on my elbows, my eyes searching for Caleb.

When he comes into view, my cheeks practically explode.

He casually jogs over to me. Despite, or maybe because of, his incessant snacking, the boy is in good-ass shape.

He waves his arms at me. "Oh, thank god. I was worried I'd have to run down to the next picnic area, which is a good two miles away. I would have, but I was hoping I wouldn't have to," he huffs out. He grabs at his knees, his back slouching in, taking a deep breath before flopping down beside me. Then he pulls a water bottle from his backpack, which I didn't know he was carrying, and takes a long, desperate sip. I watch his lips, his eyes closed as he satiates his thirst. When he stops, he glances over, and I do what I should have done several times before.

I grab his shirt collar and pull him in, halfway. His eyes meet mine, and I nod, giving him permission to fill the distance.

A mix of warm sweat and honey fuels our kiss. I keep my hand on his shoulder, and after a long moment, I pull away and lean back on my elbows, face to the sky.

"Tell me you felt that?" he says under his breath.

I nod. "Chemistry."

Chapter Twenty-Six

We head back holding hands, but as we make our way onto campus, something in me shifts. I spot Fern, and before they can speculate about what is or isn't, I gently let go of Caleb's fingers.

"Rally the troops!" Fern cries out, bouncing toward us.

"What did we miss?" Caleb asks.

Fern gives him a look, then glances toward me. "More like what did I miss?"

My face floods with embarrassment, but the good kind.

"Oh stop," Fern says. "It's just me, I've had two flings this week. But you have missed a lot. There's been some uncovering." Fern raises their eyebrows super high and dramatically.

"Go on." I nudge Fern.

Fern plants themself between me and Caleb, interlocking their arms in ours, which feels nice and comfortable. I have grown to love Fern and everything about them—their impeccable style, their wit, the way they like to sing in the morning even though my ass is still asleep. Above all, the way it's been easy to form a friendship with them, perhaps one of the easiest and most delightful relationships I've made in a long time. I have a few friends back in Santa Cruz, but I suspect once high school is over, we'll drift apart.

Between me, Caleb, and Fern, I'm the slowest walker, so I do my best to stay in line with their military march.

"Well, after lunch—where were you two, by the way?"

"Ummm . . ." Doesn't seem like exactly the right time to tell Fern I was kissing Caleb and learning how to ride a bike.

"Doesn't matter. Tell me later." Fern gives me an eye. "After lunch and stuff, we divided up into groups and figured out the clues from the benches around campus. At first it didn't make any sense, but then someone, Martin maybe, had the idea of putting the bench inscriptions in a clockwise order because of her sports romances, *Off the Bench* and *Run the Clock*, and they revealed the name of a lookout point: Grizzly Peak."

"Grizzly Peak?" It sounds familiar.

"Yeah, so folks are gathering provisions, food and drinks and blankets, and rides, with the goal of leaving campus around seven p.m. to get up there by sunset."

"I can drive us as long as Lily still has her cousin's car," Caleb offers. "Lily won't mind as long as she's allowed to be a passenger princess."

"Amazing, because riding in the car with Gina is super traumatizing." Fern shakes their head at having to relive the driving experience. "If recreational drugs are your thing, I think it could be a good place to, you know, let your hair down or whatever."

'Tis a good question. My eyes peer up as I wait for Caleb's response.

"Eh, not me, but do what's best for you."

I shake my head. "Nah, I'm neurotic enough. I can't have anything enhance that. Y'all don't want those problems."

Fern nods. "Heard. I have some mushroom chocolates, but I'm saving them for later, probably the last week. I'm making good progress on my story, and I can't have anything throwing me off my game. I *will* win a spot in the anthology."

We step into the dorm room elevators and ride to our floors in silence, thinking about the prize, Betty Quinn, or a combo of both.

Caleb gets off at the second floor and sticks out a hand to prevent the doors from closing. "How about we meet at the quad at six-forty-five?"

"Sounds good." I do my best to sound neutral.

The door closes, and Fern and I travel up the next three floors. "Oh my gosh, you two are so in love. Has anything ever been more obvious?"

We barely fit into the car, our bodies stuck to the windows, as Caleb drives Fern, a couple other students, and me up to Grizzly Peak. The roads twist and turn to the point I think I might get carsick. Thankfully I don't. Some other folks get rides with two counselors, and some even try to walk the three-mile distance. We're high up in the Berkeley Hills, tucked away in mountains, overlooking the bay. By the time we reach the lookout point, the rocks are speckled with bodies and blankets.

"Fern, over here!" someone calls out as my roommate bounces away.

Most of the retreat is here. Seems to be an outing that everyone wanted to check out, mystery solvers or not.

"Betty Quinn loved a good view. She said this particular one was the inspiration for many of her settings," Caleb says, standing beside me. In a move that has become so natural, he laces his fingers with mine.

"I get why." My eyes stare out at the vastness of the bay. The view is surreal, something that seems like it maybe isn't earthly. The early evening sky is various shades of blue and bubblegum pink. The lookout point extends all the way out to the Golden Gate and Bay Bridge. It's as if the universe and Betty are telling me to take in this very beautiful moment. Like Betty knew that we'd be asked to study "Location, Location, Location," and that it would take us a minute to get to this place, where she found the best time and place to tell *her* story.

"I brought some goodies. Join me?" Caleb asks, as if we haven't been connected at the hip, first by force and now by choice.

He lays down a red-and-black-checkered blanket from his backpack, and I take a seat. Then he pulls out a thermos and offers me a cup.

"I love tea," I say.

"I know."

My face heats up—did I tell him this? It's one thing if I told him, but it's quite another if he simply picks up on the little things about me.

The jasmine tea is warm, and I inhale it before taking a sip. "Mmmmmmm."

And because it's Caleb, he pulls out a small wood cutting board that looks suspiciously similar to the ones in the dining hall and begins placing crackers and cheese on top.

"Oh, you fancy," I say.

"Only the best for you."

"Trying to woo me, huh?"

"Is it working?"

I smirk and reach across him to grab several pieces of Ritz and cheddar cheese. Caleb does the same, only his cracker-layer combo is about three times the size of mine. We spend the next ten minutes eating and drinking in a comfortable silence. Around us, Lily is blowing bubbles that appear iridescent in the golden light, and someone's playing some Lana Del Rey on a portable speaker. Martin and Fern wave their arms to the music, their bodies floating and bending like inflatable tube people at gas stations or tire shops. The deep blue evening sky turns dark, and a half-moon appears.

"This is incredible, right? Sometimes the world is really mind-blowing." The night air is clean and cold but refreshing on my skin.

"The two bridges, the lights, the water. God really showed off," Caleb says.

"And these architects did not miss. The San Francisco sky-line, the water! Perfect tens."

Curtis, a guy I've only seen and never talked to, stands up on a rock and screams, "Betty Quinn, why did you bring us here? What do you want us to find?" his voice echoing off the rocks and going into the ether. At this, some students clap, others laugh.

"Maybe there's no answer to her clues. Maybe this is just . . . it. Inspiration. Maybe she just wants us to enjoy . . . *this*." Caleb shakes the crumbs off the cutting board and places his impromptu-but-super-cute charcuterie board back in his bag. He takes out an extra jacket, balls it up, and makes a pillow, lying down immediately.

I follow suit, eyes on the stars, the vastness of the universe holding me.

Caleb and I are close but not touching, until his fingers brush over mine and then my hand is in his.

"Is this okay?" His voice is soft.

"More than okay." I squeeze his hand as our fingers interlock.

"Out of all the writing retreats, all the pairings in the world—you're the hamburger to my fries," he says.

I let out a small laugh. "I know, right? Kinda wild. Especially since our families are like pickles and peanut butter. What do you think it means?"

He chuckles, then turns to face me. "What do you want it to mean?"

A heavy lump forms in my throat, and I swallow. "What do *you* want it to mean?" I'm so lazy for kicking the same question back to him. But his answer matters to me, maybe before I give my own. I think a little more about our families disliking one another, my mom and his dad especially. They're both very type A. Could it be awkward? We are our families in a way, aren't we?

After a beat, Caleb says, "I like you. I like being around you. I want to spend as much time with you as I can. Even though we are halfway through our stay here." Caleb is so easy and assured with his feelings.

"Me too," I say, but it doesn't hit the same. Thankfully, he doesn't mind.

"Good. Because I always wanted to be a star-crossed lover."

I laugh; his eyes are pointedly focused on the sky. "Okay, but a better ending than Romeo and Juliet? Because I'm only seventeen, which is way younger than Juliet's thirteen in our time. . . ."

He snorts. "Oh, we are for sure having a better ending." Caleb props himself up on his elbows. "Maybe it's me, but this seems like a pretty romantic spot to . . . be romantical?" He throws up his arms.

I sit up too. "This is the perfect spot to be romantical." And there's not much else that needs to be said after that. As his hand rests on my cheek, the world spins around us, people laughing, crying, doing whatever they do when they are human. Caleb and I embrace our own humanity—that desire to be swept off our feet with a single kiss.

Chapter Twenty-Seven

The good vibes from Grizzly Peak carry into the following days, so when Caleb and I head to the Writer's House, we are talking so fast, so full of energy and ideas, that we totally miss the John Green room.

"Did we really pass by three times?" Caleb asks, holding the door for me. There are about two weeks left, and the energy is high—we're coffee that's about to percolate, or buttery kernels about to pop. Whatever the metaphor, something big is about to happen. Having paid some attention during our lectures, I know that the climax is coming.

I pull out a chair and throw my bag down as Caleb sits next to me.

"So, how's your story coming along?" I ask.

"I think I figured it out, my time travelers and their mission, where they don't have enough fuel."

"Hell yeah, you did! Tell me right now," I interject.

He smiles so hard his eyes close, and then he leans in close, like he's gonna kiss me, but just touches his nose to mine, like a bunny or something. It's cute. Way cute.

"Absolutely not. You'll read it soon," he says, leaning back.

Between lectures and our rendezvous, I've spent spare moments brainstorming, writing down ideas and concepts I like. Granted, I only have 1,500 words, but I can't focus on that just yet. Get the story out. Write first. Fix later—that's week four.

I hold up my notebook. "I'm going to write some swoony stuff for my teen journalist and her hockey player. They've fallen in love after several mishaps and need to figure out how to say the big words while, you know, not looking wimpy or whatever. Dialogue is hard!"

Caleb nods and then grabs his phone and sets the timer. We stare at one another for a long moment, waiting for something else to happen, to be said. It's not just the characters in my story who are having a hard time expressing their feelings. I take a long sip from my Stanley, which is filled with iced tea.

"Eight minutes?" I ask.

He nods. "Eight minutes. Also, you got this. No bad ideas. Just ones that haven't been fully ironed out." That makes things feel slightly better. Advice that I know but often have trouble believing.

"Ready?" Caleb's voice is soft yet serious. An energy fills the room, and I know whatever is happening right now is something magical, and the best thing I can do is surrender myself to the creative process. "Let's do this."

The moment my pen lands on my paper, I'm like a writer possessed. Words race out of me. The muscles in my hand begin to tighten, but they don't win; I don't stop. For eight minutes, we write.

My latest chapter starts off a little rocky, but I push through. Essentially, I'm able to write one scene. In eight minutes, I get my characters to talk through some of their deepest fears. On the ice-skating rink, they both share their experiences with relationships, or lack thereof, because my main girl is in love for the first time. Meanwhile, the love-spurned Canadian athlete is right about to say the words she's been hoping to hear when . . . a beeping sound floods my brain. Even after the timer goes off, I write two more sentences, ending at a place I'm satisfied with.

For the first time since we've been here, I begin to think that maybe, just perhaps, there is a possibility for me as a writer. I guess the retreat is actually working. . . . I'm building up my confidence, and I have stories to tell. Which also means . . . our time here is almost up. Heat builds on my neck, and I tug at my high bun.

"I could have written more."

I nod. "Me too. Today felt . . ."

"Smooth?"

"Super." My fingers tap on my paper. "Should we, you know. Switch? Do the whole critique thing?"

Words I've only recently built up the courage to speak. But if I can learn how to ride a bike and dabble in mystery, then surely I must be able to show him what I'm working on.

Caleb slides over his notebook.

We don't make eye contact, but the switch happens. My eyes drift up to a timid Caleb.

"Go easy on me, okay?"

"I could say the same thing."

We both project nervous smiles, painfully aware of what the other person is thinking. When I begin reading his words, I'm instantly, so quickly, faster than sound, *super* into him. I didn't think someone's writing could make me want to take them on a date or change my status, but Caleb's does.

Or maybe it's because I already like him that I see all the ways his writing glows, and how his prose is such a special extension of him. It's an honor to see this side of him. His handwriting is a little messy, a mix of print and sloppy cursive that takes me a minute to decipher, but once I do, I'm immersed. I'm in his world, the depths of his artistic mind. I bite my lip. The reality of how much I like Caleb is strong in my chest.

Caleb's space couple has finally decided whose mission to complete with their remaining jet fuel. Ramon decides he's going to sacrifice his mission so that Belinda can achieve hers. Only Belinda has traded the last of her moon orbs (a valuable space currency) to help Ramon. Nearly out of time and out of money, they scramble for plan C—split up to do the right thing and save the ones who ultimately brought them together, even if it means going their separate ways. And before they part, they never get to tell each other how they truly feel about their relationship and their time together. Because Ramon's never believed in love, he has a hard time vocalizing and expressing how much he loves Belinda. And because Belinda promised she'd never fall in love again, she definitely can't tell Ramon that she's head over heels for him. The scene is fast-paced and beautifully written.

"My only note is that Ramon and Belinda should say exactly what they feel, right? Before it's too late." I pause. Who is the *they* here? "I mean, we are working on dialogue. I wonder what the story would be like if they said more rather than internalizing everything." I slide Caleb's notebook back, too afraid to look at him. There's a lot that needs to be said on and off the page. The question is, will either of us have the courage to say it?

Chapter Twenty-Eight

By the end of week three, we're back in Betty Quinn's library, on our reconnaissance grind, searching for something new. The heat is on, and time is running out.

"I hope we find more money in a book," Caleb says as he opens another storage box.

"That would be great. I would love to go on a shopping spree, but it's unlikely to happen twice." I flip through a black Moleskine full of faded blue cursive writing that lists a ton of book title ideas.

"Or, at least, something to connect us to the other night. What did she say—'Sweet endings are cake'?"

I giggle while stepping over two large boxes. "Close. 'Sweet endings are a piece of cake.'"

"Mmmm. Now I want cake. German chocolate or straw-berry. Carrot would even do." Caleb rubs his tummy while batting his eyes. I must ignore him because I could always go for a slice of cake, but if we get distracted, we'll never get back on task.

My fingers flip through another worn journal. "This should be illegal." The woman has hundreds upon hundreds of notebooks, every moment of her life written down. "I think if you find someone's notebook, the proper thing to do is close it, well, read a page or two, then close it, and then, of course, recycle it. Seems like such a violation to have it available and ready for public consumption." I face Caleb, but he's deep into another box.

He shrugs. "I don't know. She wanted this. She left it for us, even if we don't understand the reasons why. I mean, look at all these boxes. She intentionally included them." His hands wave around the room. "There are so many notebooks to peruse, at her request! Who are we to say no?"

I raise an eyebrow. "I guess. But, for the record, if anyone finds any of my notebooks, god forbid any of my journals, I deem it illegal to read them. May they immediately catch on fire if they so much as flip open a page and sneak a peek at any of my precious words. Family included." My eyes close, sealing this decree.

Yet I flip open another of her notebooks, and clearly, I'm called to the page, so I begin to read.

January 19
The reviews for The Romantics are in.
And they are bad.
Bad beyond measure.

Cruel, mean, unconscionable.

"A poor excuse of a story" and "Not her best work, but maybe her worst."

If I were less of a person, I would stop writing altogether. But I'm me, and what my readers have failed to see, which is too bad, perhaps that is my fault, is that my stories aren't for them. They are for me. Specifically, for us.

In every story, I write us, together at last. Where we can be immortal. Where my life's previous choices haven't hurt me or caused such pain.

The reviews may be terrible.

But I write for you. About us.

Always and forever.

"Who the hell is *us*?"

"What'd you say?"

"Shh." I read on.

January 23

When it rains, it pours.

When the critics have opinions of me and my work, they are so dismissive. Cold. Because I'm writing romance. And not just that fluff my cohorts write. As if they know the pain I've endured to get to the other side. As if they've lived with guilt that makes them question if they're deserving of a happily ever after.

As if I'm not a human being with a multitude of emotions. I won't let their reviews break me, although my editor thinks I'm seeking them out.

Anyway . . .
I continue to write.
I will not give up.

"You find anything?" Caleb asks, taking two steps behind me. "I think I got something you might like." I turn as he says the words, causing my heart to skip a beat.

"Lemme see." I put the journal back and head toward the binder he has open.

June 6
Dear Ms. Quinn,

I hesitate in writing you this letter, but something urged me to write—I must.

I'll be direct because, well, in truth, it is always what I am (more so who I am, but I digress). I read your most recent novel, The Romantics and I hate it. Not that I hate it, but I loathe it, I wanted to burn my copy of the book. I was so angry, so emotionally unregulated because of it, I accidentally went on a two-hour rage walk across my city. When I returned home, rather sweaty and still upset, I realized the only way for me to process what I was feeling was to write you this letter.

So here we are.

Please consider removing this book from your repertoire.

You may find that there are more people like myself, who have read this book, finding it rather loathsome but don't know how to tell you. Well, consider yourself told.

Taylor James (yes, that one)

September 28
Dear Mr. James,

Thank you for your honest letter.
I regret that I don't have much to say to you, except, well,
I'm glad that my book made you feel something.
I think it's better we feel something than nothing at all.

Yours,
Betty Quinn

PS: You've given terrible business advice. I will not be pulling
my book <u>The Romantics</u> from stores. I will be honest in saying
that I find great pleasure in letting you know that the novel has
become one of my bestsellers. Surely, this Taylor James gets the
<u>Times</u>.

October 1
Dear Ms. Quinn,

First, I am so glad you responded. I can only imagine the influx
of letters you get. When I wrote you, months ago, I was in quite a
different space. I was, simply put, depressed, angry, grieving. I read
your book <u>The Romantics</u> to escape these contradictory emotions
inside of me, and instead your novel made me experience them even
more. Tenfold. No, actually, a million.
I cannot begin to tell you how much I have found that grief
and love seem to be connected.
This is to say, I apologize. And yes, thank you for making
me feel something. Even if that something was pain. Please

continue to write your wonderful books. I will admire them from afar.

Yours in artistry,
TJ

January 2
Dear Taylor,

I think we are on a first-name basis now, wouldn't you agree? I don't usually write this much with anyone, well, except for a few authors I won't name, but here we are. Because yes, I hope that you continue to feel things. Life is meant to be experienced as fully as possible. Would you believe me if I told you most of the books I write, while they are romance, are rooted in a big loss? I can't judge my feelings anymore. Sometimes, I know what to do with them, and they end up in a book. Other times, I don't. I too have done the angry walk across the city. I've locked myself in a room, breathless, barely hanging on to life, for weeks on end. And yet. Somehow. Some way. I get back up. I continue.

Yours in artistry,
BQ

February 10
Betty,

I've been alerted that you have another book coming out. I am eager to read. After your last correspondence, I must admit that I tried to learn more about you. But I could find very little information online. I see now that it's intentional. What would you say to a day with a movie star? I could charter a plane for you. Fly you anywhere in the world. We could meet, we could talk in person. About love, and loss, and the little moments in between.

Say yes?

—TJ

February 19

TJ,

Respectfully. No.

—B

This makes me chuckle. Betty Quinn is kind of a badass? My fingers run across the pages. I wonder how old she was writing these letters. The years are marked out, so it's hard to tell.

"Caleb?" I shout over the open boxes and stacks of books.

"Mm-hmm?" he calls back. A second later, his head appears beside a large, bulky bookshelf.

"What do you know about Taylor James?"

"Funny you mention him, because I watched his documentary a couple months ago. Big Hollywood star, right? Like child actor turned writer. I believe he writes mysteries. Really handsome? Definitely a himbo, respectfully. Oh, and rich. Very, very rich. Yes, actually, it's coming back to me now. He spent a lot of his life in the spotlight, did some reckless things in his twenties, but once he started writing in middle age, he kinda became a recluse."

I can see Taylor's face in my mind's eye. Dad is obsessed with documentaries and casually leaves them on to relax, so I've probably seen snippets of this one.

Caleb reappears by my side. "Why? What did you find out?"

I hold up the letters. "Betty and Taylor were definitely pen pals. Friends? Friendly? He asked her out."

"Tell me she said no."

"She did."

A sign of relief on Caleb's face. "Men. They never know how to keep it platonic." He playfully rolls his eyes and touches the back of my upper arm, which sends a tingle down my spine.

"He wanted to know who she was, like others, like us."

Caleb reads through a letter and then peers up. "I mean, yeah. A little mystery is part of the intrigue when it comes to the laws of attraction, isn't it?"

"You are certainly an enigma, Caleb Bernard."

He steals a kiss.

"Should we go back to the cabin?"

"To commit more crimes?" he asks.

"Hardly! But maybe? What's one more crime between friends?" I say.

His eyes widen. "Friends, huh? Do friends do this?" Caleb kisses me again, and I forget about Betty and her flirtation, with a heartthrob of my own to focus on.

Chapter Twenty-Nine

That evening, Fern and I both find ourselves in our room, which is rare. Usually one of us is out hanging with other students, exploring the city, or discussing writing and craft with someone from class; and the other is out with a hot boy searching for Easter eggs left behind by a bestselling romance author.

Fern's been at their desk, hardly moving, while I've been at my desk, closet, bed, window, trying to find inspiration to write but actually doing odd tasks and showing overall avoidance behavior because my brain is full of too many thoughts to synthesize anything.

"This is over for me. I think I might actually cry," Fern says, flipping their laptop screen closed. They rub their eyes in silence, a move my dad does right before a lecture of epic proportions.

At this, I stop moving, confused. "Wait, why? What just happened?"

Fern stands up, hands on their head, eyes closed. "This is hard. Too hard for me. I can't write. I've started—and stopped—at least twenty different times. And each time I think, *Aha! This is it. This story is fire.* And then when I read it back, the story is anything but fire. It's more like, dire." Fern opens their eyes. "Get it? From fire to dire?"

"Oh, believe me, I get it."

"Then you have to laugh! Even if it was super cheesy." Fern's eyes widen as I fall out of my chair, faking a hearty and quite vocal laugh.

"Thank you, that's much better," Fern says, sitting back down in their chair. I roll onto my side and then sit up. "Maybe that should be the title of my memoir. *From Fire to Dire* by Fern Aztlan Garcia-Alvarado That has a ring to it, right?"

"Stop! For real. You're doing a great job. I know you are. There is nothing easy about any of this. There's so much pressure to write the greatest story ever."

"Ugh. Why does everyone else make it seem so easy?"

"Pfft. Who is everyone?"

"I don't know—just everyone. Half of the other students I've talked to are damn near finished with their second drafts. Some are even talking about writing full novels and querying agents and adding their attendance here to their college applications and doing all this stuff that I hadn't even thought about."

Really? Yeesh. I've been working on my story. I just . . . need the extra week allotted. "Well, you've got to tune out the noise and just focus on you and your words."

"Hmmm." Fern flips their laptop back open. "How about you? How's it going?"

"Okay? Sorta? I'm at like five thousand words now. I probably could do a little more writing, but Caleb and I—" I stop when I notice Fern's expression. "What?"

Fern continues to stare at me.

"What?" I say again.

"You don't want to know," Fern says flatly.

I shift in my seat. "Well, now I absolutely want to know." At least I think I want to know.

Fern bites their bottom lip. "Promise not to get mad or upset?"

"I absolutely cannot promise that, but I'll do my best because you're still my roommate and that face you're making right now is slightly scary. Intense? I can't live with you walking around making that face." I raise my eyebrows as Fern nods.

"Point." Fern exhales and then winks at me. "All right. I don't mean any harm with this, but, and correct me if I'm wrong, maybe because of your parents, or despite them, you're not taking your work here as seriously? I'm not trying to read you, but just as an outsider looking in, I hope that you can, you know, really make the most out of your time here. And not just with Caleb. He's cool and all. Actually, I really like him, but I think you came here to do stuff for you. Not for Betty, not for Caleb or your parents, but for you."

My mouth falls open. "When you say it like that . . ." I'm not sure how to respond, so I sit back at my desk. After a moment, I turn to Fern. "Thank you for sharing that with me. I'm not mad. I just need to sit with it a little more."

Fern nods.

My fingertips wake up my computer screen just as Fern seems to have woken me up. Maybe there is a bit of me that hasn't been able to take myself seriously as a writer because I have my parents to fall back on. Caleb and I have been spending a good amount of time together, but also, I'm young, and we only have a little over a week left. My heart flip-flops at that—soon Caleb and I will go back to our worlds. We haven't even discussed what'll happen to us next. Maybe Fern is right, maybe I need to focus on what it is I came here to do, which is write. Everything is confusing.

"I mean, I've been doing sorta the same thing, so that drag is for both of us. It's hard finding a work-and-play balance, but I'm recommitting now. Last thing"—Fern and I both turn from our chairs—"I love you, and I hope that wasn't too harsh. But I've read some of the others' stories, and they are good. Objectively good. So, let's use that as fuel for our fire or whatever? My pity party is over. I'm ready to do this. Are you?" Fern stretches out their arms and cracks their fingers, filling the room with the tip-tap of keys.

"I'm ready." I think. No, I am. "But, Fern? Just how objectively good?"

Chapter Thirty

Caleb thinks he has an idea for how to cure his writer's block once and for all. I'm hesitant at first to leave campus again, really wanting to be studious since it's week four—revision week—and I finally got the remaining two thousand words on the page last night. But then he does this thing where his eyes get all droopy and his shoulders look like they might fall off his body, he's so dejected, so I agree.

He's silent in our rideshare, which is fine. I zone out for a moment before the car stops.

"The beach?" I ask, confused as hell.

"The beach."

He doesn't say much else, just hops out of the car. I give the area a quick scan and deem it normal enough before I step outside, back arching in a small stretch, kinda wishing I had dressed accordingly. Caleb's already on a bench, taking off his Crocs and crew socks.

I also need to sit down and focus to take off my platform Dr. Martens and the two pairs of thick socks I wear with them to prevent blisters. Caleb waits patiently while I free my feet and then place my shoes in my bag.

"Ready?" He stands eagerly.

"Ready as I'll ever be."

Two small steps lead us to the entrance, which is sprinkled with people. The sand is warm on my toes, and for a brief second, I'm a kid again, full of joy and wonder. There's something super soothing about being near the ocean. The air smells crisp and clean, and the sound of the waves rushing back and forth against the shore is calming, meditative almost. Caleb and I hold hands as we walk along.

We take several more steps, and Caleb, who was once on my left side, closest to the water, scoots around me, his face suddenly full of fear. Now he's like a kid . . . but one who's just seen a tarantula or something. My head swivels.

He fakes a smile. "Okay, so don't laugh. Or do. But full confession, I'm actually terrified of the ocean. Ter-ri-fied."

This stops me because the Pacific Ocean is *right there*, close enough that a high tide could touch our toes, close enough that I can taste the salt from the sea.

Caleb throws up his arms. "I know. In my defense, I thought this would be a good idea. You kinda inspired me."

"Me?"

"Yeah, with the biking—because you're practically a biker now. I really enjoyed seeing you try something you know you hate and just get over it."

I shake my head. "If anything, that was all because of you. And Betty Quinn."

He thinks for a moment. "Either way, we are here. Let me be one with nature? Let me try to understand the beauty of the ocean? And get over my terrifying-but-slightly-rational fear of getting swallowed whole by the sea?"

I pause. "Okay, but tell me if you get too afraid and need to leave or something," I offer.

Caleb sorta relaxes his shoulders, and he adds with a small smile, "Plus, isn't this like a required location to check out on this retreat? Aren't romance stories good for a nice, long walk on the beach?"

He grabs my hand, and our arms intertwine as we fall into an easy stroll.

"I mean, I see why. It's hella romantic. . . ." My eyes glance up at his. "Unless you're deathly afraid of the ocean, of course."

"I can't be the only one! The ocean is just so large and vast and practically all-consuming. The waves alone are menacing. Tell me that doesn't look scary." He points to a small wave splashing at the shore.

I snort. "So, no surfing for you? Boogie boarding?"

"No, ma'am. I'll leave that for somebody else."

We walk a little farther, passing a group of volleyball players and several sunbathers.

Caleb squeezes my hand. "You know, this isn't terrible. I don't think that the ocean is going to swallow me whole. At least not yet. Maybe if we walked closer."

I laugh. "I'm sorry. Do we want to be swallowed whole?"

Something calms in Caleb as we continue our nice, slow rhythm. The waves sound relaxing, and the ocean looks peaceful to me, but we all have our things we gotta work through.

When I was younger, Dad would make me take swimming lessons, against my will, for this reason—so I could be confident at the beaches in Santa Cruz, or around any body of water anywhere, for that matter.

"How are you doing? Is this phobia overcome?" I ask.

"Mmmm . . ."

"Come on. Let's get our feet wet."

After a little tug, we glide forward and allow our toes to sink into the wet sand as we stare out at the blue waves. One time at the beach, I lost my retainer trying to bodysurf. I was afraid to tell my dad, thinking he'd be pissed at me, but he just laughed. Made a joke about mermaids and overbites.

Caleb tells me about how he's been afraid of the ocean ever since a bad experience one summer in Haiti when he was six. He closes his eyes when he talks about it, so I don't press with questions. When small sweat beads begin to build on my face, I point to an open bench nearby.

"Wanna sit?" I ask. It's on a slight hill, so Caleb holds my arm up as I do my best to not tumble over. When we plop down, I reach for my water bottle, and Caleb immediately pulls out an Uncrustable.

"So, we've got a couple of days left of this retreat," he says after a medium-sized bite. I've been putting this thought off. There's not much time left for, well, anything. We haven't found Betty Quinn's lost manuscript, which I was hoping to

181

use as a guide for my own work. I definitely can't ask my parents to help me revise. Now I'm second-guessing whether I've written something worthy of submitting for a spot in the anthology. Caleb and I haven't whispered a word about what will become of us once we are back in the real world, when he goes to New Orleans and I return to Santa Cruz.

"Yep," I mutter as a way to mask what I'm holding back.

"But I did a Google Alert for Taylor James, and guess who is doing a book signing tomorrow night? In Berkeley?"

I slap the bench. "Shut up!"

"I know. I almost couldn't believe it either. Maybe he can help us, I don't know, tie up loose ends before this is all over."

"Yeah, exactly. I don't know what to make of this puzzle."

"I think that's because we aren't finished finding the big pieces yet."

I nod. "True."

He clicks on his phone, pulling up a flashy graphic for tomorrow's event.

"A tell-all of the literary world?" I read the tagline and admire his photo. "Taylor James has still got it. He's pretty handsome for—"

"Macy, he's like seventy. . . ."

"Don't be ageist! He looks great." He gives hot grandpa for sure. Like Pierce Brosnan.

Caleb rolls his eyes and, in one last bite, devours the remaining two-thirds of the Uncrustable. I don't know if he even chews his food.

"So, what's our plan?" I ask.

"We go tomorrow night. . . ."

"We prepare our questions. We bring our receipts. We figure out as much as we can with the time we have left."

He traces a small circle on my hand. "Yes, we figure out as much as we can with the time we have left."

The time we have left . . . which, if we're counting down days, isn't a lot. The way Caleb's face falls like he's saying goodbye makes me wonder if he's thinking about more than Taylor James.

Chapter Thirty-One

The next evening, Caleb and I walk down Telegraph Avenue, one of my favorite streets in the city, if not the world. There's something about the energy of this part of town that makes me come alive more than any other place I visit. Maybe it's the secondhand weed smoke, or the political activism by the young and the old, or the hot college kids flooding the streets, eager to change the world. Telegraph Ave is quirky and vibrant and authentic in a way that other places try to emulate but can't ever pull off.

"Are you nervous?" Caleb asks.

I nod as he releases my hand but links our pinkie fingers together.

"I'm nervous," I say.

He tugs on my pinkie, and we stop in front of a new kebab restaurant with a bright neon sign. Caleb appears animated, like something out of a video game, the way the lights shine on him.

"Why are you nervous?"

"Are we digging too deep into Betty's personal life?" I wonder aloud.

He tilts his head to the side. "This place smells good. Should we get food after? Probably, right?"

"Caleb! Focus! Is this even our business and our place to be, you know, asking these questions? But also, if it's not our place, why did she leave so much of herself exposed?"

He grabs my hands again, zipping our fingers. "That is the mystery, isn't it?"

My eyes close for a moment. He's right. *Stay invested, Macy. You've come this far.* My eyes open. "Okay. And also, yes, food after. This place smells exceptional."

"Right?" He runs a thumb along the side of my chin. "Let's get out of here before I order something to-go." A smooth smile settles across his face, and heat creeps up my neck. He's pulling me closer, and just like a million other times today, we kiss.

One arm slides up my back for support.

"Honk, honk!" Voices from a kid on a skateboard and his friend on a BMX bike behind him pull us apart. "You're like in the middle of the road."

Cheeks burning, Caleb and I separate and scurry down the last block to Moe's Books, a place I've loved and visited my whole life because of my parents and their book events. Three packed floors of books (duh), CDs, vinyl, college students, hippies, and lovers dispersed throughout the aisles.

Caleb opens the door for me and a gust of warm air hits my face. "This way." He points up toward the large poster of

Taylor James, his book cover, and an arrow guiding us to the second floor.

My legs make it up the stairs without burning. That's progress.

The second floor opens to a packed room, full of bodies.

"Oh shit. The man has fans," Caleb whispers. We grab a spot in the back.

"Too bad I can't see anything." I wobble up on tippy-toes but only grow enough to see the tops of heads. Lots and lots of tops of heads. Mostly gray hairs, but some light purple, and a few too many fedoras for my liking.

Caleb lightly grabs my waist. "It's my fault we're so far back. All because I wanted to make out in front of a delicious restaurant."

"I wanted it just as much." I smirk.

Caleb relaxes into the wall. "Well, this event will have to be heard only. We'll listen and let the conversation fill our souls."

We stand, connected in a deep moment of cheesy love for a beat, before the room is overcome with applause.

"Ladies and gentlemen, Taylor James is in the building," the bookseller hosting the event says.

The applause continues, and for a moment, I'm a little starstruck. Even though I've gone to countless author signings for my parents and the writers they actually like, and I've been nearish to some pretty famous people, my jaw is unhinged. This is an important creator to some, if not many.

The crowd shifts forward, and two feet of space suddenly

opens up in front of us. We step forward, and I can steal a few glances of Taylor—his black-rimmed glasses, his wispy gray hair, his salt-and-pepper mustache.

For the next thirty minutes, Caleb and I listen to him speak, mostly about his life in the public eye, as an actor and then as a writer. He tells a few funny stories as they relate to his latest book. His voice is soft but stern, very grandfatherly.

Thankfully, he doesn't talk too long, and before my knees give up on me, he begins signing books and taking pictures.

This is the part that requires patience.

Slowly but surely, Caleb and I inch forward, the line to Taylor moving, albeit turtle-like. Another twentyish minutes, and there are two people in front of us. My fingers can touch his table.

"We got this," Caleb whispers into my ear.

Go time.

Taylor smiles as we approach. "Well, hello there." Up close he looks familiar—maybe it's because I've spent the last several days reading his letters to Betty, so I think I know him. "How are we doing this evening?"

I clear my throat. "Hello, huge fans. We, um—"

"We don't have a book!" Caleb exclaims. Oh shit. I guess we forgot to buy one.

Taylor lets out a small laugh. "You got in the book-signing line without a book? Kids today. Thankfully, you can buy one downstairs. You'll just have to bring it back up again. And pray that I'm still here." He winks but motions to the last few people in the line behind us.

It's truly now or never. "We're going to get a book, but we, um—we have a few questions. We were hoping we could talk to you about . . ." My voice catches in my throat. "Betty Quinn."

Taylor's eyes flutter closed. After a quick moment, he opens them again, I'm sure wishing that we'll be gone, but no such luck. "Young lady, I don't . . ." Another pause, like he's getting into character. "I have absolutely no idea who you're talking about."

Caleb inches forward. "You sure you don't remember talking to one of the most prolific romance writers of this century?"

Nothing.

"Sir, it would really mean a lot to us if we could just ask you about Betty. We are students at Penovation, the writing retreat, and we've been following her clues. Well, we think they're clues. They definitely can't be coincidental. We only have a few questions. About your letters to each other."

A devilish grin takes over his face, and Taylor stands. He's almost as tall as Caleb. He smooths the wrinkles of his khaki pants and pulls a hat from the inside of his jacket, also khaki. "Lenora, the car please, dear. We are done here." He raises a hand, a perfect beauty-pageant-queen goodbye. "Thank you all so much for coming. I'm afraid I must leave early. Something's come up. The pleasure has absolutely been all mine." He bows at the waist, and I almost want to applaud. The man is charming.

One last try. "Mr. James, please. Please! You could save a life." Dramatic, I know, but if not now, when?

He pauses, perhaps considering how generous to be. He steps around the table and, in a low, deep voice, says to me, "Betty was my friend. A very good friend. And I've lost her. I'm not sure if you know about loss quite yet, or the way it can linger in your bones. So, you'll have to forgive me if I don't care to open up old wounds because you added a *please*. She was a person, my person, who I won't be able to call again. Whose laughter I'll never hear. You'll . . ." We lock eyes, his glassy. "You'll have to forgive me if at this very moment I don't drive straight into a deep hurt."

Goose bumps cover my skin.

There were so many reactions I prepared for, answers I was hoping to receive. This was not one of them.

Caleb tugs on my arm, my body rustling like a floating leaf. "Macy, I think we better go." And that's when I realize that everyone in the room is staring at us. "Let's go downstairs for a moment and catch our breath."

I nod. We make it to the first floor.

"Come here," Caleb says, wrapping my body in a tight hug. The embrace is comforting, and he smells so good, it distracts me from my shock. "Okay, so that didn't go exactly as planned." He pulls his head back, and I stare at him. "You okay?"

I release from the embrace. "Yeah, I think so. I didn't mean to be insensitive. I guess I wasn't thinking. I was just super focused on getting answers."

"That makes two of us. Ugh, his reaction gutted me, talking about loss. I know that pain."

Now it's my turn to grab Caleb's hand. "Shit, I'm sorry. I

didn't mean to stir up another conversation around grief. Are *you* okay?"

He nods, but I can tell by the lines around his mouth and the heaviness in his eyes that this is one of those situations where he's doing his best to keep pushing along. "I'm good." He nods again. "Should we get out of here?" He points to the back exit.

"Please. Let's get some kebabs and pretend this never happened."

He's got my hand and we're already at the door. "Say less."

Chapter Thirty-Two

As soon as we exit the bookstore, the night air, cold and frigid, slaps us across our faces.

"Oh shit," I say, startled by the person in front of us.

Taylor James exhales, and a large white cloud covers him, as if he's a ghost who can disappear.

"You're a smoker?" I ask, immediately wanting to take the words back.

"It's a vape, and it's legal here." He puffs again. "I haven't smoked a cigarette since the late nineties." He leans his head back, hat off, as his hair tosses in the wind.

Then he sticks an arm out, offering his pen. Caleb inches forward, like he might consider it, until I pull him back.

"You're probably right," Taylor mutters. "That would be weird. And maybe illegal?"

Behind Taylor, a big black Cadillac stalls, headlights on. "Lenora, turn the car off, will you?" The engine shuts off and the world goes silent.

Taylor stuffs the pen in his jacket pocket. He rubs his chin as Caleb and I hold a collective breath.

Take two.

Taylor closes his eyes and says softly, "I would like to begin again, if you wouldn't mind. And apologize for my behavior up there. I was . . . caught off guard. You must understand that I am still hurting."

I nod. "I want to apologize too. I didn't mean to come across as insensitive. I am truly sorry for your loss."

A small smile crosses his face. "I will give you two minutes to ask your questions, and I will answer as I deem appropriate. Betty's privacy was important to her. But she also loved puzzles and riddles and whatnot. I know she left some things behind because she wanted to share a more personal piece of herself with you kids. In her own way, I believe she wanted to be found, to be discovered."

"Were you together like romantically?" Caleb blurts out, and my mouth unhinges itself. Sometimes he's filtered water, and sometimes, like right now, he's so unserious.

Thankfully, Taylor laughs. "Why, because of my handsome face?"

I turn to Caleb. "Dude."

"That's not a no?" Caleb insists. His sleuthing skills are questionable at best.

Taylor's shoulders rise to his chin. "We have a long and interesting history. Did I try, once or twice, to become lovers? Of course, it was my nature at the time. But not hers. It took years to convince her to go on a coffee date with me. Luckily for me, we became friends, the best of friends. And for that, I'm a better person. But in a way, I guess I like to think that we were soulmates, that our relationship was deeper than anything lovers could build. But we did love each other, spiritually and emotionally, just not physically." He inhales and closes his eyes. "You two look like a young couple in love." He smiles and my cheeks flush.

"I think we could be over time," Caleb says easily. "Is that intense? Strike my words from the record, unless . . ."

Hmmm. I've never wondered if my soul has a mate or if I've ever known real love. And I haven't truly considered if Caleb could be my person. I suppose he's an excellent contender. The few weeks with him have been better than I ever could have imagined. . . .

I have to stop myself before my thoughts trail off to his hands on the small of my back and what kissing him feels like.

With a clap of his hands, Taylor pulls me out of my lusty thoughts. "Has the game been enjoyable?"

So he knows about Betty's quest. Of course he knows.

"Eh. Kinda and kinda not," I respond. "But I'm curious to know why she did this. Why the unpublished manuscript? What exactly can you tell us about it?"

Taylor doesn't budge.

"It's just that, you know, we only have so much time left."

"Well, isn't that life?" Taylor interjects.

I huff as Taylor checks his watch, a nice big-and-round silver face with diamonds around it.

"Some things become too unbearable to say out loud. Some things she wanted to share on paper, on the page."

"Care to be a little more specific?" Caleb sputters.

Taylor sighs. "There are some things she let me know and others that remained a secret. You'll discover exactly what she wanted you to." He reaches for his vape again, places it at his mouth, and gives it one big pull. "You—you look familiar." Taylor places a finger to his chin.

"Me or her?" Caleb asks.

Oh, let's just save us both time. "I'm Mina Descanso's daughter, the famous writer. And Allen Descanso. Those are my parents."

"I already know you're Mina's daughter. You're walking around with her face on. I meant him." Taylor points to Caleb.

"Um, like Macy's parents, my parents are writers too."

"You're the Bernard boy, aren't you?" Taylor asks.

Caleb nods.

"I know exactly who you are."

"You do?" I cut in. Why the hell does Taylor know Caleb or his family?

Taylor throws up a hand, and the car turns on. He takes small steps toward the car without looking back at us.

"Wait," I practically scream. "You can't leave like this. What's going on?"

Taylor pauses as Lenora comes around and opens his door. "I'm thinking about how much I should reveal and if the truth really sets you free." He looks up at the sky, and then at Caleb and me. "You're saying a Bernard and a Descanso are

canoodling? Oh, Betty would have gotten a kick out of this."
He rubs his chin.

Umm, okay. What?

"Find the foundation." Taylor's eyes are super sincere, which makes my chest tighten.

"What foundation?"

"Betty Quinn has a foundation. Try to find the archives. The *real* archives. Or, at least the unpublished things. Not the ones she sent to Penovation. Find the stories written, lost, and kept. I think you'll both be pleased that your families' legacies are a part of them. Especially yours." He points to Caleb. "And the password is *futura forever* should Emery ask!"

Taylor knows he's leaving at the worst moment, a second before a big bomb goes off.

I step forward just as Taylor slides into the car and closes the door, a villain leaving a crime scene. The tinted black window rolls down, only Taylor's eyes visible through the small gap.

"Be well, young writers. Don't give up. You'll find exactly what you need to." Fingertips wave goodbye as Taylor drives off.

Chapter Thirty-Three

My insides are twisting and turning, and not in a pleasant way.

Caleb, on the other hand, seems to be revitalized by this news. "A foundation? What do you think is there? And futura? Like the font?" He's talking too fast. "At least we know there's more to discover, and we gotta get on it before time runs out." Which is soon.

The entire walk back, Caleb keeps repeating the same sentences over and over again.

What else did Betty leave behind?
What do you think we'll find at the foundation?
How is the foundation connected to the locations?
Futura forever?
And who is Emery?

When we finally reach campus, Caleb grabs my hands, but even his touch feels out of place.

"What are you thinking? Do you want to come up to my room? Or should we try to sneak into the library to see what more we can find?"

"What time is it?"

He pulls out his phone, the light illuminating his face. "Almost nine-thirty. I think the main stacks close at eleven? This is . . . unreal. We're getting close. We could have this thing solved and wrapped up before we leave if we stay focused." He's speaking so fast; my thoughts can't keep up. "What do you say?" He wraps an arm around my waist.

I shake my head. "Taylor James was a lot for me. I want to do our homework and think about this later." I wasn't expecting him to know our families, but maybe I've been naive. Or maybe I've been caught up and distracted in finding the wrong things. My actual story is like patches of a quilt that need to be sewn together.

Caleb's nose wrinkles, a pout on his face. He's debating if he should argue with me or not. I take two steps away, making the answer easy for him.

"I'm gonna go up and try to write. We can talk later, okay?" I run up to him and kiss him on the cheek, hoping my voice hides any trepidation brewing inside of me. Without turning back, I head to the door.

When I reach our room, for the first time maybe ever, I sit at my computer, and I don't think about anyone or anything else—not what my parents write, not Betty's work. I close my eyes and focus on crafting my story before time runs out.

Chapter Thirty-Four

The next afternoon, Caleb is bursting with energy and excitement, having searched and found the address to the Betty Quinn Foundation.

We're in North Berkeley now, walking up a steep hill. Each step forward burns my legs and makes my heart pump loudly in my chest. After our third epic incline, I begin to slow to a stop. Caleb pulls on my arm to help me, to move me, but I just can't.

"Save yourself, Jack. Get on the raft and go without me." Dramatic, always, I throw up a hand as my torso falls over my knees so I can catch a breath.

Slightly amused, Caleb lets me have my Oscar-worthy moment before tugging on my arm again. "We're so close. It's right up here." He motions to a two-story building half a block away.

I stand and my knees wobble for a moment before we begin to walk again.

"These Berkeley hills are annoying," I grumble. Just when I think we've reached the top, another hill appears.

As soon as we make it to the front of the building, I flop down onto the cold concrete.

Caleb sits next to me and pulls out a KIND bar and his water bottle.

"You want some?" he offers.

"Can't eat." Can barely talk.

Caleb takes a huge bite of the bar, almost devouring it whole.

I turn and stare at the building. It's nothing impressive— old, two stories, with chipped white paint and blurry windows to keep the outside world at bay. I stand to get a better view, and Caleb follows. There's an intercom to the side of the door, but the buttons are so worn and slightly unhinged, they don't appear to work, and nothing's labeled. If it weren't for GPS, I wouldn't even know that this was the right address, as the numbers on the side are peeling off and hardly visible.

Caleb takes a large gulp of water. He stayed up all night, scouring the internet. At first the only thing he could find was the foundation's PO box, until finally, after making some weird connections, he found the blog of a book reviewer who also happened to be a big fan of Betty Quinn and who somehow won a signed copy of one of her first editions but never received it. The blogger was ripping on Betty, her work, and just about everything she'd ever done because he never received the book. Until finally, deep in the comments, someone responded with an address if he could stop being a jerk online. My words, not the foundation's. Why Betty would make her foundation hard to find is beyond me, but it's very in line with everything I've learned about her. Kudos to Caleb for his great sleuth work.

Softly, I tap on the door in front of me. Once, and then again, with gusto. I can hear the echo of my knocks from inside the room.

"I don't mind waiting for someone to show up," I say. "We can play a game." Plus, I'm too tired to try to walk right now.

Caleb and I sit on the ground, back-to-back, supporting one another.

"A kissing game?" he says.

"Tempting. But I'm too stressed. Not to mention, a little hungry. I have a serious craving for a really big sandwich." Once my mind decides it wants food, there's no changing directions.

Caleb laughs, then squeezes my shoulder. His touches are warm and electric every time. "A girl after my own heart. Let's wait a bit longer. After we get the intel, we can grab a sub. I know an excellent local spot that is also nice on the wallet."

I nod, my brain and stomach approving of this plan. "Say less, say less."

So, we sit, cuddled up, for the next thirty minutes, counting the number of Teslas we see (twenty-five). When that gets too boring, Caleb starts whistling songs that I'm supposed to guess, but I'm only halfway decent at that because my playlists mainly consist of nineties rock and Broadway musicals, so it isn't much fun. Then he tries his best to teach me how to whistle, but I get nowhere, unable to produce even the smallest sound. We agree that whistling might just be genetic. Some folks got it, and some folks don't.

When my stomach growls louder than the bus that passes us by, I know it's time to call it.

"Are you sure we can't give it another five minutes?" he begs.

"I give up. Maybe we'll find something else about the foundation on campus. Or maybe in her notebooks; there're so many boxes, I'm sure we missed something." I stand and dust off my butt. We should really be writing anyway. We only have a few days left, and I am so close to finishing the final assignment, I can practically kiss the anthology prize. Caleb is clearly using this mystery as a distraction to not finish his, but I can't let him do that to himself or his mom. And while kissing Caleb has been enjoyable, that's about the only thing we've done today. Fern and my mom pop into my brain—they both told me to stay focused! Now look at me.

My head points toward the street. He frowns but agrees.

We're walking down the hill in silence when I realize I can't find my phone. I do a quick pat—butt, pockets—but nothing. I swivel on my feet, and of course I don't see her, a woman walking briskly up the street just as I spin around. We bump, our shoulders knocking each other.

"Oh, pardon," she says.

"My bad." I take a step back and peer up at the person my bony frame has unintentionally attacked. She's good-looking, with full, shapely eyebrows, high cheekbones, and flawless brown skin that's so smooth it must get a twelve-step skin-care routine day and night. She's striking. I stare at her like Taylor James did with Caleb.

She holds my gaze.

Now, how do I *know* her?

Beautiful and familiar, but my brain can't place her. After a beat, she drops her eyes and turns on her platform wedges, taking long strides up the hill.

My feet don't know which way to move, like I'm stuck in mud and unsure of what to do next. Bumping into her is like déjà vu bodychecked me.

"You good?" Caleb asks. I shake my head, waiting for my brain to connect something. Caleb hands me my phone, which must have fallen on the ground.

"I feel like I recognize her, but I'm not sure from where." Over our shoulders, we glance up the hill.

"We have to go back," Caleb says.

"What? Why? No. I can't climb that mountain again."

"I have a gut feeling. You have déjà vu. I think I know her from somewhere too . . . from book events, with my family." Caleb and his long legs are already ten steps up the hill.

"But I'm tired! And hungry! She could have one of those faces, you know, hot so you think you know them, but you're just taken by beauty."

"Macy." Caleb points a finger. "She went inside the building."

Chapter Thirty-Five

"Oooof," I grumble, curious about what I might be walking into as we return to the foundation, my legs surprising me with an unknown strength on this hike back.

"The lights are on inside," Caleb whispers. "I'm going to knock." Caleb's eyes are giddy with excitement. He takes a tiny inhale to steady himself and then brings his closed fist to the door. His knock is powerful, so much so that it bounces off the walls, causing the window to rattle. "Oops, too much."

"You better be extremely important!" a voice from inside shouts. Caleb's head whips toward me, panic flooding both our faces.

"My arms are super strong! Sorry! A blessing and a curse," he calls back. He smirks, one eyebrow raised. He does have nice arms.

Before I can respond, the door swings open, and in front of us, in her five-foot-eleven glory, is the woman I so carelessly bumped into on the street moments ago.

"Well?" She props a manicured hand on her hip.

My mouth falls open, and Caleb is silent.

I'm starting to think that we should rehearse these kinds of situations a bit more.

Another second and we still don't speak. Definitely should have come up with a plan, talking points at least.

"No soliciting. Please don't come again." The door is nearly closed when I throw my arm into the last open inch. Risky, very risky. My fingers could have gotten chopped off.

"Wait, please. We are here about Betty Quinn." Once I say the words, Caleb wakes up and jumps in.

"Yes, sorry. We are from Penovation, you know, the writing retreat up the road, and we have questions about . . . well, we have lots of questions, let's say that."

It takes a moment, her eyes assessing us both, before she opens the door wider. Her neck cranes, and she scans the street. There doesn't seem to be anyone out there.

"Quickly." She shoos us in. "Before I change my mind."

We take two steps inside the building, doing our best to assess the situation. Under his breath, Caleb says what I'm thinking. Hell, what anyone who came inside would be thinking. "Or perhaps we should ask to chat outside? I don't do haunted houses." He tries to whisper, but I'm sure she can hear us.

She walks in front of us to a long, narrow room, which is relatively empty. This whole place is screaming for a makeover, or any kind of attention. Our footsteps are heavy against the old varnished wood floors that are covered in a good number of dust bunnies. She takes a seat at a large wooden desk and points her hand at the two chairs opposite hers.

The beautiful unknown woman digs through the desk and pulls out a large white Diptyque candle and lights it with a fancy rechargeable lighter, which is good because the room does have an old, antique-y scent.

"There. That should balance us out," she says, taking a deep breath. "My name is Emery. How may I help you two? I'll try my best, but no guarantees."

Emery. Taylor's words from last night come to mind. Shit, we must be super close to getting answers.

Caleb sits up straight. "I'll let my associate get us started?"

I stifle a laugh. *Associate?* Really?

"My name is Macy, and this is Caleb. And like he mentioned before, we're students at Penovation this summer."

Emery nods. "Congratulations. I know how prestigious that retreat is."

"We've also, um, found some of the clues left behind by Betty Quinn. Not just us, other students too."

"How exciting" is all Emery says.

"Well, yes. Somewhat. I mean, I think so." I'm stumbling over my words.

Emery just nods. "Yes, Betty Quinn loved to leave little surprises and things for her readers, as I'm sure you're aware. Not uncommon if you know what you're looking for. Artists do that kind of thing all the time. Easter eggs as they are so-called. My favorite is finding them in paintings and video games. Betty enjoyed those of Taylor Swift." Her voice is so matter-of-fact.

Caleb scoots his chair in closer. "It's definitely provided a new layer of intrigue to the program. This adventure has led us to do some things we wouldn't normally do." He smiles at me, all teeth, in a way that lets her know we are together.

Emery raises her eyebrows as if to say, *Get to the point.*

"We, um, we were able to go through some of Betty's stuff—her wishes, not ours. And we found letters from Taylor James. Last night we actually met Taylor at his book signing down the street. And we asked him some questions too—we thought he'd have more answers for us. He was kinda nice, kinda grumpy," Caleb says. "He also knew something about our families' history."

I jump in to try and save Caleb. "We both come from literary families—our parents write fiction." Of all the times I've cringed when others mentioned my family, here I am, hoping this info will help me out. "We are aspiring writers, like they were. Taylor told us to find the foundation, which we did, but it wasn't easy, as you know."

This makes Emery smile. "There are several authors, myself included, who go to great lengths to be . . . off the beaten path. Makes things more . . . interesting."

"Well, it's working." Caleb matches her energy, which gets her to relax a bit.

"What do you do here, if I may?" I ask, trying to smile so she will ignore the fact that I'm being nosy.

"I manage Betty Quinn's estate. Mostly from my private

home office, but it's good to have a base in the city too." Emery stands up and her chair grates against the floor. This must be our signal.

"Listen. We only have a few more days until we go back to our respective homes, I have insane writer's block, and Macy thinks whatever Betty's left can help her become a better romance writer since she only read obnoxiously highbrow literature before. We were hoping for something that would lead us to Betty's unfinished manuscript. It's all anyone can talk about. Is there anything you can share to help a few kids out? Taylor said to find you and to mention—futura—"

"Futura forever," I finish. "Like the font."

Emery softens, and the muscles in her face relax. "Taylor gave you the code, did he? That man is getting soft in his old age."

"Umm?" is all I can let out.

"Give me a second." Emery walks to the back corner of the room and pulls on a wall fixture that resembles a light, which of course, because we are dealing with Betty Quinn, opens to a small cabinet. I can't see what's in there, but Emery rustles through some papers and pulls out a small bound book.

"I only have one, so you'll have to share. But maybe you can find something of use in here." She extends her hand, and before Caleb can grab it, my arm is out.

"*Untitled Anthology on Love*," I say, reading the title. "*A Collection of Authors and Their Stories About the Art of Writing and the Art of Love.*"

"Betty and some new authors she admired or mentored

worked on this project for quite some time years ago. Nothing ever came of it, for various reasons. People and art and collaboration can be a funny mix. I always thought the book had potential, though."

"Let me see." Caleb peers over my shoulder, eager as ever, so I hand him the copy. A soft harp sound beeps, and Emery grabs her phone and steps to the other side of the room. With her hand over the receiver, she whispers, "You've got two minutes with that before I need it back and you have to go."

I turn to Caleb, and without another word, we are back at the desk with the book sitting before us. Because of the plastic protective cover, the pages are preserved nicely.

Of all the things we've found and learned about Betty in these last three and a half weeks, to be here, actually here with *the* manuscript, is unthinkable. Or maybe we are exactly where she wanted us to be.

We lean in, scanning the cover. At the bottom left-hand corner there is a list of names.

"Holy shit—Linh Tien." Caleb points. "Do you think that's our Dr. Tien?"

"Gotta be, right? It explains why she's been following the clues."

Caleb's eyebrows pinch, then he taps on the book.

My eyes dart back and—"My parents?" I yelp, spotting Mina and Allen Descanso listed as contributors.

Caleb brings his face practically on top of the book. "And mine." He backs up and then points to their names—Pierre and Brenda Bernard.

"Wow, wow, wow. Stop the train. Why would my parents never mention being a part of this anthology? My mom loves talking about her work!" I grab the book, passing it to Caleb. I have to stand and pace because it's what people in big discovery situations do.

"I've never seen my parents' stories either." Caleb rustles through the pages. It's what I'd do if I had the guts, maybe another time. "Here, I'll take pics," he says, one hand on the book and the other fumbling with his phone.

"I thought our parents didn't like each other. Why would they write together?" I say, but Caleb isn't paying attention to me. His phone is out, and he's hovering over the desk.

Caleb moves quickly despite taking a lot of photos.

"Got it." Caleb quietly cheers at the right moment. He closes the book just as Emery walks toward us, hand out.

"I hope you got everything you were looking for." Her eyebrows arch, and she smiles, suddenly in a much better mood than when we arrived.

"Yes, we appreciate your help," Caleb responds. "We got everything we needed. Right, Macy?" Caleb and Emery turn to me.

"Absolutely. Again, thank you so much for your time." My fingers twist into themselves. "We got everything and more."

Chapter Thirty-Six

With the new discovery, Caleb has completely forgotten about the sub spot he promised to take me to earlier. Which is probably for the best, as everything inside of me is bubbling, acid in my stomach and sweat building on my forehead. Not a cute look. Instead, he calls a rideshare to take us to campus, which is nice, the fifteen-minute walk trimmed to a three-minute drive. Caleb, meanwhile, is upbeat, drumming his fingers on his thighs.

When we get near the dorms and snag an empty table outside, Caleb fiddles with his phone for a moment while my mind spins. My parents are the last two people on earth who should be providing love advice, let alone dispersing advice in print, on the record, and for a book! Maybe over an intimate dinner with their respective besties, immediately followed up with "but I'm no expert" or something like that. Giving advice for the masses seems so out of their range.

"Okay, I've sent you your parents' pages. Should we read together? Or should it be more of a personal thing? Probably a personal thing." He's talking so fast I can hardly keep up. "Personal sounds right. I'll just go over there, and then when we are done, we can regroup. Sound good?" But he doesn't wait for me to respond; he's up and walking to the bench across from mine, nose practically touching his screen.

I unlock my phone and stare at photo attachments from Caleb. I guess there's no time like the present. Taylor James seemed to think we should have access to this, so it can't be that bad, can it?

Another quick glance, and Caleb looks like he's studying for the SATs, concentrating hard, all focus. His legs are crossed, and he's hunched over, immersed in whatever he's reading, the rest of the world totally tuned out. I get it. I can only imagine how exciting and intense it must be to read something new from a parent you never thought you'd hear from again.

I smile in empathy before going back to my phone.

I start with Dad's story first; the beginning words make me miss him. His part is so on-brand, so very Dad, that reading it immediately gives me comfort. The story is about a man and an older dog and their adventures together one boring summer in Vermont. Very homely. Very tender. Glad to know that Dad, in his writing and in his life, has more or less always been . . . Dad.

There are so many different types of love—family, friends, pets; platonic, romantic, something in between. If we're lucky, we'll get to experience them all. Dad's writing has always been good about highlighting the various relationships we have in our lives and how they can shape us. Respect.

Pulling up Mom's story makes my heartbeat pick up.

Several clicks on my phone and then I enlarge the text. From the very first word, Mom's story is vulnerable, raw, open, in a way that makes me blink repeatedly in confusion— this is *my* mother? Essentially, her story is a conversation between Mom and her mother, my grandmother, right before my grandmother dies. They have a very honest talk about love, and Mom gets to do the yelling and pleading while my grandma just listens. The story is very expressive and beautiful in a way that only Mom can write. This is very much her. The story goes on to describe love, a mother's love, and the ways it can shape a person. It's good—make-you-cry good.

That's always been Mom's specialty in her writing, her ability to pull at all your emotions and then surprise you with a good teary eye as you finish the page. As the story continues, Mom gets to ask her mother why she was left behind from her other siblings, how a mother could let her daughter go. Worse, what kind of mother could do that? Angrily, she discusses all the ways in which being left made her feel, and the grandmother is silent. You almost want the grandmother to jump up and say something, to respond, to get angry, but she doesn't. And that makes the story even more intense. See? Powerful. Mom has always been good at writing.

I don't know much about my grandmother; I never met her. There are no photographs of her in our house. I don't even know her birthday, and she probably didn't know mine. Mom doesn't say much about her. In fact, "grandma" is one of those "do not bring up" topics with my mom.

Mom was chosen to write about love, and she wrote about her mother—is their relationship a love story? My stomach twists again. It's not often I think of my mom as a child, and here, in this story, on the page, she seems so helpless, so lonely. So why did she choose to write about her mother? To process years of resentment? If so, why would she want to share that? Is this Mom being brave? My head begins to throb, and my heart aches. Another question pulls at me—why would Mom want to share this story with the world and not me?

For the millionth time in my life, I'm upset with her. I wonder why this story didn't get published. Caleb said my parents were responsible for the whole book being canceled. Did my mother decide she didn't want to go public about her childhood? Now I want to know more about Grandma.

My throat tightens, as a bigger thought crosses my mind— how much of my grandmother's influence affected my mom, and most important, how much of that is a part of me? How did their relationship impact ours? Generational trauma drips down.

I'm about to have an existential crisis when Caleb comes bouncing over with a jolly smile stuck to his face.

"I could kiss Emery, and I'm officially in love with Betty Quinn. I don't even—wait, do you want to go first?" He sits next to me, tapping his feet; the sleeves of his shirt brush my skin. I don't know if I've ever seen him so happy.

"Care to share?" I ask.

He bounces up. "Not yet, but soon! Very, very soon." He starts walking backward, and I fake a smile. No news is good news, right? Because I'm not sure I can take any more surprises.

Chapter Thirty-Seven

"Today is going to be an epic day. I'm calling it right now," I say as we walk through the dining hall. Fern and I meditated last night, and when I went to sleep, I promised myself to keep that same calm, cool energy during my last days here. No matter what.

"How can you be so sure?" Fern asks. Caleb also gives me a suspicious glare, like I might be going too far, but I'm not.

"Because ta-da"—and then I point to the most beautiful, delicious, enticing thing to have been developed in the dining hall—"a pancake and waffle bar."

Fern laughs. "That's your predictor?"

"Yes, I'm better than a groundhog. The days here are determined by what breakfast is served in the morning, that's just fact."

Caleb squints his eyes and pauses. "Actually, you may be on to something. When the breakfast is popping, we do have better lectures."

"See, a solid breakfast is how we start the day off right."

We grab our black trays and slide them against the metal as we've done several times a day for the last four weeks. I make sure not to forget a napkin and some silverware while the others do the same.

"I'm obviously starting with the pancakes." I am salivating.

"Ditto," Caleb says. Though, let's be real, this boy will eat at least five full plates of just about anything for breakfast.

Fern grabs their tray and heads toward the cereal station. "Table by the window?"

We nod in agreement.

The pancake bar is probably the most grandiose thing that has ever blessed the dining hall, with all the sugary toppings one might imagine. I go for a chocolate chip, a blueberry, a plain, and one pancake with granola for good measure. I also get some English breakfast tea to wash it down.

Fern and Caleb, with their trays just as full, join me as I'm about to take my first bite.

"What's with all these balloons?" Caleb asks as he cuts into a waffle drizzled with blueberry sauce.

"They brought out the big ballers. Today is going to be good-good." I ting my fork and knife together.

"It's Alumni Day," Fern says matter-of-factly.

"We have an alumni day?" I ask between the best and most syrupy bites of chocolate chip pancake.

"Duh, Alumni Day is like super active. All the famous people associated with the retreat come. They do talks, workshops, and signings, so the organizers put up balloons—"

"And bring out the pancake breakfast bar."

Fern points a piece of watermelon on a fork at me. "Exactly."

"I wonder who will be here." The thought comes as fast as it goes because I'm mostly too obsessed with these pancakes to focus on anything else.

"Well, let me just say this right now, if Elise Bryant or Maurene Goo happen to be in attendance, don't worry about my thotty behavior, m'kay? I have an insane crush on both of them, and I will do anything to make it work." Now Fern has their butter knife up.

"Okay, chill. We hear you," I chime in. Over the past few weeks, Fern has turned me into an Elise Bryant fan.

Caleb picks up his fork and taps it lightly on his plate. "I'm just saying, you're not the only one. Who doesn't have a crush on Bryant and Goo? Like it would be absolute chaos if they showed up."

"Chaos squared," Fern agrees. "Sigh. Maybe one day."

"But if they bring some crusty old authors out here and make us listen to them wax poetic about literary canon or something, I will absolutely lose my mind," I say.

We all giggle because as much as we'd hate to see it, it very well could be our reality in the next hour.

The rest of breakfast is comfy and casual, as if nothing strange has happened. Super full, I pass on getting my morning Froyo. We drop our trays off in the dishwashing section, and as soon as we step outside, Caleb's hand brushes against mine.

"The sun is shining, birds are chirping. You're right, Macy, this is going to be an excellent day." Fern echoes my sentiments from earlier.

"What should we get into later? We can go to San Francisco?" Caleb asks.

"Oooh. That could be fun! I know it's cheesy, but I really want to get a bread bowl with clam chowder, and then take a picture by that big tower, and maybe run across the Golden Gate Bridge before we go," Fern says.

"Ambitious. Sounds fantastic, though," Caleb says before I can.

The path toward the main auditorium is something out of a Disneyland parade, full of balloons and streamers. I think I even hear marching band music coming out of speakers I didn't know were on campus.

"They are really doing it big," I observe.

"I hope these decorations are biodegradable," Fern adds. In front of us, at a distance, a crowd of adults in suits walks our way.

"This must be the alumni now." Caleb points his chin in their direction.

We walk toward each other down the main walkway.

Caleb runs his thumb over my knuckles, a small gesture that sets a fire in me.

The group walking toward us isn't just any group. My breath hitches in my throat. Their eyes find me first, which throws me off a little. I'm surprised my legs still work. They hold my gaze as we are pulled closer and closer together. Our respective groups are about to bump into one another.

I cannot believe it.

When we are about a foot apart, one in particular fakes a smile. "Macy?"

My insides flip, twist, and turn. I drop Caleb's hand and do my best to stand up straight. Why haven't I figured out how to make myself disappear yet?

"Mom?"

Chapter Thirty-Eight

"In the flesh." Her voice is singsongy. She throws up her arms and reveals an outfit not unlike my usual style. Hers is more glamorous and more expensive, of course. She's Nordstrom, and I'm Nordstrom Rack . . . clearance aisle. She's even wearing platform shoes, which she knows is my thing. Except hers have the iconic Prada logo on them, and today my platforms are just black Vans with a small hole growing on the side.

"Wh-what are you doing here?" The words barely escape my mouth. Fern and Caleb are silent as they stand by, watching.

"No *Hi, hello*? *Nice to see you*?" Sarcasm drips from Mom's voice. "I was invited, sweetheart. I wanted to surprise you," she says the moment Dr. Tien strolls up beside her with a large grin on her face.

"You two know each other?" I ask.

"Macy, please." Mom's tone is condescending, but she's

right, of course Mom and Dr. Tien know each other. I momentarily forgot how I got into Penovation.

Mom crosses her arms, her gold Tiffany bracelets shining as she smiles mischievously. "Well, are you going to introduce me?" Her eyes toggle between Fern and Caleb. Mom sticks out a hand, and I remember the few manners I have.

"Sorry. Um, Mom, this is my roommate, Fern. Their pronouns are they/them. They're like my best friend here—"

"Hi!" Caleb cuts in.

I shoot him a look that says *chill* as Mom and Fern shake hands. "It's a pleasure to meet you, Ms. Descanso. I loved *After August*," Fern says.

"Likewise. Any friend of Macy's is a friend of mine." Mom lays it on thick.

I scratch the back of my neck. "And, Mom, this is . . ."

Mom gives me another look, her left eyebrow a perfect arch, like she, once again, knows all.

"A Bernard, yes? Caleb, correct?" she says.

Caleb sticks out his hand. "Yes. It is a pleasure to meet you, ma'am." He and Mom shake hands, and excuse me? What episode of *Black Mirror* is this? Caleb doesn't seem fazed, nor does Mom, which weirds me out even more. When Caleb releases his grip, he steps beside me, but we don't hold hands.

"We have about two more minutes before the morning session starts." Dr. Tien taps her watch. "And I'd hate for any of us to miss the opening speaker." Dr. Tien gives my mom a loving glance.

Is Mom going to give opening remarks? I mean, this last

week is about revisions, and I have seen her revise a novel in only a few days.

My stomach tightens.

Mom stares at me until Dr. Tien turns on her heels and waves us all to follow.

We trail behind their group and soon hear footsteps running behind us. Caleb, in slow motion, turns and says the words to totally solidify this as the exact opposite of the best day ever.

"Dad?" Caleb's voice squeaks. "What are you doing here?"

"Son." Caleb's dad stops in front of us, and it takes an awkward moment, but Caleb leans in and they hug. I notice my mom stops at hearing Mr. Bernard's voice, but then she just continues inside.

When Caleb steps back, I try not to stare at his dad, but it's hard. Mr. Bernard is slightly taller than Caleb, with the same flawless dark brown skin. He's got a salt-and-pepper beard that goes all the way around his face, above his lip, and even dangles off of his chin. Where Caleb is soft T-shirts and shorts, Mr. Bernard is dapper. Well, maybe not all the time, because this is our first interaction, but everything about him in this moment screams proper, refined, elegant.

They pause and then both take off in a fast-paced Haitian Creole. Fern and I turn to one another briefly before our eyes dart back to them.

Never mind an introduction. I can stand here, I guess.

Around us, folks trickle into the auditorium. I swear I hear whispers about our parents, but I'm not sure; I could just be paranoid.

Fern tugs on my sleeve while Caleb and his dad keep talking, as if nothing else exists. I'm a little disappointed that after six years of French, I can pick up nothing of what they are saying.

Until, finally, Caleb's dad smiles big and waves bye.

Is he leaving?

He walks toward the side of the building and goes in a different entrance than the students.

Ummm.

"Sorry, I'll explain more later," Caleb says, not even looking at me. He nods to Fern, and we fall into step with the others toward the open auditorium doors.

"Were you even going to introduce me?" That comes out more upset than I'd like. Up until a minute ago, I wasn't even sure I wanted to be introduced, but hello, at the very least it's just manners. Or would it have stung more if he had introduced me and called me a *friend*? Suddenly, at the appearance of our parents, a lot of relationship pressure is piled on us, and I don't like it. Especially after last night's rocky conversation.

"Macy, yes. When the time is right," he states matter-of-factly.

"Did I say that when you were yelling hi and cheesing at my mother?"

"Come on. Don't be like that."

We shuffle into the last row, and then I put Fern between us as we sit.

Something is going on, and apparently, I'm the last to know about it.

Inside, I seethe. The lights dim so Caleb can't see the resting bitch face he's brought on. I'm beyond annoyed at him and this surprise family reunion.

All of the auditorium lights go out, then the stage lights come on, nice and bright. From stage right, a line of well-known authors walk out as the crowd begins to clap.

"Welcome to Alumni Day!" Dr. Tien's voice rings out over the microphone.

There are seven people onstage, including a Pulitzer winner. I notice that Mom is the first in line and Caleb's dad the last. Are they intentionally sitting apart? Just like me and Caleb?

Chapter Thirty-Nine

After several opening remarks and an uplifting speech I only catch bits of, Dr. Tien passes out notecards with fruits on them to divide us for our small group sessions with the guest authors. I don't know why the universe is so intent upon pairing me with people who make my life slightly chaotic, but it is.

"If you have a blueberry on your card, follow me!" Mom's voice is strong and commanding and slightly bubbly.

I turn over my notecard and, of course: a blueberry.

With a quick step, I turn to Fern. "I need you to switch cards with me. Please?"

Ferns eyes widen, but they don't blink. "Sure." They stuff their notecard in my hand. "No questions asked."

Stealthily, I pass Fern my notecard, and a wave of relief washes over me.

"A literal hero. Thank you so much."

Fern nods, but my anxiety comes back the moment I flip over Fern's, well, now my, card. "A blueberry?" I wail.

Fern shrugs. "What did you—" Fern turns their card over. "Ha! You also had blueberry! What are the odds? No escaping your mom now." Fern laughs, linking their arm in mine. They pull us toward the door.

We're split into six different fruits, or groups. With about six students in each, led by alumni. When we get to the small study room, Mom has placed the chairs in a circle, with a small opening near the front dry-erase board.

The other four students trickle in, and for once, I'm glad Caleb isn't one of them.

Fern grabs a seat closest to the board and motions for me to sit next to them, but I can't. I grab the farthest seat away from Fern, but that doesn't help, because even with an out-stretched arm I could touch Mom. Close. Everyone in this room is entirely too close.

"Hello, everyone. I'm Mina, Mina Descanso. Feel free to call me Mina." Mom turns off the overhead light and plugs in a diffuser and a yellow sun lamp. "There." A lavender mist fills the room. Mom hops up on the desk and crosses her ankles. "Much better. I don't know why the lighting in learning insti-tutions always has to be so insufferable."

The other students laugh, but I've got on a straight face. Mom is charming today. But she's also . . . Mom.

"And yes, full disclosure, that is my daughter." She points my way, and the group turns to glance at me.

See. Mom.

As if they didn't already know!

"Shall we get started? Pens and paper out now, please. Let's begin with a warm-up exercise to get your creative juices flowing today, followed by some time for you to revise your short stories, and then we can do a question-and-answer session. How does that sound?"

"Sounds great!" Fern exclaims, leaning off of their seat, super engaged. I shoot them a look, but they just shrug it off. It be your own friends.

"Great!" Mom echoes back. "Everyone shout out words or phrases, and I'll write them on the board. This can be anything, whatever comes to you."

The group wastes no time.

"Dogs!"

"Nobel Prize."

"Venus."

"Cotton candy."

"NASA."

"Family secrets," I chime in. Mom glares at me but writes my words down anyway. The list on the board looks all out of place, but we're silent as we wait for Mom to guide us.

"I'm going to write each of these topics down on a sheet of paper. Then I'll give a paper to each of you, where you will write one sentence. Then you'll pass your paper to the right, and the next person will add on to your sentence with another sentence. We will do this for several minutes until we have the beginnings of a story. Sound good?"

Everyone is game.

Mom scribbles on the papers and sets a timer as we begin. I start with NASA. The activity is interesting, I'll give her that. The papers spin around the room until the stories are born.

About twenty minutes after our warm-up and a timed

revision session, where people asked for Mom's feedback, she begins to wrap things up.

"We have ten minutes left. How about some questions? Ask anything that's on your mind, and I'll be as honest as possible. Industry, revisions, agents—anything that comes to you."

"Do you think it's ethical to write stories about family members without their knowledge?" I blurt out, thinking about my unknown grandmother, someone who I can't even talk about but who my mom intended to share with the world. Mom frowns and makes a disapproving face, her mouth twisting on something sour.

"What would make it unethical? Is that the correct word? Do you want to try again?" Mom speaks but doesn't look at me.

"How do you know when you're ready for an agent?" Lily asks.

But I speak over her. "Fine. Do you think if you're writing about your family members that other family members have a right to read those stories?" I'm frazzled. "I don't know the right context, but what the hell was that anthology story about? You and Grandma?" I'm huffing out words, confused about Mom and Grandma and the last seventeen years, annoyed that I found that damn story, frustrated at myself for wanting to unearth Betty's final work so bad.

"Macy. Language." Mom hates cussing—she thinks cuss words lack imagination. She especially hates when I cuss. But I do it from time to time, I guess when I want her attention, or to irritate her, or a little of both.

"I thought this was your time to be honest?" I stand, grabbing the paper on my desk, painfully aware of all the eyes on me. I'm making a scene. Another thing Mom hates.

"Students, let's take a quick pause while Macy and I reset and—"

"No need." I stomp away. "I'm leaving." I grab the door and let it slam shut behind me.

Chapter Forty

To: MrDescanso@gmail.com
From: MacyMania911@gmail.com
Subject: Et tu, Dad?

Ummmm. You're so fake. Why didn't you tell me Mom was going to be here? You must have known. A heads up would have been decent.

::::::Cries in mom trauma:::::and dad betrayal:::::::

From: MrDescanso@gmail.com
To: MacyMania911@gmail.com
Subject: Cry havoc and let slip the dogs of war!

Hi Sweetie,

So, she decided to actually go, eh? To clarify and perhaps absolve myself, I knew it was a *possibility*, but I didn't know if she'd attend for certain. I'm sorry if you felt blindsided or ambushed, definitely wasn't my plan to betray you. I haven't heard from your mother since I've been at sea, so I assumed her interest in being at Penovation was gone.

But now that she's there . . . would I be wrong to suggest that you two make the best of it? You know, she is a wonderful writing teacher, even if she also happens to be your mom. Could she be a helpful sounding board? Perhaps!

How are your final days? Bittersweet?

I haven't heard from you recently (outside of this angst, of course).

What's going on? Anything you need to tell me? Anything I should know?

Unrelated, but now I think I'd like to do a rereading of *Julius Caesar*. One of my top five Shakespeare plays. Do you have favorites of the old Bard? If so, I'd like to know about them. Can't wait to show you the free "swag" I got.

Love you. Miss you.

Favorite Shakespeare plays! Swag?! Dad is completely missing the point right now. I bite my bottom lip, unsure if this requires another response or if he's just going to pry more. Which makes me wonder . . . why is he asking so many questions? Did Mom email Dad that she saw me and Caleb holding hands? Is that what he wants to know? I close my eyes and take a deep breath, doing my best to settle myself.

From: MacyMania911@gmail.com
To: MrDescanso@gmail.com
Subject: Re: Cry havoc and let slip the dogs of war!

She did show up. I've been dating the Bernard boy.
We found an old story of yours from that Betty Quinn
anthology. Also found Mom's story with stuff about
Grandma that I never knew about. Kinda a weird
way to find out about family drama, no? I get that
it's tough for Mom, but a little warning woulda been
nice. You and Mom are both fired, relieved of your
parental duties effective immediately, until further
notice.

    I stormed out of Mom's writing session, which,
okay, was extra, but I have good reason. I guess I
have no choice but to talk to her. Light a candle, wish
us luck. You know we'll need it.

    I forgive you, but I won't forget ,

M

Chapter Forty-One

The groups break for lunch, which is two local taco trucks and a churro cart, but I am too upset, too confused, too hurt to eat, which is even more disappointing given that Mexican cuisine is my favorite. From Mom's ambush to Caleb's non-existent introduction this morning to Dad's emails, I'm not feeling any bit of this day. No amount of pancakes could have prepared me for the wrath building inside of me.

My phone buzzes from my back pocket. Please be something good.

Caleb: nvalskdfjo&^%31#@!!!!!

Caleb: I've got great news. Can you meet in front of the dorms ASAP?

Macy: ?

Caleb: tell you there

Macy: but tacos?

Caleb: I know. Believe it or not, the good news > tacos

Caleb: I don't even recognize myself rn, lol 😹

I stuff down the grab bag of emotions that brews inside of me at even hearing the words *good news.* But maybe his happiness will rub off on me; maybe he can transfer his good energy, and I can wash away this morning. I stomp toward our usual bench, ignoring the birds chirping and the perfect blue sky.

Thankfully, it's relatively quiet when I arrive. Everyone has the better sense to be at lunch and is probably five tacos deep or in a much-deserved food coma.

"You're here!" Caleb rushes toward me and plants a soft kiss on my cheek.

Okay, that's nice. I cool down one degree.

"What's the good news?" I ask, doing my best to sound normal.

"So, I spoke with my dad, and I told him about what we found."

"Go on."

"Well, first I filled him in about everything that's been happening since we arrived."

"About us?" I blurt out.

Caleb half frowns but is way better at keeping calm than I am, clearly. "To an extent, yes, I told him about us." He raises his eyebrows, a move that should make me smile but only makes me itch.

"What did he say?"

"Uhh? Not much. But I was thinking, maybe we could all go out to dinner? Since we're all here. Tonight?"

Not much is all I hear. I'm digging, searching for something or someone to unleash my anger on. Caleb looks me in the eyes, and I exhale. Okay, Caleb is not the appropriate target.

"Sorry, I'm just feeling off. Go on. I won't interrupt. Promise."

I close my eyes and shake my head, doing my best to be an effective listener. "Please continue." When I open my eyes again, he's still smiling.

Caleb claps his hands. "Last night, reading my mom's story, I found buried treasure, or—or, even better, like a lost conversation with my mom. I could hear her voice while reading and I . . ." Caleb pauses and then stares at something in the distance. "I'm going to submit her story for the competition."

"Wait, what? Can you even do that?"

He chuckles. "Why not? These words, her words, deserve to be read by others. That's why she wrote this, I'm sure. It's way too much of a loss for all of us if it just—what? Lives in some file cabinet in some crusty old building." He pauses, nodding to himself, hopeful. "Dad had kind of forgotten about

Mom's old story and thinks that maybe me using some, if not all, of her work for the anthology submission could be a nice tribute. I would obviously credit her—I'm not trying to pass her work off as my own. I just want her stories to live on. Words can be immortal, you know?"

"I get that, but also, the submission—your submission—should be your own writing. I don't mean to be the one to remind you of the rules or whatever—"

"So then don't? You're my critique partner, not the critique police."

I frown and stand up. "Really, Caleb?"

His face softens. "Sorry, I'm not trying to be mean. I thought you'd be happy for me."

"I am happy for you, but that's just not what this retreat is about."

He grunts. "Never mind. I shouldn't have expected you to understand."

I don't even try to hide the irritation in my voice. Every cell in my body is ready to attack. "What does that mean?"

"What is this retreat about, then? You can't even comprehend losing the two most important things in your life."

"No, I can't, but—"

"Writing was our thing. It's our family thing. And maybe I can't write anymore, which sucks, but I need to keep moving. And I need to do what I can to honor her."

"But you *can* write!" I practically scream.

"Stop saying that! You don't know what I had before—you could never know."

"What does that even mean? Actually, I don't want to

know." I'm huffing out the words, practically out of breath I'm so exasperated.

Caleb stands and crosses his arms. "You know what it means."

I frown. "I don't."

"The relationship I had with my mom is different than the one you have with your mom. Maybe you're not really upset about me using my mom's story, maybe you're actually upset about your own mom stuff. And since we are being real, your mom is still here. Don't take that for granted. Figure your relationship out, stop acting like a brat, and make it work."

"A brat?!" I wail. "Don't go there just because you want to justify taking a shortcut. We still have a few days left. Finish writing your own story and see about winning a spot in the anthology like everyone else. Honest, authentic, and original, that's what we were told from the very beginning." I cross my arms to match his.

"A shortcut?" he takes a step back, face contorted, evidently ignoring everything else I said.

He's suddenly hit every nerve, every unresolved issue that's been bubbling and brewing inside of me.

"You don't know anything about my mom—or me." Whatever little control I had is gone. I have officially entered the unhinged, anger-is-a-natural-and-necessary-emotion phase. "No need to even suggest dinner with your dad, since apparently now it's fine to break bread together but not be introduced?"

"It wasn't even like that."

I cut back in. "Oh, but it was."

He's cold. "Fine, if you think it was, then it was."

Even though I brought it up, the reality of it all begins to sting. Did I actually want to go to dinner with his dad? Maybe he's right and I don't know how to navigate fighting through writer's block while dealing with the pain that comes with losing a parent. I know I can be difficult with Mom, but she's difficult with me. Beyond guarded. He's not wrong, though; life is flimsy. I'm not the rule police, but damn, I know he can write. I've seen his work.

Pressure builds behind my eyes. "Well, you know what this brat thinks this is?"

Caleb throws his hands up. "I said 'acting like.' You know what? Whatever. I think we both know."

Over.

But neither of us has the guts to say it.

"That's fine. I need to go." I spin. I can't see through my anger haze.

"No, I need to go first." Caleb huffs, turns on his heels, and begins heading toward the dorm.

I pause—I wanted to go to my dorm room, to curl up in bed and cry, of course, but if Caleb is going that way, I can't follow him. My feet start walking. I can figure it out after.

"Actually, I'm going over there." Caleb is suddenly beside me, muttering. "Those tacos are sounding good right now."

"Great, I'll go this way." I turn again and try not to glare at him as I do my best to head in what I hope is finally the right direction.

Chapter Forty-Two

After an emotional afternoon, I find myself doing the unthinkable—meeting up with Mom.

"I'm surprised you showed up." As soon as I say the words, I immediately regret them. I don't love that she can activate my heinous, grumpy side, but it's been that way for years. It's like she has something in her that brings out the monster in me. I don't like it, but I also don't know how to quell it.

"How about you try that again?" Mom responds on beat. Rightfully so. Her head tilts, and her bangs, which need to be trimmed, fall into her eyes.

"Sorry, I just—I never know when I'll see you." My gaze finds the ground for this last bit because it is true, I never know with her. Mom was always the type to have something come up last-minute and miss recitals. And don't let her be on pickup duty, because she's *always late.* I can count ten times in my life where she like just forgot to show up. Entirely.

So, I'm not making up the sass. But to be fair, that was a long time ago.

This is now.

But components of our relationship still sting. Some wounds take so long to heal.

"Hey, Mom. Thanks for meeting me here," I say, one arm open for a side hug. She matches my move, and suddenly I'm a little kid, hanging on to her mother. Her scent, roses, always roses, fills my nose, and as much as I want to ignore it, there's a part of this embrace that feels like home.

She motions toward the bright, flashing lights of the diner. "Shall we?"

I nod as we step inside.

Glenn's is an iconic twenty-four-hour diner that has an extensive menu, and the portions are usually too large, like the Cheesecake Factory but less fancy. Mom and I snag a booth, while most of the other patrons sit at the counter on those spinny chairs near the line cooks. Something sizzles in the background, and immediately my nose picks up the aroma of grilled onions and garlic and my mouth waters.

Mom removes her glasses from atop her head and puts them on, where they sit on the bridge of her nose. She squints, considering the options.

Out of habit, I bite my bottom lip. I'm trying to recall the last time Mom and I actually went out to dinner or just hung out like this. It must've been six months ago, when she drove from Los Angeles to an authors' panel in Santa Cruz. Betty Quinn did the unthinkable and brought us together, I guess.

"No sucking, Macy," Mom says, tapping her own lip. She's always hated this weird tic.

I let that thought come and go when an older man approaches our table. "Drinks, ladies?" he asks through wire-framed glasses.

"Coffee, black," Mom says before handing the menu to the server.

"I'll have the same." Mom shoots me a glance. "Actually, never mind. I'll take a vanilla milkshake, please, extra whipped cream, and a side of fries."

He gives us a nod and disappears for a moment before returning with two glasses of water.

I take a big sip of mine, the ice-cold really hitting. All the while, Mom watches my movements, like I'm some kind of art installation at a museum.

"What?"

She responds, "I'm just admiring you. You've changed so much since the last time we saw each other."

"I looked great this morning."

"You know that's not what I mean."

The alumni workshop was a complete mess, but I push the memory to the side. If I dwell on our history too much, I'll never get to the heart of why our relationship is where it is. Even though it's more talk of the past, it will help me to understand some things about me and . . . us.

I take a moment to recalibrate my thoughts. I need to be straightforward but not accusatory. Last thing I need is for Mom to get upset and leave. Who knows how long it'll take for me to see her again.

"And here we are," our server says, placing a hot basket of fries and our drinks down. Mom grabs the white porcelain and cradles it like she's done her whole life, long fingers wrapping around the mug. I'm not sure if she loves hot coffee or hot cups in her hand.

I eye my fries while I finally muster up the courage to ask. "So, Mom. Betty Quinn? I didn't expect to get caught up, entangled, but here I am."

One eyebrow arched and raised, she pulls the mug close to her face and takes a loud sip. "You surprise me still, Macy."

I don't know how to answer that, so instead I take a handful of fries and use them as a spoon in my milkshake.

Mom gently puts her mug down, and a soft-but-sad smile forms on her face. "I . . . Why don't you tell me what you know? And I'll do my best to remember what I, well, remember. That way we can both do our best to clear up what happened earlier. And figure out a path forward."

"Is that what you want? A path forward?"

Mom takes a sip of her coffee and smiles but doesn't answer.

The way Mom is staring at me makes me a little uneasy. She's hardly ever one to be startled, or caught off guard, no matter what she says. She's always prepared for an emergency, and nothing surprises her. Whatever it is, though, it's clear now: my mom is a mystery.

Maybe that's because her mom was a mystery.

My brow furrows and I think about the next step—

"Just say it, Macy. I'll be okay." There she goes again, in my head, even when she shouldn't be.

"Fine," I mumble. "I think she—Betty Quinn—there were rumors that she had an unpublished manuscript hidden in Berkeley. And she left a lot of clues around for us to find it. She told us to be clever. Caleb and I, well, we got close, but we also began to answer these mysteries, and we found"—my stomach tightens, and the last four weeks of searching and even Caleb rush to my mind—"we found an old anthology, met Taylor James and a woman named Emery, and I read your story—the one about grandma."

Mom doesn't blink, doesn't move as she processes the information. We sit in silence for a moment, and then another before I want to ask her if she heard me, but from the way her expression lingers between a smile and a frown, and the way her eyes seem heavy, like they're fighting back something more than she wants to say, I know she's trying to figure out how much to tell me.

To calm the awkward silence, I take a large gulp of my milkshake, the cold shocking my teeth but the taste delightful and refreshing.

"Why didn't you ever mention the book? I had to hear about it from dad's publicist's son. Or about Grandma? Why were you working with the Bernards if you dislike them? Why didn't the story collection ever get published—I don't understand." I can't look at my mom when I ask these questions. I'm almost afraid of the answers.

"Oh, Macy. Where to start?" A tear builds in her eye, reflective and bright, and in the quick instant she blinks, it's gone.

"I don't want to complicate anything. I only . . . I want

to know. I think I deserve to know. Finding out about you and our family by accident is . . . kinda hurtful." My face falls when I realize what I've actually been feeling is hurt. Maybe for some time now. Maybe I wish that Mom and I could have had these conversations more. That speaking to her wouldn't be so hard. That she felt she could tell me things.

And then Mom does something that completely stuns me. "No, I'm sorry. You're curious. I know you don't mean any harm or hurt. And you're right—you deserve to know. That story is as much about me as it is about you."

The apology is enough to send me into a tizzy. My brain is about to freeze, and it's not from the ice cream. The thing about having a stone-cold, super-intense mom is that apologies usually don't come this easily or freely. But the way it just rolled off her tongue has me shook.

She grabs a fry and stuffs it into her mouth.

"Are you kidding me right now?" I gasp. In addition to being anti-fries, she prefers to live off of almonds and oat milk and does everything in her power to keep her "Black don't crack" and "Asian don't raisin" skin youthful. Which she has been successful at; her face is smooth like porcelain and we often, unjokingly, get mistaken for sisters.

She shrugs and grabs another fry from the mound.

"Where to start?" she asks again. "I was born, as you know. And when I was about ten, things got a little rocky at home. Mind you, there were four of us kids already. We were poor, probably poorer than most. Mom got an opportunity from her second cousin that allowed me to go live with them. At ten, I thought I was doing the family a favor, so I went. But I was ten, I was too young to make those kinds of decisions. And living with that cousin . . . that wasn't great. I never saw much of my parents or siblings after that." Mom doesn't look at me. She nods, and her eyes get glassy.

Then Mom does the unthinkable. She takes a long sip from my shake, closing her eyes as the sugar hits her lips.

"My goodness, that's delicious."

She slides the drink back to me.

I nod, seeing her in a new light. This might be what cities feel like after an earthquake happens, small movements that bring about big change. I feel like the plates between us, or whatever was keeping us apart, are now pulling us together.

"Did you see your mom again? How, um, autobiographical is the story? And why didn't it get published?" I finally ask.

Mom grabs another handful of fries and stuffs them into her mouth. Then she washes it down with a sip of coffee, my soul in disbelief. That feels like a crime against humanity.

"I saw her a handful of times when I was a teenager, but I was too upset with her then. They were failed attempts at connecting. When I started writing, or I should say when I started to get paid to write, several of us new authors were brought together for an anthology, the one I'm guessing you found. In a strange turn of events, I went to visit your grandmother—she was very sick at the time—to try to clear the air, but . . . the conversation wasn't productive. I wrote the story you read, and . . . she died shortly after. I was devastated, to say the least. And I, for reasons I won't get into, was the reason the anthology was pulled." She pauses, taking a big, deep breath. "Well?"

My mouth wants to fall off of my face. Mom and I have never had open conversations, and having them now feels like . . . I don't even know. Exploring space, or something just as wild and nebulous.

Mom raises an eyebrow. "Your expression says it all."

At that, we both laugh.

We sit in a soft and comfortable silence for a few moments, the fries slowly disappearing. Mom has a refill of coffee and finishes that quickly too.

"I never really had a mother, so I've never really known how to be a mother—it's all been a mystery to me. Maybe that's why I am the way I am. But I've always been proud— proud to be connected to you." She leans in and our hands touch. "Anything else you want to eat?" she asks.

I shake my head, and she smiles deep, the lines around her eyes showing but still revealing her beauty. I can't eat anything else. I'm still digesting what my mom has served. Not only that, but coming to the realization that Mom is . . . Mom is *human*. She was once a young girl, figuring it out. Once a young writer, figuring it out. And now a mom figuring it out.

"Anything else I should know about your retreat or . . . Betty Quinn?"

I whip out my notebook. I tell her about the clues, the things Betty Quinn left behind that we've found. And then I tell her about Betty's writing, years of rejection, years of what people would call failure and then, boom—success. So many stories, so many books.

At this, Mom's face lights up. "In writing, we become immortal."

"I guess so."

Mom pays the check with a crisp one-hundred-dollar bill and tells the server to keep the change. She grabs my hand again. "I guess this might explain why I'm the way I am? Maybe you come from a line of women who do things a little bit differently."

My eyes begin to sting, and then a tear runs down my face. "I guess so."

And then Mom makes sure I see her fully. "Different doesn't necessarily mean bad, you know. Different is just . . . different. Special. Unique."

I can hear what she's asking me, and maybe I've made different mean so many things, but she's right—different doesn't mean bad. It just means different. So, I throw my arms around my mom, and we hug, and for the first time in a long time, the embrace is wrapped in love and forgiveness, and it fills me up in a way that only a mother's hug could.

Chapter Forty-Three

We walk outside to Mom's car, a gray Mercedes with personalized plates.

"So, you want to tell me about this boy?"

At this, I freeze.

"How did you—"

Mom's eyes pierce me, the brown like lasers even in the dark. "There are some things we say with words, and some we say with our bodies." Then she lets her shoulders slump and makes a super mopey face, which I guess is a fairly accurate representation of me since Caleb and I had our fight.

I pull at my sweater sleeves. "It's not going to work out between us." And my eyes heat up again. Because it's one thing to think that something won't work, but as soon as I say it out loud, I don't know, it becomes real. Realer than it was before as a quiet thought in my brain.

She pulls me in close, and I feel so small in her arms.

"Oh, sweetie. I know it can be tough," she says softly. "Love is—"

"I didn't say anything about love," I say defensively, blowing my cover even more.

"You're right. You didn't. Relationships, love, everything in between. They are never perfect, but they are ours. They teach us, they help us grow. They guide our souls."

My face warms up, and as much as I want to fight back the tears that are building, I don't. I close my eyes and let one sneak down my face. "Ugh. It's so annoying," I whine.

She tightens her grip and gives my arm a squeeze. This is most definitely our record for affection in like, my whole life? I guess today is as good a place as any to start.

"It's annoying. Yes. But life is both frustrating and exhilarating. I think those peaks and valleys make a good life, a great life, even."

I open my eyes as she releases me. Finally, we see one another. As mother and daughter, sure. But just as people, connected. Forever.

So I decide that this is the best time to take a chance. "I think we're cursed," I say. "Like our family. We are all just shitty in love. It's like a dominant, genetic thing. Why would it skip a generation? Of course I have it, of course." I think about Caleb, and how he and I should be together right now, preferably kissing. But I don't know, I've kinda messed that up.

Mom's body stiffens. "Oh, Macy. I never took you to be, what's the word? Superstitious?"

I scoff. "How could you not? I mean, where in our family is there representation of like a normal relationship? Stuff with Grandma was left unresolved. Exhibit A, you and Dad! I mean, who gets married and divorced not just once but twice in a lifetime?"

"Oh, sweetie," she says again. Softer, her voice almost childlike. Mom bites her bottom lip, something I do that I know she hates, so this must mean she's thinking, or calculating her next words with care. "Love stories are never perfect. Haven't you learned that yet from this retreat? They aren't packaged a certain way, they just . . . are."

I frown and so does she.

"Let me try that again. There is no one way a love story should look. I think there are elements and qualities to *loving* someone—respect, honesty, care, those types of things. But two people are going to have a love story unique to them and their identities. Does that make sense?"

I nod. I mean, I guess.

She continues, looking intently into my eyes. "Your father and I didn't get a lot of things right, outside of you."

This comment makes me both cringe and overflow with love at the same time.

"What? It's true. We both learned a lot about ourselves in the process of being together. And I know it's unconventional. We met and got married so young. And then divorced. And then to do it again? Trust me, people thought we were out of our minds. And maybe we were, maybe we just had to see how much time had changed things. But we were just doing us. And guess what? I'd do it all over again, in a heart-beat. Your father is a good man. Some people are destined for happily-ever-afters. We got two happily-for-nows."

Mom says it all so casually, but living through it, their extreme ups and downs, was hard. I remember for a full month, Dad would come home from work, put on the same sad, sulky playlist, and lock himself in his room. He'd reappear for dinner, his eyes red and puffy from the crying he'd been doing. Meanwhile, Mom was off, wherever she was. I had to make sure he'd drink his water, leave soup by his door. I cared for him like he was the child and I was the adult.

"Dad was like super wrecked, just so you know, after the second time."

Mom stares off into the distance. Several cars pull into the parking lot as the diner fills up. "I know. I never said love came without pain."

Which brings me back to my original point. "So why do we do it, then? If we know there are no perfect stories, and we know that there is a possibility of hurt on the other end? Why would anyone try?" And not just anyone. Me? Why did I think I could be immune to the follies of a relationship?

"That's the question. Perhaps, and I'm going to be cliché here, perhaps the journey is more important than the destination. All relationships will have different destinations, but the journey that you make with a person, that might be the real joy of it all."

Hmmm. I let Mom's words sink into my brain, like a seed that's just been planted. Maybe she's right. What did I think would happen with Caleb anyway? We both knew this was a four-week situation. Our relationship always had an end date. We both knew this. We gave it a go anyway. And even though we aren't talking now, even though I sure as hell would like to, I'm glad we tried.

"It's getting late. I'll drive you back to campus. Oh, also, not that the issue is any of your concern, but I was able to talk to Pierre Bernard. One benefit of this emotionally charged day was that I was also able to express our condolences, in person, about Brenda to Pierre. I'm glad I had the chance to do that. She was a lovely woman. And, well, things are resolved. We're not besties, but we don't have . . . ?"

"Beef?" I offer.

Mom chews the side of her cheek for a short moment. "Beef . . ." She closes her eyes, calculating her next move.

"Oh, come on, just tell me! You're soooo close, spill the tea, Mina."

Mom's eyes check me, quick. "You know I hate when you do that."

I smile. I do know that.

"Fine. But only this once. This is probably the sugar and dairy talking." Mom frowns. "A long time ago, oh, I was probably your age, when I was just starting out as a writer, I met Brenda at a writing program, just like yours. We worked under Betty for a summer; the three of us had a unique bond. Years went by, as they do, and Betty sprang the anthology idea on us, and we were just beginning our literary careers, mind you. But Betty kept tabs on us and was impressed with our debut novels. And she was determined to show the world the power of a good romance story. I agreed to do it because of the money and because she was so excited to bring different perspectives together. So I wrote my short story and then your grandmother passed, and . . . in my grief, I did a lot of things I regret, I see that now. I wasn't pleasant to be around. I got a lot of pushback from some of the authors of the anthology, including Brenda, about how I had interpreted the anthology submission, and how that kinda changed the whole tone of the book. There are specific beats and tropes in romance that you just can't mess with." She exhales while I'm hanging on her words.

"And?"

"You have to remember this was before social media, okay?"

"So, you were using carrier pigeons?"

Mom just rolls her eyes. "Something like that. I'm not proud of what I did . . . but I was a mean girl. My second book had just become a literary success, I was doing well, and I was bitter. Basically, I said that romance writing, romance books, were a waste of time. Fluff. Essentially downplaying all the work Betty and Brenda had done, especially. Then I backed out of the project. I got some of my editor friends and other authors in the anthology to rethink the romance genre as a whole. Suggested they weren't doing *serious* writing, whatever that means. Betty, of course, was pissed at me."

Mom rubs her temples for a moment. "For a short period of time, Betty was the closest thing to a mother, a mentor, that I'd ever had. I know my lashing out hurt her; I know it did. But me downplaying the genre, that was—*tsk*. That was me being nasty. With all the commotion, Betty shelved the manuscript. People had passed up other opportunities to do this project and lost sizable pay. The book had already been signed, so we had to give back that initial payment. The editor couldn't publish it because they only did romance, not the literary mom-daughter story I'd written. And, in support of me, your father had also turned in a story about a man's love for a dog. Perhaps this was the catalyst for the Bernards disliking me. Pierre stood up for his wife, as he should have." Mom inhales, breath shaky. "Of all the writing I've done, romance was the most challenging. So, I'm proud of you for not letting my opinions and teachings stop you from engaging with the genre."

My mouth falls open. "Well, damn!"

"Language. But yes, I know." A pained look crosses Mom's face. "Trust me, I know."

We sit in silence for the short ride, and when she pulls into the campus parking lot, I almost want to tell her to turn the car around, that I want to go home, back to Santa Cruz. That I can't face any more unknowns. Instead, my fingers pull at the lock.

"And what you mentioned earlier, about your father . . . I cried too. I cried a lot," Mom says. The words sting my eyes, and maybe I might cry again. I nod. I don't know why I feel better knowing that losing my dad, our family unit, was as hard for her as it was for us.

"Thanks, Mom. I love you," I say.

"You more." She swallows as her eyes mist.

"It only took a mediocre essay for Penovation, an author's cryptic clues, a hot guy from a family that my family was beefing with, a little breaking and entering, and some overdue honesty, but I'm glad we got here, Mom."

"Hold on. What breaking and entering?"

Chapter Forty-Four

Fern's alarm clock blares exactly when I think I'm about to finally get some rest. It's our final day of class, and in forty-eight hours, we'll be going home.

"Morning already?" I turn my head into my pillow, but the sound, whatever this horrific sound is, has already infiltrated my brain and penetrated my peaceful world. "Also, what is that noise? Is that new?" Their alarm continues to blare, some hip-hop mash-up that feels way too offensive before breakfast.

Fern jumps. "I'm so excited for today! Also, morning!" Their voice is too chipper.

"Fern. Alarm. Please." Against my better judgment, I open my eyes and prop myself up on my elbows.

Fern holds up their phone. Everything that was blurry comes into focus. Fern. Our dorm room. This retreat. Caleb. My life in shambles.

In two quick steps, Fern is beside my bed. "This is a remix of the *Bridgerton* theme song. It puts me in such a good mood." Fern hops up again and twirls. Actual in-the-air twirls, like a figure skater on land. "Today is going to be an excellent last day, indeed!"

My head falls back into my pillow. I said the same ahead of Alumni Day, and we saw what happened.

"I have a feeling that something big is going to go down. Something will give on the last day of classes. Last day to wrap it up, last day to say I love you, or I lust you, last day to get off our bullshit and do what we need to do to win."

I roll my eyes, but Fern can't see.

"Have breakfast with me? Maybe read over our stories one last time? Oh, but you have to come out tonight. Say you will. I have a friend who knows a guy who can get us into this very exclusive lounge and serve us drinks if we go when he's working the door or the bar."

I pause, my brain taking a moment to process. "To be honest, I'm ready to get back home."

Fern's face falls, and their shoulders slump, making me feel bad.

I try again. "Imagine! You'd have this whole space to yourself."

Fern gives me a glare. "For like two days? You belong here. I need you here. Don't give up right before the finish line because of a boy." The sincerity in their voice tugs at my insides, and my eyes begin to feel like I've just diced an onion.

"Okay, we absolutely cannot do this now. You get ready,

go eat. I'll see you at morning session." I throw up a hand and shoo Fern away. Fern gives me a long, cold stare before grabbing their towel and leaving the room. I'm slow to get out of bed, but I do. I grab my clothes and am beginning to get ready when I see myself in the mirror. I lean in close, the freckles on my nose larger than I remember. "Just get through today, okay?"

"Our final session, and I thought, why not do something new?" Dr. Tien stands in front of the whole group, her silver jumpsuit and silver jewelry almost blinding. Her outfits are always surprising, and I've learned she likes shiny material, but hey, she looks good. "A freewrite. I encourage you to incorporate what you've learned and what we've discussed in the last four weeks. You have your stories for submission, but push yourselves further, write more. Absolutely anything you want." The room is silent, but laptops are open, and pens are put to paper. We are ready.

She sets a timer, and before the countdown begins, I've already started. I think I've been waiting to write this story my whole life but didn't know where to go because I didn't see the full picture. Now I do.

Macy Descanso
Freewrite

TRUTH TALKS

"Whoa, where am I?" The room is all white, with bright, offensive hospital lighting.

"You don't know?" a computerized male voice responds. "You brought us here."

"Wait, who are you?" A quick glance down tells me that I am me—these are my hands. I touch my face, the earrings in my ears, even though I don't entirely know what's happening. "Wait, am I dreaming? Is this my brain?"

"Something like that," the voice responds.

"The narrator in my brain is male?!"

It can't be.

"Technically, I am without gender. This is just the tone you've selected. But feel free to change the timbre if you'd like. Though I should remind you that time is running out."

"Time for what?"

A bang. Smoke fills the room.

There's a swivel chair and the back of someone's head. "Mom?"

"Yes. Hello, Macy," she responds.

"What are you doing here?" I ask, but I know the answer.

Another bang like before, smoke following.

"Mom?!" my mom parrots me.

"Grandma?" I follow. I've never seen the woman next to my mom in real life, but I wear her face, her dark eyes and her cheekbones.

"Yes, yes. I am here." Grandma has short black-and-gray hair, wavy wrinkles on her skin, and a calm-but-chilling expression. I can't tell if she's happy or annoyed.

I stand up. "What is going on—what is this?"

But I already know. I have this thing where I ask questions even though I know the answer. I don't know why, but then again, I suspect I kinda do.

Next to Mom, there's a small table with three empty vials that read "truth serum." If we've somehow taken that, things are about to get real. I guess I did ask for this.

"You have four minutes left. Please ask any questions of each other that you'd like. Questions must be answered, but they won't be remembered," my brain narrator says.

"Wait, what?" I spin on my heels, hoping to see this person, but there's no one.

Mom twists toward me and tugs at my hand. "Have a seat, honey."

So, I sit.

Mom turns again, this time toward her mother. "Why did you let me go? How could you let me go?" To anyone else, Mom's voice would sound strong.

But because she's my mom, and I know just about everything about her, I can pick up on the quiver, the uncertainty hanging off her words.

My grandmother closes her eyes for a brief moment. "I knew you were going to ask this."

A long moment of silence.

Growing up, my mom would just say she never knew her mother and leave it at that. I guess because I was little, too busy playing with my toys, I never wondered much about the woman who raised my mom or, in this case, didn't raise her. I never thought much about how my mom's mom and their relationship would somehow have an effect on me.

Grandma scratches the inside of her palm and lets out an exhausted sigh. "You deserve to know. You're right, you deserve to know." She pauses and grabs my mom's hand. "I let you go because I thought you would have a better life without me."

Someone quivers, maybe my mom, maybe my grandma, possibly both. A strong part of me wants to see my mom's face at this moment, but her back toward me is probably best because I know I won't be able to handle her raw emotions. Mom never cries, but if she were to cry right now, I'd lose it too.

"It was a mistake, you know. A mistake I paid for every day of my life. . . ." Grandma pauses, probably waiting for my mom to forgive her or something, but Mom doesn't speak. "We were so poor, so poor. It was

hard to see any way out. I thought sending you—
I thought sending you would be best."

"But keeping my other brothers and sisters
together? Why was I . . . why was I expendable?" Mom's
voice holds a lifetime of sadness.

"I know. I was wrong. You were . . . you were the
oldest, and I thought . . . I suffered every day on earth
for it." Grandma leans over and grabs Mom's hand. "I
never stopped loving you, and I never forgave myself
for letting you leave." She sniffles. "You don't have
to forgive me, but please know I love you. You are so
strong and so successful. We see what you've become.
You are . . . the best thing I've ever done."

Mom leans into Grandma's chest as Grandma wraps
her arms around her.

"I needed you. I needed a mom."

"You deserve so much more than I could have ever
given you." My grandma's voice is soft, and after a beat,
tears begin to crash down her face. My mom is silent,
but I know she's crying too. I know her; she's deep in my
bones.

"Two minutes," the voice calls out.

"Mina, what else?" my grandmother asks, still
holding on to Mom's hand.

"What . . . what is your favorite memory of us?" The
crying in Mom's voice is apparent now.

"Oh, that's easy." Grandma doesn't hesitate. "We
used to take these evening walks, just you and me . . ."

". . . and the singing . . ."

"Yes, we would walk and sing without anyone interrupting us," Grandma adds.

Never in my life on earth have I known Mom to sing a song. I'm too shocked to speak, to move, to even breathe.

My mom stands up and Grandma follows. "That's my favorite memory of us too."

And like that, I can see Grandma's arms around my mom again. There's gentle sobbing, and then a moment of silence. Grandma cuffs her hand around my mom's ear and whispers something that makes my mom pull back, lock eyes with Grandma, and laugh. I want in on the joke, but that same smoke from earlier appears, and my grandmother vanishes before I can interrupt.

"One minute," the voice calls out again.

"Wait, but that's not fair!" I try to protest, but again, I know the answer. We always need more time with those we love. The time we get will never be enough.

Mom turns to me, her face damp with tears. Her eyes are bright, glowing, a little happy and a little sad.

"Your turn," she says.

We stare at each other for a moment, mother and daughter. In my mother's face, I see so much of my future, and in mine, I'm sure she sees so much of her past.

"Not a question." The words barely escape. If not

here, then when? "I'm . . . I guess what I'm trying to say is, I'm sorry I'm not better. I'll be a better writer and possibly human. I . . . I need more time. It's hard following in your footsteps, you know! You didn't make it easy."

"Oh, honey, I—"

"You and Dad are weird? Complicated? I mean, I love you both. I just . . . sometimes I want to be like you and other times I can't stand that I am like you—it's confusing." I pause because under any other circumstances, I would never be so open and honest with my mom, but right now, wherever we are, I don't hold back. "Why don't you ever say 'I love you'?" The words are hot acid out of my mouth. A question I thought I'd buried, only to come back from the depths of my subconscious.

Big tears roll down Mom's face. "They are the hardest words for me to say. Even with your father, I had . . . I had a hard time expressing them to your father. But I always tried to show you, I always put my love on paper for you. Every book, every word, I wrote for you."

My chest tightens, and it feels hard to breathe, to move, to think. It's true, Mom always dedicates each of her stories to me.

I never thought much of it.

A mist. Grandma appears and places a hand on Mom's shoulder.

"I love you, Macy. I'm sorry that those words are hard for me to say—I'm still figuring out this human thing too."

Mom grabs my hand, and I feel connected to her, to the grandma that I've never met, to every woman in my maternal line that has come before me.

"And we're about fifteen seconds out." That damn voice.

"Wait. I need to keep this. I need to remember." I'm pleading with myself. "I can't go back thinking that . . . that . . ." Shit, why is there never enough time? "I don't want to go back with some untrue story of us. . . ." I'm frantic in my own mind and I hate it.

"Five seconds."

Grandma rubs Mom's shoulder. "The heart will never let you forget, Macy. We love—"

Chapter Forty-Five

Caleb is one chapter that requires an ending.

As much as I'd like to avoid him and pretend that these last four weeks didn't happen, I can't. It wouldn't be right. Not for myself or for the relationship we had.

I don't need to call him, because I think I know where I can find him. Hopefully.

The path toward Lake Rose feels harder this time. With each step, I'm pushed into a conversation that I already know I hate.

This time, the path seems longer, the afternoon sun meaner. Even the greenery seems to be angry.

But the closer I get to the lake, the more I realize the path is the same, the sun is shining, and nature is not mad at me for screwing things up with a cute boy, even though that might be the story I want to tell myself.

With the last steps before the lake, I take a big, deep

breath to steady my body. And just as I had hoped, maybe even dreamed of, he's there, on our bench from that first, or second, depending on which one of us you'd ask, meet-cute.

Perhaps he was waiting for me too, because he glances up at just the right moment. His fingers wave hello as I make my way over to him.

"Mind if I join you?"

"I was hoping to see you here." Caleb gives the bench a double pat, so I sit.

"This is . . . What's the opposite of a meet-cute?" I mutter. "Sorry, that was supposed to be funny."

"No, it's funny. The opposite of a meet-cute? I think we might have missed that lecture." He dons a smile, fake, but kind.

I rub my hands against my jeans. "I guess we should have thought this through a bit more. At least, yeah, maybe talked about us being together a little. Or at all."

"Oh, definitely. What would you have said, if you could get a do-over, if you had your time machine, or something like that?" Caleb takes a rock from his pocket and flings it into the lake.

I frown. "That's the funny thing about this, isn't it? I thought I was saying and doing the right things in the moment. But in hindsight, I wish I could have been more honest about my mom and our family stuff, but I didn't even know how much of our rocky relationship was building and brewing in me until this summer. It's kinda a weird thing to finally realize that your parents are . . . human. Just regular people, trying to sort through life too." I pause, tears welling in my eyes. "Oh, and I would have mentioned how hot I thought you were at our first meeting."

This gets Caleb to laugh, genuinely. "Oh yeah?"

"Yeah." That day seems like an eternity ago, even though it was only four weeks. Time is strange.

Caleb leans back, his arms atop the bench. "Well, since we're being honest, I will say I saw you and your dad the first day. I was hoping we'd be paired together."

"You were?" I'm shocked. "Why?"

"Even though there's drama between our families, I knew that you would understand what it's like to be at a writing retreat having parents like ours."

"Having parents like ours," I echo.

"But yeah. I guess our story . . ." He can't say it, so I guess I will.

"I guess this is the final chapter?"

He nods. "Louisiana and California are so far apart."

"Right. Plus, school . . ."

"Yeah, and the time zones."

"Exactly. Not to mention writing, and extracurriculars"

"It would be a lot."

"Too much—distance would probably remind us being together isn't a good idea."

"Exactly."

"So, we agree?"

"Mutual agreement."

Has a mutual agreement ever felt so shitty? Probably.

Doesn't this happen in most romance novels? The breakup. Though, in our case, there won't be any big moment where we get back together. Because that's not real life.

Neither of us makes eye contact, which is good, because if he saw me any more clearly than he has these last four weeks, he'd see pain.

He leans in. "I'm sorry about the other day—about what I said."

"About me being the worst critique partner in the universe? My brat-like tendencies?"

He scratches the back of his neck. "I wasn't thinking clearly when I said those things about you. I was just mad, being mean. I'm glad we found our parents' drafts together, but I'm not going to try to use my mom's words for submission."

I nod. "I'm sorry too. I was so upset that my mom was almost willing to share herself with the world before me."

"I get it."

Another long pause.

Caleb turns to me, his eyes a little red. "But there's good news. I was able to write. I have to thank you for that."

"Me? No way. You're the one doing the hard job of working through grief. Your mom would be so proud, I'm sure of it." I allow myself to sneak a small glance at his face. I do my best to remember this moment, a happy moment. An ending, but make it somewhat cute.

"Well, you were the best. An excellent friend, partner in crime, detective, purveyor of fine snacks. The list could go on."

How could I not smile at that?

"And you, kind sir? An absolute dream. Even if I had a time machine, I wouldn't change a thing about our story." My eyes begin to water again, and my face feels hot, so before either of us is foolish enough to say something more, to try to make the impossible possible . . .

I stand. Yes, this moment here, although this is a good-bye, this is how you end a chapter, even if it's a love story. No guidebook in the world could have helped us. Because sometimes when you love someone, you just have to say goodbye.

Chapter Forty-Six

The last night of the retreat, and of course it happens. Martin finds a clue that he thinks will lead to the actual missing draft from Betty Quinn.

Go figure.

After Caleb and I blew up, talking to anyone else about what we saw at the foundation felt too personal. Better to stay quiet and out of grown folks' business. If our parents and the others want to do something with that manuscript, they will. But I'm not surprised that Martin found something we missed. Knowing Betty, I'm sure there are lots more clues waiting to be discovered. The woman was good at this mystery thing.

"Okay, I'm almost ready. I think. Two more seconds." Fern is on a loop, going between their desk, halfway-packed suitcase, and closet. Looking for what? I dunno.

"It's time to wrap this party up. Game over. For the most part, I'm ready to go home. To my bed and my bathroom that

I don't share. The packing cubes were cute coming in, but going out, I'm leaving with whatever makes it into my suitcase. I can't believe we're finished tomorrow."

"I know, right? Time can't be real." Fern pops back up. "Got 'em!" Fern's eyes are beaming with nefarious teenage shenanigans.

"Why do we need those?" I yelp.

Fern holds up two extra-large black Sharpies and grins. "I never leave home without them. Nor should you." Fern throws their head back, and an actual high-pitched evil-villain laugh escapes their mouth. "Okay. Let's go. Martin said to meet on the quad two minutes ago."

We rush downstairs as Martin and every other person form a line, heading out. Every other person except Caleb. Most of me is relieved—we've already said goodbye, why undo any of that good forward-moving progress by being next to one another again?

But something small in me glances across the group, not once, but three times, to see if he's here.

"Martin, where are we going? Are you sure?" someone calls out, which stops Martin in his tracks.

The group forms a circle, and Martin steps into the middle. "My esteemed peers, am I sure? Absolutely. After I found the money, which I wasn't allowed to keep"—the crowd boos—"after that, I knew there was a lot left to uncover. With the cunning of some of y'all—thanks for the tip about the website—I learned I was right." Martin pauses, and we all stare at him, transfixed. *Finish what I started*? That could mean anything. So, while some of y'all were canoodling, some of y'all writing—shout-out to you, do-gooders—I went back to the library and through Betty Quinn's stuff. And guess what I found?"

I hold my breath. I'm guessing this time it's not debilitating heartache or family secrets.

"I found the actual book from her website, you know, the one that said, *Finish what I started.* Something told me to look for it in her library, so I did, and I found the damn thing." Someone gasps. "Yeah, tell me about it. Where was I? Oh duh, so about thirty minutes into my hunt, I find the green book from her website. Naturally, I started to freak. I'm giving the book an inspection, and then boom! On the back? One address. And that address, sweet friends, is where we are going now." More murmurs in the crowd.

"Well, let's move. It's getting cold!" Fern calls out, and everyone laughs.

We follow Martin off campus in a single-file, ants-marching line. The evening sky is a medium-deep blue, the streetlights providing enough light for us to see three feet in front of us.

The walk should probably take only three minutes, but because some of the group misses the green light on the cross-walk, we get separated on different blocks, so three minutes becomes fifteen, which is when folks start to get antsy.

"Are we there yet? I'm in heels!" Gina calls out.

"Okay, okay. I think we have arrived." Martin stops at the end of the block, does a quick run around the corner, and returns to the front of the group. "Yep. We are here. Ta-da." He extends his hands in a great reveal, but impressing teenagers is hard.

"Wait, are you sure?"

"Umm." Martin throws his hands up again.

How sure can anyone really be with these kinds of . . . *adventures*?

"This was the address she left," Martin exclaims.

The group steps forward.

"The Berkeley Public Library, though?"

The lights are off inside the old brick building because it's almost eight p.m. and it's obviously closed. One little but mighty streetlamp beams onto the library sign.

"Is there more?" Luke asks.

"Uhhh . . . this was all I found," Martin replies, deflated.

"Womp, womp. Kinda mid. Let's go."

At that, the group breaks up and fades away, as if we were never here.

Fern goes up to Martin and gives him a pat on the back. "Thanks, fearless leader. I think it's cool."

"Wait! Come check this out," Lily calls from around the corner.

We walk toward the building, and perhaps this is actually what we were meant to find. The back wall of the library is worth a view.

Fern places a hand on their hip as Martin shakes his head.

"You came through," Fern declares.

The large wall has a spray-painted picture of several different authors, including Toni Morrison and her iconic quote

"If there's a book that you want to read, but it hasn't been written yet, then you must write it."

Fern slaps my back. "Well, that's clear to me. *Finish what I started*? Not us actually finishing her last book, but finish our stories? Continue to be a part of a long legacy of writers?" Fern pauses but then lifts a finger to the sky. "Betty is saying to write and obviously support your local libraries. Kinda an elaborate way to tell us, but I'm down. Too down."

Martin was clearly hoping to find more. "That's it?" he whines. I guess he'll have to figure out how to dominate publishing on his own merit. He'll be fine.

"Not quite." Fern walks up to the back wall, and we follow.

It's Berkeley, not the Sistine Chapel, so the bottom third of the building is already populated with a modest amount of local graffiti.

"Betty Quinn was here," I offer.

Fern pulls out their Sharpies and waves them in my face. "And so were we."

Martin stands guard while each of us scribbles our initials; Fern draws a plant next to theirs.

We link arms, admiring our work.

"Not too bad," Martin says. Fern nods in agreement, stuffing the pens back in their backpack.

My eyes scan the back wall, the mural, the graffiti, and the picture collage in the office window. "Wait, check it." I point, my feet already moving toward the glass. There must be hundreds of photos from over the years taped up. Young kids at story time, workers shelving books, birthday parties.

Fern flips out their phone and shines a light in my direction. And that's when their eyes catch mine. I step closer. The photo is faded from time and sun exposure, but that's them all right. There are three rows of faces—in the bottom row, I spot Mom immediately. She's sitting next to Brenda, who is next to Mr. Bernard, or Pierre. In the second row, there are two people; one person has a hand over their face, and the other hand holds an open book, making them hard to distinguish. Next to them is a young but tall girl, if I had to guess, Emery. In the last row, Dad stands with three other guys I've never seen before but have probably heard of. My eyes squint. I do my best to see more but can't.

"Fern, what book is this person holding?"

Fern brings their phone closer, but at this angle in the dark the light only makes things blurrier. "Hard to tell. Why? Who is that?"

Martin leans over Fern's shoulder, resting his chin.

I tap twice on the woman holding the book over her face, her tiny Afro the most visible part of her.

"We finally found Betty Quinn."

Chapter Forty-Seven

"I can't believe we're going to meet everyone's parents," Fern says as we walk to the main auditorium. Our arms are linked, and even though we've promised to keep in touch, we both know the truth: Fern is going to college in New York, which is basically galaxies away from California. Fern has become, dare I say, a good—nah, scratch that—an incredible friend this summer. I'm going to miss them.

"I can't believe you got ready before me." I tug on their arm.

"Pfft. Believe it!" Fern stops as we approach the large door to the building. I know what Fern is thinking, what we are all thinking, about how much four weeks can change a person, about how much we've grown since we started. How, if we're lucky, we'll keep going.

Fern pulls me in for a big hug, their arms tight around my body.

"Fern, do not cry," I declare.

Fern sniffles. "I won't. But I might. The start to my summer of yes was so good. And you as a roomie, and Betty Quinn as a third wheel, I just . . ."

I can practically feel the tears building on their face. "Seriously. Don't you dare. If you start, it'll lead to a chain reaction. I need to leave with the last of my emotions intact, okay?" I break the hug and give Fern a hard glance. But it's too late, Fern is misty in the eyes, top lip quivering.

"For fuck's sake," I mutter. Ugh, I'm going to miss Fern. I pull them in for one more hug while Fern lets their tears flow.

Inside the auditorium, Dr. Tien shares photos and highlights from the last four weeks; she even showcases some of the graduating seniors who are heading off to college in the fall.

After an hour of this, the lights go up, and it is really, truly over.

"Friendly reminder, your anthology submissions are due by three p.m. today. Best of luck to you all," Dr. Tien says again, like she needs to remind us.

As a group, we give ourselves and the staff a round of applause. Then the back doors open, and we are flooded with familiar adult faces. Fern finds their family immediately. Their dad is super tall, with long, thick, curly hair. What I imagine Fern's would be like if they let their locks go wild. Fern's mom is super short but also possesses the same long, thick, model-like hair. Fern's hair genes are no joke.

The auditorium is almost too stuffy and hot, so I slink outside to the cold air.

"Something told me you'd be out here." I know that voice. The one, the only. I turn and my body warms. I've missed him.

Dad's got a big grin on his newly super-tanned face.

"Dad!" I shriek.

"DAD?" I say again when Mom appears behind him, holding on to his arm.

"Hi, Macy," Mom utters.

My mouth falls open, and all the air in the entire universe flows in and out.

They are both equally my parents. And they can technically both pick me up. But didn't I see Mom the other day?

"Now, don't go thinking too many thoughts at once," Dad says, pulling me in for a hug. "It's been nice to catch up with your mother. I heard you two finally spoke as well?"

I catch Mom's eye from the side of our embrace. "Yeah, it was time."

Dad releases me, his arms outstretched as he holds on to my shoulders. One of his favorite moves. "I was thinking we could all go have dinner? Hear about the retreat and your writing before Mom heads back to Los Angeles?"

If this had been another time, last year, I would have thrown such a fit. Or simply seethed internally about the suggestion, saying nothing at all.

But things are different now.

"I know a good spot," I say, linking my arm with Dad's. "Mom?" I extend my other arm, and she takes it.

One quick glance over my shoulder as I whisper bye to the space. A lot can happen in four weeks, and for me, a lot did. I found friendship, love, and perhaps the most important thing of all—the courage to use my voice as a writer.

Chapter Forty-Eight

"I just need ten minutes," I yell to Dad as I rush into the library. I flip open my laptop and look at my latest draft. I need to change the final chapter. What I had before was only okay, but after the last two days, I think I know how I want at least one love story to end.

"Ten minutes," I tell myself. Which is good, because in fifteen minutes, our final story submissions are due.

Macy Descanso
Anthology Submission

LOVE ON PAPER

Tasha had finally solved the case. Four weeks of undercover investigative work, and she'd found what she was looking for—love. Well, love and the reason behind Jazzy's mysterious concussion: fainting from low blood sugar and not the suspected foul play at Robert's party. Turned out Jazzy was prediabetic, but with some modifications in his diet, he should be back to his normal Jazzy self.

"Are you sure you wanna do this? And for a boy?" Jazzy whined in the passenger seat of Tasha's mom's new Tesla. Driving it felt like piloting a spaceship. A very cool, fast, computer-like spaceship.

"He's not just a boy," Tasha replied.

"Said every girl ever," Jazzy said, running his hands through his locs.

He's my boy, Tasha thought. *And I'm not going to let him get away.*

"Wow, slow down!" Jazzy grabbed the side of the car, but Tasha didn't slow down. She wouldn't slow down. Seth's hockey game would be ending any minute, and then he would be on a bus back to Canada for spring break. What? Was she supposed to just let him leave, let him go without saying the words in her heart? Why hadn't she told him in person? Why hadn't she whispered *I love you* into his ear when she'd had the chance? Too caught up in a mystery when love, true love, was right in her face! It was painful how perfect Seth was. Well, not perfect, because no one is perfect, but perfect for Tasha. Who else understood that she acted the way she did because she had detectives as parents? And the fact that they'd bumped into each other so many times at multiple points in this school year? No, it wasn't a coincidence. It was Cupid, the universe, the Millionaire Matchmaker signing off on their union.

But noooooo.

Their last time together and Tasha was too afraid to even suggest long distance after graduation. Pathetic. Too afraid to even suggest that they suggest ways to make their relationship work.

The parking lot to their stadium was full, so Tasha drove the car to the front and stopped in a red zone. "Stay here and don't get us towed, Jeffrey!" she hollered at Jazzy, who was too busy scrolling on his phone to notice his friend fleeing like a kid on the last day of school.

Tasha did not stay to wait for a response. Instead, she was running as fast as her out-of-shape legs would take her, bolting through the stadium.

"Seth! Where are you?" she called out. The game had just finished; people poured out from every direction. Tasha felt lost, but she had to keep going. "Excuse me, so sorry, pardon me," she said on repeat to everybody she accidentally bumped into, which was a lot.

When she got to the ice rink, a cold covered her face. What if she had really missed him? Looking at the glistening ice made her think back to the first time they'd met, when she was taking a beginner's skating lesson. Tasha hadn't realized her class was intended for kids, but Seth didn't make it awkward. In fact, he'd taught her how to happily float across the ice she had always feared. Then, the more Seth became insistent on helping her solve Jazzy's mystery, the more Tasha realized how much she liked—wait, loved—this person. Her person.

"Seth!" she called out again, right as three bodies appeared on the ice.

"Seth! Where are you?"

Before she knew it, he'd skated up to the divider. "Tasha? What are you doing here? I thought—"

"I know, I was wrong! If solving this mystery taught me anything, it's, well, how to ice-skate, and that sweet endings are a piece of cake! You're my cake, you're my partner in light crime, you're my sweet ending! I don't need any more clues to figure out how I feel about you. I love you!"

It only took a moment before his hands were on her waist, pulling her in for a long-awaited kiss.

"I love you too. Since the moment I met you. You're my cake, my ice cream, my Froyo buffet. Everything good in the world leads me back to you."

They kissed again.

Case closed.

A smirk hangs on my lips. I've done it. It's a love story, one that challenged me as a writer, one that I created with care. A story that helped me process my feelings. The best I could do with where I'm at in life, grateful that writing could get me here. *My* kinda love story, with a beginning, a middle, and now an end. And I'm proud of myself. There was a lot I had to say, a lot I had to feel, so I took it and put it on paper. With a minute to spare, I exhale, and then I press send.

Epilogue

There are several things you need on your first book-promo tour. Sharpies to sign books, should anyone ask you. Thick or fine point, classic black or your favorite color will work, up to you. Gum or mints, obviously and without explanation. A request for a Chanel purse to carry said items. Your parents will laugh and ask if you have Chanel money, which you don't (but it is good to at least ask, because hey, you'll never know unless you ask). And lastly, you need courage. The first three items you can, luckily, buy; the courage thing you gotta work on. But I'm finding the older I get, the more courageous I'm becoming.

And at nineteen, my life is exponentially better than at seventeen. A lot has changed in two years—I've grown so much that sometimes when I reflect back on who I was, I'm imagining two different people. Take the relationship with my mom, for example—way better. Not perfect, but stronger and kinder every day. I think that's probably because nine-teen is so close to twenty, which is totally not a teenager. Adult me gets Mom in a way teen me would gasp at. The cool thing about change is that I'm curious about who I'll continue to evolve into next. Time and growth are powerful, especially as life keeps moving forward.

Berkeley, thankfully, is still the same. Like Moe's, the local indie bookstore, hasn't changed much, which is kinda wild and comforting at the same time. They have, however, given the inside a nice little facelift (everyone needs a little work done from time to time). There's a fresh coat of off-white paint that makes the lights glisten. The various plants that they keep around the store windows are larger, more in charge.

Book lovers dance around the first floor, where the best-sellers section holds something special that I got to see at various stages—Betty Quinn's final anthology. I'm not sure how it happened, but Dr. Tien was able to do the impossible and finally get the sorta-hidden manuscript published. I take two steps and crane my neck at the cover, proud of the names I recognize, authors I've become lucky enough to know. My parents, Emery, Taylor James, the Bernards, all finally together. As it should be. I nod to myself before heading up to the second floor to celebrate our work.

Slowly, as if I've done these bookish events before, I make my way to the front of the room, where a long, rectangular table is set up. I rub the navy blue pencil skirt and matching jacket Mom let me borrow, finger waving to the others in the room.

Fern spots me first, grabbing my shoulder. "From FaceTime to in real life!" Before I can respond, we are in a tight hug, rocking our bodies to from side to side in excitement.

"Wow, I am so happy to see you I might explode into a million, bajillion little pieces!"

"I know, right? Better than any HD screen? Better than any iPhone could convey, right?"

"Better times infinity." We hug again because duh. Best friends and long-distance relationships call for this type of reunion. I'm often surprised at how easily Fern and I were able to keep in touch. I've heard horror stories about friends falling apart because of distance, but somehow, with Fern, or maybe because of our dynamic, distance made us closer.

We took the time to send each other articles and videos, to make sure we responded to texts, and even though we probably had ten different conversations going across our various social media apps, we made the time to really check in with one another, asking how are you? No, *like HOW ARE YOU?* And not shying away when one of us had to answer that we weren't so good. That life got tough once we left our parents' homes. That things felt confusing after high school. That maybe we'd made the wrong decision about college or that we had, indeed, fucked up. We held space for one another, and I dunno, that's kinda made all the difference.

Fern and I release from the hug, but our arms stay connected. Fern's moved on from knitting beanies to larger items, like the oversized rainbow poncho with fringe they are wearing now.

Dr. Tien grazes by before stopping to greet us. "Lovely,

isn't it? Should be a nice-sized crowd for your first book launch. And a *San Francisco Chronicle* reporter will be in the audience." She dons a smile worthy of the PR gods. She's in an expensive-looking fitted black suit, with newly gray strands of hair that make her even more beautiful and more intimidating than before. Which I didn't think was possible. I'm into it.

"Okay, but feast your eyes." Fern points to the front where there are several copies of the anthology propped on the table.

Our book.

My book. With my words inside. In print, for people to love and hate and everything in between.

Each copy looks like it has a ring light in front of it, glowing and shining.

"Oh my," I can only whisper. Two steps forward, and I reach out to touch the cover, my fingers running over the embossed title, *I'm Into You,* with little doodles of cupids, emojis, and hearts decorating the front, plus the glossy spine and all the other components that come together to make the magic in my hands.

I've always loved books, always. Maybe my parents gave me that love, and honestly, for that I'm not mad. As a kid, when I needed to be transported, which I often did, books were the vehicle to get me out of my head.

And in my hands, I have a story that got me back to myself.

Wild.

The paper is cold but electric to the touch as I flip the pages. I'm inspecting every inch of the damn thing, like it's a newborn baby, checking every crack and crevice. "She's perfect. Absolutely perfect."

The back cover of the book features the five lead YA romance authors. And, of course, there are the five Penovation students whose work got chosen to be part of the anthology. Below our name cloud is praise from authors I've long admired.

Seeing my name in print like this makes my chest tighten.

My lips tug up, a smile imminent, when I read through our bios. There's one my heart has been looking for.

Caleb Bernard hails from a family of writers. He's currently studying English in college, where he is always eating a snack. This is his first published piece, but definitely not his last.

Naturally, he had a great love story in him. If our four weeks together taught us anything, it was how to love, and how to put love on the page. My heart beats loudly, the racing pulse inside of me reminding me of our moments together. Funny how it only takes one period of time to help shape who you'll become.

"Good evening, good evening." Dr. Tien taps at a wireless mic, her voice all power and omnipotent, and folks immediately begin to sit. Fern pulls at my sleeve, and we take two seats near the aisle, toward the back, so we can giggle should we need to. And because no one is paying attention, I take a copy of the book with me. What's one more?

I did help write it, after all.

The lights dim, soft and low orange, as Dr. Tien begins a slideshow about the retreat and the importance of telling our stories.

I tuck the book in my lap and flip the pages until I find his words.

"Operation Cinnamon Roll" by Caleb Bernard.

My lips part, and my eyes widen. Maybe reading this here isn't a good idea. But I can't help myself. I have to know what he's written about, what still lives in his heart. So I let myself skim.

Life would never be easy as a vigilante time traveler. Ramon had come to accept that as his fate. But life would always be sweet if he had Belinda by his side. . . .

Ramon tugged at his collar, afraid to give her the bad news, that their rocket was almost out of fuel. Operation Cinnamon Roll would most likely be incomplete. Four weeks hadn't been enough time. . . .

After what felt like an eternity apart, Ramon had discovered that Belinda, his Belinda, was living on another planet. Not with her ex, fortunately, though he was very much alive. Ramon went to Lake Rose immediately, with one intention—never losing her again. . . .

The clapping and laughter in the room pull me out of the trance from his story. The boy can write. But I always knew that. I'll annotate and highlight later, in the privacy of my own home, where I can geek out over his storytelling. His piece is everything I imagine from that summer—the complex emotions we often hold, all at once. *Proud* might not be the right word, but it's what I am. Proud that he had the courage to sift through his feelings, even if he had to do that away from me.

"Food, time for food." Fern points toward the back of the room, where everyone is lurching at a chocolate fountain.

I stand, the blood and oxygen rushing to my legs and head. Emotions build inside of me too, like Caleb said, happy and sad at the same damn time.

Air. I need air. Breathing for my body.

I wasn't expecting to be flooded with emotions, from our stories to this book event, hell, even to thinking back on those four weeks Caleb and I spent together two years ago. I need several business days to process.

My legs wobble as I make my way to the back toward the exit.

Two heavy steps, and there he is, in all his glory.

He's changed, a more handsome change, which is apparently possible. He's gone from a hot ten to a searing twelve. I kinda expected to see him in a location T-shirt, but instead he's in a fitted and soft gray cotton shirt that tugs at the hems because of all the pull the shirt endures over the hilly shapes of his muscles. He's not even flexing, but his arm muscles are showing off.

"I was hoping to see you here." His voice is the same but a little more mature, comforting and soft, husky and sweet, distinctly his. "You look beautiful."

"Your story . . ." is all I can let out.

"YOUR story," he responds with emphasis. "You are incredibly witty, and your voice is . . ."

"Well, you wrote the most beautiful piece. Your mom would be so happy. . . ." I pause, unsure if I'm allowed to speak about her, his family. Perhaps it's all the time that's gone by, or how we can channel our grief into something else and what we allow it to morph into, or a mixture of both that pulls at me, deep in my belly, making me brave. "I know she would absolutely love your story, your way with words. Without a doubt."

"I hope so. No—I've learned to say that I *know* she's proud of me." He runs a hand along his fresh fade.

"So, where are you going to school right now?" I ask.

"Tulane, you know of it?"

I'm doing my best to keep my cool, but that's practically impossible. "Stop. I'm actually transferring there next semester. I can't believe this."

He grins. "Us both being here right now . . . our writing bringing us together after so much time . . . Are we in a rom-com?" Caleb asks.

"There's only one way to find out." I smirk.

"Oh yeah? How so?"

"Are you getting rusty? By our ki—" One of Caleb's hands cups my face, and the other is on the back of my neck as he pulls me in. Our lips meet, soft and slow at first and then with a lot more intensity, clearly making up for lost time. Two star-crossed lovers reunited by the universe, or at least, reunited by Betty Quinn, who is probably begging us all to create our own love story.

PENOVATION Suggested Reading List

1000 Words: A Writer's Guide to Staying Creative, Focused, and Productive All Year Round
Jami Attenberg

Along for the Ride
Sarah Dessen

The Bodyguard
Katherine Center

The City We Became
N. K. Jemisin

Dreyer's English: An Utterly Correct Guide to Clarity and Style
Benjamin Dreyer

The Fault in Our Stars
John Green

The Heartbreakers
Betty Quinn

Happily Ever Afters
Elise Bryant

I Believe in a Thing Called Love
Maurene Goo

Persuasion
Jane Austen

The Romantics
Betty Quinn

Romeo and Juliet
William Shakespeare

Something Clever
Betty Quinn

A Swim in a Pond in the Rain: In Which Four Russians Give a Master Class on Writing, Reading, and Life
George Saunders

When Dimple Met Rishi
Sandhya Menon

Acknowledgments

How special, challenging, rewarding, and surreal to be writing acknowledgments again! I am forever grateful to all those who've helped make this book possible.

Big thanks to:

Pete Knapp for wisdom and guidance.

All the lovelies who make up the Park and Fine Media and Literary for publishing and business acumen.

Bria Ragin for grace.

Vi-An Nguyen, Liz Dresner, and Cathy Bobak for the stunning art, cover design, and interior design, respectively. I love this cover and layout so very much.

David and Nicola Yoon for hope.

The entire Random House Children's Books team—Wendy Loggia, Beverly Horowitz, Barbara Marcus, Colleen Fellingham, JoAnna Kremer, Cindy Durand, Shameiza Ally, Sarah Lawrence, and Shannon Pender—for bookmaking ingenuity.

Jade Adia for sisterhood.

Kristy Boyce, Myah Hollis, and Justine Pucella Winans for kindness. Your blurbs helped carry me to the finish line. I hope our paths cross soon so I can woo you with cake.

Elise Bryant, Isadore Hendrix, Myah Hollis, justin a. reynolds, Lisa Springer, and Brittany N. Williams for check-ins and industry chats.

Tina Canonigo for care.

Rachel, Angel, Meli, Mina, and Tuss for BFFship.

Berkeley for being Berkeley. Stay weird.

Mini canned Coke for thrills.

Romance writers for swoons.

Walker, Miles, and Carter for heaven on earth.

And anyone I may have forgotten, sorry! I'm writing this postpartum.

Love you, thank you again.

About the Author

Danielle Parker was born and raised in sunny California. A former English teacher, she loves to talk books. When she's not reading or writing, Danielle can be found looking for a pool to splash in, eating dessert, or taking a quick nap. *You Bet Your Heart* was her debut novel; this is her second.

danielleparkerbooks.com

Turn the page for a sneak peek at . . .

"Romantic, real, and tender."
        —Elise Bryant, author of *Happily Ever Afters*

"Your next favorite rom-com."
        —Maurene Goo, author of *Somewhere Only We Know*

"An affirming love story for the anxious, the driven, the color-coordinated-pencil-case-loving reluctant romantics everywhere."
                        —Jade Adia, award-winning author of
                        There Goes the Neighborhood

CHAPTER 1

I'VE BEEN SUMMONED.

Every student at Skyline High School knows the principal's calling card—that infamous wallet-sized light green piece of paper. So when Marcus Scott, the self-declared Hermes of school messengers, busts into my AP English class like he's walking onto a Broadway stage, I don't pay him any mind. Instead, I grow an inch taller in my seat, extending my raised hand high in the air.

"Why, Sasha, yes, please," Mrs. Gregg says. Her eyes dart between Marcus and me. She nods for me to proceed and we both smile. We've been doing this exchange all senior year. She asks the tough questions, and while other students are thinking, I stay ready to answer. Like right now, my fingertips flutter in the air as I wait to respond to her question about Shakespeare and his influence on modern media.

But that moment never comes, because Marcus walks up to Mrs. Gregg, hands her the summons slip, and then points at me. It's not until Marcus leaves that Mrs. Gregg slides the flimsy paper across my desk and I realize what's happening. All eyes in the room shift to me, and my body stiffens. I know what they're thinking, because it's what I'm thinking too: What the hell is this about?

I've been called to the principal's office all of once, and it was because my perfect-attendance certificate needed to be picked up. Without making too much of a fuss, I grab my bag and place my pencils, pens, and highlighters in their respective pouches—yes, they each have their own homes. Then I gather the rest of my things and go. Quickly. Trying not to overanalyze how the word *now* is circled three times in black ink.

In the main office, a small bell on the door dings, announcing my presence. I take another step and am met with a mix of familiarity—I've been going to Skyline since freshman year, and the school is like my second home—and newness, because I'm never actually in the main office. The walls are adorned with student photos from the last three decades, with a sea star, a sea otter, a sea lion, and my personal favorite, waves (because we are, you know, making waves here as the second-best public high school in Monterey), as a backdrop. When you go to school this close to the Pacific Ocean, the themes are always gonna be nautical. Mrs. Brown, the world's nicest office attendant, perks up.

"There's our number-one girl," she calls from behind the counter. "Sasha, sweetie, it's so nice to see you. Whatcha doing here?"

I inch toward her and hold up my summons slip so she can see I've been *called* to the office—I'm not just walking around, loitering, wasting class time. As if I would do that anyway. Her eyes dart across the paper and then back at me before breaking into a warm smile, like the sun. I swear, if every high school in America had a Mrs. Brown, student productivity would increase by, like, a lot. People would just be better.

"Have a seat, honey. Principal Newton is finishing up a meeting and then he'll be right with you." She leans on the counter, closing the space between us. Up close, her brown skin glistens. Her straight black hair is in her signature short bob, and her bangs have a streak of gray that makes her look badass, like how I imagine Storm would be in her fifties. Or forties, or thirties? Maybe? Mrs. B is one of those women with flawless skin and a playful personality who seem to defy age.

I try to return her kindness with a smile.

"Knowing you, I bet this is something good—exceptional, even." Then she flashes me a wink.

I can't help but feel . . . thrilled. Being swept out of class to the principal's office. I've been on point all senior year—scratch that, my whole high school career—and maybe this meeting is about that.

For once, the main office is empty, so I take the seat closest to Principal Newton's door. I shut my eyes and savor the peace. Silence. A little mental vacation, if you will. But as soon as I begin to relax, the bell rings.

"There she is. Hey, Mrs. B—that's *B* for *beautiful*." A deep voice interrupts my peace. Moment gone. I open my eyes and turn my head.

Mrs. B rests her elbows on the counter. "Here you go," she says, that infectious smile still on her face. "Ezra, honey, you've been called to the office? Don't tell me you're in trouble, now."

From my chair, he doesn't see me, but I have a full view of him. He's wearing a fitted white tee and white jeans, which make his brown skin pop. His curly black hair is pulled up in a small but high ponytail, and he's got a medium-sized gold chain around his neck that lies on top of his shirt. A small diamond sparkles from his ear, and his black camera hangs across his chest like the sheath of a sword. I take one last gaze and notice the outline of his face, his nose and jaw, which are prominent. He stands so tall and straight it makes the bones in my back follow. I really need to work on my posture.

Ezra.

He must be able to sense me staring at him, because he does a small pivot, and our eyes connect like magnets. I blink nervously and avert my gaze.

He turns and holds up his summons. "I was hoping you could tell me. You know what this is about, Mrs. B?" he asks, his voice a lot deeper than I remember.

"No idea, honey. But go ahead and have a seat by Sasha. Shouldn't be long now." She motions for Ezra to sit in one of the two empty chairs next to me. Ezra gives them a quick glance, but decides against it. Instead, he stands awkwardly, lingering by the doorway.

If Ezra is Mr. Fashionista right now, I'm the opposite. I have a strong urge to slink down in my seat and blend in with the wooly fabric. Today I'm in my black Nikes—but not like sneaker head Air Maxes or Jordans, just regular, degular, old-man running shoes with worn laces tied a little too tight. My long locs are pulled back in a messy bun, giving end-of-school-day vibes. I didn't have time to do anything special with my hair this morning. Okay, I never do. Who has that much time? I'm too busy with school. I mean, this isn't New York Fashion Week, right? Who cares that I'm not wearing makeup? I huff and catch a whiff of . . . Wait . . . am I wearing deodorant?

I'm in my favorite baggy, ripped blue jeans and a black tank top, layered underneath a holey, loose green-and-red flannel with the sleeves rolled up. I give myself a quick once-over and . . . what am I? Going to go work on the railroad? What is this—pioneer chic? Not that I care what Ezra thinks, but I know I have better outfits than this. I peek down at my arms, my umber skin is a little, okay, maybe a lot, dry, with tiny white flakes speckled across my arms. Did I put on lotion? Out of habit, I pat the side of my hair. *This is fine, I am fine.*

I gaze back to Ezra, who hooks his thumbs in the front of his pockets.

Has he been staring at me this whole time?

He raises his eyebrows and says, his voice soft and deep, "Hey, you."

CHAPTER 2

MY CHEST TIGHTENS. I WISH I HAD MY HEADPHONES ON, SO I could pretend to be listening to NPR and avoid any type of conversation with him. Before I can respond, two tearstained freshmen walk out of Principal Newton's office.

"All righty, then. Who's next?" Principal Newton's voice bounces off the walls. That just happens to be his energy—he's like the Energizer Bunny, but with eyeglasses and a big smile. Skyline High is totally his Disneyland, the happiest place on earth. But I guess if you're going to be working with kids, it's the right kind of energy to have. He appears, then holds open the door and makes a big "come on in" gesture with his other hand. I blink out of my trance and stand. Ezra takes a step back, and I scoot past him.

"Oh, you too, Ezra. Both of you, come inside. Have a seat, please," Principal Newton says.

Come again?

Both of us?

We enter his office, which consists of four large black chairs, a tall lamp, and a desk that is an absolute mess, with multiple piles of papers, pens, and books in disarray. I cannot with this chaotic energy. Just give me five minutes in here, some color-coded folders, and a label maker and I know I could make this room shine. Sparkle. Sing. But that's not why I'm here, so I snag a seat and ignore the mess.

"Sasha, this is Ezra. Ezra, this is Sasha, another senior. Do you two know each other?" Principal Newton asks.

"No." "Yes." We speak at the same time.

"No," I say again, with a little more authority in my voice.

So maybe that's not entirely true. I guess if we're going to get technical about it, Ezra and I have met. We *used* to be friends—best friends, actually—but that was years ago. I don't know him now. I *knew* him. Past tense.

"Okay, fine. We've met," I say, doing my best to ignore the glare I know Ezra is giving me.

Ezra sits down, leaving an empty spot between us. Principal Newton tugs at his green bow tie and then rubs his bald head. He smiles as he sits up in his big, rolly chair. He clears his throat, and his cheeks turn a light pink.

"Is this where the kids would say 'it's complicated'? Is that the relationship status update here? Verified? Green check mark?" His voice booms as he laughs at his own joke and welcomes us to do the same. I wait for Ezra to respond, but he doesn't. So I don't either. At least we both can agree on silence.

"Well, then." He coughs, annoyed by our lack of enthusiasm for his comedy routine. He brings his face to his laptop screen as he pecks at the keys with his index fingers. He finds what he needs because he presses his hands together and his eyes light up. "Let's talk about why you're both here." He leans away from his screen, his blue eyes dart from me to Ezra. The only sound in the room is the fluorescent lights from above, crackling as if insects are being fried inside.

"As you know, it's late April, and senior year is wrapping up. There are several things on my radar, of course." Principal Newton takes a long pause. Apparently, he's a master of the art of suspense. "Teachers and administrators are beginning to prepare for end-of-the-year activities and whatnot. You both know that senior year has lots of moving parts, don't you?" He perks up in his chair, waiting for an answer. I'm doing everything in my power not to scream, so I keep quiet. I'm not one for surprises. Ezra just shakes his head like he has no idea, like he's genuinely interested in this buildup.

"Yes, lots of moving parts, lots to plan. Prom, Senior Legacy Night, and, of course, graduation. This is a special time for seniors, so much happening, there's so much good stuff on the horizon. But I digress. This is all to say that, as of today, we have two people tied for the position of valedictorian and the accompanying scholarship."

Okay, now I'm really listening.

The scholarship. $30,000.

"This is new for Skyline High School and for me. I've never seen such rigor academically. Same classes, same grades, two different people." Mr. Newton points to me and then Ezra. "One, two."

"What?!" The shout comes louder than I'd like, but his words awaken everything inside of me. I've never missed a day of school, I've never turned in a late assignment, I've made sure to give everything the proverbial 110 percent.

Before either of us can utter another word, Principal Newton continues, his voice becoming more serious, like he's about to give a lecture . . . or a eulogy. "This is rare, of course, and anything can happen by June, but I wanted to let you two know because—"

Ezra shifts in his seat, agitated. "I'm sorry. Are you sure?"

"Positive. I actually wanted to discuss this with you both today so that we can—" But before Principal Newton can finish, I'm on my feet, backpack falling on the floor.

"It should be me!" The words fly out.

"Excuse me?" Principal Newton slides back, his chair squeaking.

"With all due respect, Principal Newton"—I lower my tone and sit down again—"it should be me for valedictorian. I've worked extremely hard these last four years and . . . and . . . when is the last time the school has had a valedictorian who was not only a woman, but Black and Korean? I think I—"

Ezra jumps in and cuts me off. "Whoa, whoa. Hold up. You think *you* should get it because of your gender and ethnicity?" He fakes a laugh, the space between us narrowing. Our brown eyes lock. "In that case, I think *I'm* more deserving. Being both Black and Jewish, I can say that I am very underrepresented, not only in—"

"Oh my god, you can't be serious right now," I clap back.

Ezra's eyes widen, the incredulousness on his face hard to ignore. "Serious about how I identify? Yeah, actually, I am. It's literally what you did three seconds ago," Ezra replies.

"Okay, but it's different—"

"How is it different?"

"Enough," Principal Newton barks. The room goes painfully silent. "The last thing I want to do is get either of you upset or worked up about what *could be*. There are lots of hypotheticals here. So please, let me continue." He pauses and softens his voice. "I am so proud of you both. You've done something amazing, truly. Your hard work is a testament to this, to your grades. Absolutely outstanding. Historically, the person with the highest GPA is valedictorian, and the second highest is salutatorian. Both positions are, again, very impressive, and both people will have the opportunity to speak at graduation." The energy in the room is heavy. "But unfortunately, per the stipulations of the award, only one wins the scholarship," he says.

The scholarship. The one thing that means everything to me.

My central nervous system shudders, and I dig my nails into the arm of the chair. I'm suddenly faint, queasy. This is not the good news I was anticipating; this is certainly not something exceptionally good. This is its evil twin. Tied? With Ezra? Of all twenty-five hundred students at Skyline, I'm tied with *him*? I bite the inside of my lip so hard I'm sure I draw blood.

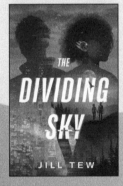